W9-AHY-303

For Agent William Craig

End of Watch: September 3, 1902

1

★ The nation's capital had come undone. The news from Appomattox Court House, in Virginia—General Lee's surrender, after four long, bloody years of civil war—had pitched the city into raucous celebration that was still ongoing, five days after the announcement. Schools and offices had closed, along with many shops, spilling most of Washington's eighty-odd thousand residents into the streets. Taverns were open, going strong—at least, the ones that still had beer and whiskey left to sell—though some apparently had been drunk dry.

Gideon Ryder, sober at the moment, moved amidst the crush of bodies thronging Pennsylvania Avenue. One of the city's steam-powered fire engines passed him, draped in flags and bunting, its whistle hooting to clear the road of buggies and horsemen. Behind it marched a motley choir of some two dozen workmen, black and white together, tipsy voices grappling with "The Battle Hymn of the Republic."

No one seemed concerned that celebration of the war's end might be premature. They either didn't know or didn't care that Joe Johnston's Army of Tennessee was still leading General Sherman on a merry chase through North Carolina; that Rebel forces in Alabama and Mississippi were fighting on as if Lee had never surrendered; that Quantrill's Raiders were still raising hell in Missouri; or that Jefferson Davis had given Ulysses Grant the slip in Richmond, vanishing to who knew where. In every part of Washington, from the White House to the Potomac, it seemed to be an article of faith that peace was guaranteed.

Gideon Ryder, short on faith, wasn't prepared to count his chickens yet.

More to the point, he had been summoned to report before his boss, Ward Hill Lamon, United States marshal for the District of Columbia. Despite the celebration going on around him—or because of it—Ryder could not suppress a feeling that there might be trouble in the wind.

Lamon had known President Lincoln since they partnered up as lawyers back in Illinois, during the 1850s, then had gone his own way as a federal prosecutor in the Eighth Judicial District, operating out of Bloomington. In 1860, despite his abhorrence of abolitionism, Lamon had joined the Republican Party to campaign for Lincoln's election based on their friendship alone. That May, at the party's convention in Chicago, he'd outwitted rival William Seward by printing extra tickets and packing the hall with Lincoln supporters. Rumor had it that he hoped for an appointment overseas, as an ambassador to France or England, but Honest Abe wanted his right-hand man closer to home.

In February 1861, serving as Lincoln's bodyguard, Lamon had traveled with the president-elect from Illinois to Washington, with whistle stops in seventy-odd towns and cities along the way. The railroad had commissioned Allan Pinkerton to take charge of security on their account, and he'd announced discovery of a conspiracy to kill Lincoln in Baltimore, before he reached the capital for his inauguration on the fourth of March. Pinkerton wanted Lincoln's stop in Baltimore cut from the schedule. Lamon countered with the offer of a pistol and a Bowie knife—which Lincoln had declined—while Pinkerton lambasted Lamon as a "brainless, egotistical fool." Lincoln agreed to pass through Baltimore without delivering his scheduled speech, and Pinkerton had cut the city's telegraph lines to frustrate would-be assassins. Lamon told the press that Pinkerton had fabricated the conspiracy to reap publicity for his detective agency.

In fact, as Ryder knew, one man *had* been detained for questioning in Baltimore—a Corsican barber by the name of Cipriano Ferrandini, who worked in the basement of Barnum's Hotel, on Calvert Street. He'd been grilled and then released, no charges filed, no evidence produced that he had harbored any wish to harm the president-elect.

The episode might well have damaged Lamon's reputation, but his old friend didn't seem to mind. Immediately after his inauguration, Lincoln had appointed Lamon as the capital's top U.S. marshal, then sent him to Fort Sumter in South Carolina, on the eve of its bombardment by Rebel artillery. Throughout the war, Lamon had personally prowled the White House grounds at night, once accosting a prowler armed with two pistols and two daggers, knocking him dead on the spot with a blow between the eyes.

Ryder would not be meeting Lamon at the White House, but rather at the Baltimore and Ohio Railroad's depot, north of the Capitol building, at the corner of New Jersey Avenue and C Street. Lamon had been ordered down to Richmond by the president but wanted words with Ryder prior to leaving town.

The reason would be anybody's guess.

Ryder found Lamon pacing outside the Italian-style depot, with its four-sided clock tower looming a hundred feet overhead. Even without the air of agitation that surrounded him, Lamon was an imposing figure, three inches taller than Ryder's own six feet and heavyset, dark hair worn long over his collar, and a bristling Van Dyke beard. A bulge beneath the left side of his long coat signaled he was armed.

Lamon saw Ryder coming, and his scowl relaxed into its normal frown. "I had begun to think I'd miss you, Deputy," he said.

"The crowds, sir. By the time I got your message—"

"Never mind. I have a train to catch, although I have to say it goes against my better judgment. Leaving Washington just now . . . I fear the threat is greater than the president allows."

"Sir, if you want me to patrol around the White House—"

"I'm afraid that task must fall to someone else," Lamon cut Ryder short. "We need to talk about the work you did in Maryland, last week."

"The counterfeiting ring."

A nest of Rebel sympathizers had been flooding Washington with phony Union greenbacks for the past year and a half, turning a tidy profit from their bid to undermine the government of the United States. They weren't the only operators in the field, by any means—some estimates proposed that fully half the paper currency in circulation had been printed up by counterfeiters—but they'd made a slip at last, sold some of their pernicious paper to an undercover deputy of Lamon's, and a raid was organized, with Ryder on the team.

"You shot one of the suspects," Lamon said.

"Yes, sir. After he fired at me."

"Apparently, his weapon was a single-shot Palmetto pistol?"

"Sir, I didn't stop to ask. He missed me by an inch or two, and I returned fire."

"With the end result, I'm led to understand, that he may never walk again."

"He's lucky to be breathing. They can wheel him into court for trial, sir."

"I am more concerned about the subject's father than his health," said Lamon.

"Oh?"

"As luck would have it, he's the junior senator from Maryland."

"A copperhead," Ryder replied, using the common name for Democrats who favored the Confederacy, though their states had lacked the gumption to secede.

"No doubt," Lamon acknowledged. "But the president still hopes for his support in reuniting Dixie with the Union."

Ryder could feel his stomach churning, apprehension sliding into something more like dread.

"So, what am I supposed to do?" he asked. "Apologize because the little bastard missed his chance to kill me?"

Lamon's scowl came back, full force. "There's nothing you *can* do," he said. "And nothing further I can do for you."

"Sir, I don't follow you."

"You're terminated as a deputy, effective from this moment. Prosecution for assault with the intent to kill may thereby be averted."

"Prosecution! When I fired in self-defense?"

"It's Washington," Lamon reminded him. "Nothing is ever quite the way it seems."

"Sir, this is—"

"I require your badge."

Fuming and speechless, Ryder reached inside his jacket and removed the tin star from his vest. He handed it to Lamon, felt a tremor in his hand, and hoped it wasn't visible.

"If you require a reference—"

"I'll ask someone I trust," said Ryder. "You don't want to miss your train."

He turned and left Ward Lamon on the depot's platform, and moved off in search of a saloon.

Ryder picked the Yankee Doodle, known for watering its liquor less than certain other dives in Washington—and for the sporting ladies who were housed upstairs. The place was packed, like every other tavern in the capital that still had liquor stock on hand. He shouldered through the press of bodies, made it to the bar, and ordered whiskey from the harried bartender. It cost a dime, which seemed excessive, but he didn't feel like quibbling.

The amber liquid scorched his throat and settled in his stomach, mingling with the acid that his curt dismissal had released there. Ryder thought of half a dozen things he might have said, ranging from furious retorts to pleading, but he knew that nothing would have saved his job. He'd run afoul of politics, and that meant everything in Washington.

Ryder was on his third shot, feeling it a little in that swimmy way, the tight fist of his anger loosening, when someone edged up to the bar beside him. Ryder felt the new arrival watching him and turned to meet his level gaze. The man was average in every way, clean-shaven, graying hair combed neatly, wearing a gray suit and black string tie. Ryder put him somewhere in his middle forties, fairly trim and fit.

One corner of the stranger's mouth ticked upward for a heartbeat, in what could have been a smile cut short. "Gideon Ryder?"

"All depends."

"Until this afternoon, a member of the U.S. Marshals Service?"

"Who in hell are you?" Ryder demanded.

"William Patrick Wood."

"I never heard of you."

"No reason why you should have, unless you'd done time at the Old Capitol Prison. I was its warden, during the war."

"War's still going on, from what I hear," Ryder replied.

"It's down to mopping up now. You know that as well as I do, Mr. Ryder."

"So?"

"So, I've been chosen for a new position," Wood informed him. "Unofficial at the moment, but it's soon to be confirmed."

"Congratulations."

Ryder raised his empty glass to get the bartender's attention, just as half a dozen drunks nearby burst into a discordant song. Wood grimaced at the racket, leaning closer to be heard, and asked him, "Can we talk outside? I'd hate to shout our private business in the midst of fools."

"We don't have any private business," Ryder said.

"But there's a chance we might," Wood said. "And to our mutual advantage, I believe."

The bartender was coming back, but Ryder waved him off. "All right," he said, "but make it quick. I plan on being drunk within the hour."

"An admirable sentiment, I'm sure. This way?"

Ryder followed Wood outside and stopped a dozen paces from the Yankee Doodle's bat-wing doors.

"All right," said Ryder. "What's this private business?"

Wood responded with a question of his own. "Have you heard anything from Marshal Lamon about coming changes at the Treasury Department?"

"No. Last information that I got from him involved my walking papers."

"Ah. Well, the department is establishing a new division called the Secret Service. Starting in a few weeks' time— right after Independence Day, in fact—the unit will be acti- vated. I have been selected as its chief."

"The Secret Service," Ryder echoed. "What is that, a bunch of spies?"

"No, sir. Our brief is to investigate and halt all forms of fraud against the U.S. government wherever they occur. One part of that is counterfeiting, which I understand you've dealt with in the past."

"Not very well, apparently," said Ryder.

"Some would disagree. Other responsibilities extend to tax evasion, smuggling, theft of mail, election fraud, finan- cial crimes that have an impact on the government—who knows what we'll be called on to examine, over time."

"I wish you luck," Ryder replied.

"I'd rather have your service than your wishes," Wood informed him.

"Why?"

"Because you're capable and have experience."

"You know I lost one badge today, because I shot a man in self-defense."

"I am familiar with your case—from Marshal Lamon, as it happens."

"How's that?" Ryder flashed on Lamon's offer of a reference, his cutting answer.

"He regrets dismissing you. The matter was beyond his personal control."

"And now you're throwing me a bone?"

"Much more than that, I hope. A golden opportunity."

"To do the same job for the same folks, more or less."

"I'm not Ward Lamon," Wood assured him.

"But your boss is—who, again?"

"That would be Mr. Hugh McCulloch, secretary of the Treasury. Who answers, in his turn, to Mr. Lincoln at the White House."

"So, more politics," said Ryder.

"Were you expecting independence, working for the government?"

"You must've missed the part where I *stopped* working for the government."

"I understand your anger, Mr. Ryder. You believe you were betrayed, and I can't argue that you're wrong."

"Or guarantee the same thing won't happen again."

"No, sir. You're absolutely right. I plan on building up an agency to serve this government and serve it well. No man is indispensable, and that includes myself. I *will* say this: if I believe one of my men is in the right, I will use every means at my disposal to defend him. If I find the agency to be corrupted by the whims of politics beyond its ordinary usage, I'll resign as chief."

"Sounds good," Ryder admitted. "But you're wasting time on me."

"And why is that?"

"I'm finished hunting men. I'm looking for a line of work where folks aren't out to kill me all the time."

"You're not a coward, Mr. Ryder. I can see that, plain as day."

"Then let's just say I'm tired of carrying a badge."

"Is that your final word, sir?"

"So it is."

"In that case, I apologize for taking up your time." Wood reached inside his coat, pulled out a printed business card, and handed it to Ryder. "Take this, if you don't mind. Just in case."

The card went into Ryder's pocket, unexamined. "Good luck with your Secret Service," Ryder said. "I reckon that you'll need it."

"I'll take that, with thanks, and hope to hear from you."

"Don't hold your breath," said Ryder, as he turned back toward the Yankee Doodle and the sweet goal of oblivion.

You want to go again?" the redhead asked, rolling against him so that one of her soft breasts nuzzled his ribs.

"Give me a minute," Ryder said. "That last one wore me out."

"Take all the time you need," she told him, wearing a seductive smile and nothing else. "You're paid up for the night."

"Good thing I planned ahead."

"I like a man who knows his mind," she said. Her fingers teased him underneath the sheet that pooled around his waist.

Ryder was drunk, no doubt about it, though the whiskey hadn't managed to erase the memory of his dismissal. Dolly, as she called herself, had done a better job distracting him, but in between their bouts of tussling—two, so far, and he was hoping for a third if he could manage it somehow—the anger still came back at him, setting his teeth on edge. The offer of another law enforcement job did nothing to defuse his sense of being sacrificed to please a copperhead whose preference, if truth be told, would have been Grant surrendering to Lee, and not the other way around.

Instead of locking up the traitors, mealy-mouthed appeasers catered to them, offering forgiveness when they should have felt an iron boot on their necks. Ryder had lost a childhood friend to Rebel guns at Chickamauga, and another in a firestorm at the Battle of the Wilderness. For what? So that the politicians who had voted for secession could be welcomed back to Congress as if not a drop of blood had spilled over the past four years?

And what about the slave states that had sided with the Union out of cowardice, as Ryder saw it? They had harbored spies and saboteurs and cutthroats posing as "irregulars" to cast their crimes as acts of war. He thought of Lawrence, Kansas, sacked and burned by Quantrill's butchers, well over a hundred innocent civilians slaughtered in the ruins. Why forgive, much less forget?

"I think we're getting somewhere," Dolly murmured, and he felt that she was right. Her nimble fingers brought him back to here and now, from battlegrounds he'd never personally seen.

Ryder had planned to join the Union Army after Shiloh, back in April '62, but Marshal Lamon had reminded all his deputies that they were vital to the war effort at home, hunting the enemies who lurked in Washington and everywhere across the country, from Manhattan with its draft riots to Arizona Territory, where Confederates vied with Apaches under war chief Mangas Coloradas to harass and murder loyal settlers. Ryder had agreed to stay in harness with the U.S. Marshals Service, maybe saved his life that way, but now he had nothing to show for it beyond a sense of being crumpled up and thrown away.

"That's it," purred Dolly, as she climbed on top of him. "I'll just . . . okay, now . . . there it is."

She settled on him, squirmed a little, getting comfy. Ryder raised his hips to meet her, and she placed a hand flat on his lower stomach to restrain him.

"No, you don't! Let me take care of you."

Whore talk, he realized, but what else did he ever get in Washington? At least with Dolly, there was a reward for being used. And at the moment, Ryder didn't mind a bit. In fact . . .

She clenched him somehow, rose a little, made him catch his breath. "I don't know whether I can wait," he said.

Dolly relaxed, quit moving. Asked him out of nowhere, "How'd you get a name like Gideon?"

"Some kind of angel," Ryder said, thankful for the distraction. "Never thought it fit, myself."

"I woulda guessed a devil," Dolly said, starting to roll her hips again. "Oh, yeah. Like that," she purred. "Just stay right there. Don't move a muscle till I tell you."

Ryder bit his lip, resisting the impulse to help her out. She obviously knew what she was doing, had already proved as much to his complete, exhausted satisfaction, and he didn't plan to spoil the moment. To distract himself a little, Ryder turned his head to glimpse his pocket watch, propped open on the nightstand to his left. He saw that it was ten thirteen, then Dolly gripped his chin with one hand, turned his face back up toward her, and bent to let her nipples graze his lips.

Why not?

"Okay, that's good. *Now* move, damn you! Like that. Oh, Jesus, fill me up!"

He aimed to please, still trying not to tip over the edge too soon. Outside, through Dolly's open window, voices reached them from the street. Men shouting back and forth, a woman's laughter, children giggling as they ran pell-mell along the sidewalk, celebrating the indefinite suspension of their normal bedtime. No one seemed to give a damn for rules in Washington tonight, and if they heard Dolly cry out in satisfaction from her upstairs crib, nobody cared.

Ryder collapsed into the featherbed beneath him, spent, with Dolly draped across him, barely conscious of her weight but feeling every dewy inch of skin that pressed against him. He was on the verge of drifting off when something changed about the voices rising from outside. From celebration sliding downhill into weariness, a note of panic spiked the tones coming to Ryder's ear. A woman's tipsy cackling spiraled up into a kind of squeal. A man passing below the open window started cursing vehemently, raging.

"Dear God, no!" somebody shouted, from perhaps a block away.

As someone else cried out, "They've shot the president!"

Ryder was instantly awake; he rolled Dolly's slender form away from him and bolted out of bed. Naked, he leaned out of her window, saw a stout man reeling past, his face florid by lamplight, streaked with tears. Ryder called down to him, "Hey, you! Yes, you! What's happening?"

"Some bastard's shot the president," the heavy man sobbed out. "He may be dying."

Ryder clutched the windowsill to keep the room from tilting under him and pitching him headlong into the street. "A shooting at the White House?"

"No, during the play. Ford's Theatre."

"What is it?" Dolly asked him, lolling on the bed, still half asleep.

"The president," said Ryder, as he scrambled to retrieve his scattered clothes.

"Well, what about him?"

"He's been shot."

"The hell you say!"

By then, he had his pants on and had stepped into his boots. Grappling with his shirt, he heard one of the seams rip and ignored it. Pistol. Jacket. Hat.

Dolly's voice reached out to catch him at the door. "You come back any time, now, hear?"

"I hear," he called over his shoulder, racing to the nearby stairs and pounding down them, toward the street.

2

★ **F**ord's Theatre was located on Tenth Street, four long blocks from where Ryder emerged onto the sidewalk. He started running west on E Street, weaving in and out past people in his way, jostling a few who lurched into his path, deaf to their protests as he passed. The word was out already, women weeping—and a few men, too— while others walked around with stunned expressions on their faces, shock and alcohol colliding in their brains. Ryder was out of patience by the time he'd covered two blocks, close to lashing out at human roadblocks as he closed the distance.

Lincoln, shot!

The fear of such a thing had been a constant from the first days of the war. The District of Columbia was more or less a southern city, geographically and in its attitudes, although it was the Union capital. It lay next door to Virginia, where Richmond served as the Confederate seat of government until one week before Appomattox—barely a hundred miles from Washington, but worlds apart in terms of politics.

Or was it? Congress had waited a year past Fort Sumter to ban slavery inside the District itself, when President Lincoln signed the Compensated Emancipation Act in April 1862. Under that law, more than three thousand slaves had been freed, while their owners received three hundred dollars per head for their lost property. Newly freed bondsmen were encouraged to leave the country by a standing offer of one hundred dollars each for those who emigrated to Haiti or Liberia. How many actually left was anybody's guess.

And now, the worst had happened. Lincoln *had* been shot, but was he dead?

Ryder stopped short outside Ford's Theatre, facing a crowd of several thousand Washingtonians. Taking a chance, he climbed a streetlamp's cast-iron pole and hung onto the crossbar set below the square glass lantern, placed there to support a lamplighter's ladder. Clutching the bar, legs wrapped around the fluted pole, he hung there, face warmed by the lamp, watching to see what happened next.

It took some time. Ryder's muscles were trembling and burning by the time a group of solemn men emerged from the theater, passing through white arches from the entryway. Behind them came five soldiers in full uniform, supporting the familiar form of Lincoln in their arms. Familiar, yes, but also *different,* face slack and pale, hair matted on one side by blood, and stains of crimson on his open shirt collar.

A head shot, then. Ryder could feel his stomach clench and twist.

More soldiers spilled out of Ford's Theatre—where were they, when the shooting happened?—and ran past the party carrying the president. Two of them started pushing through the crowd, while a young civilian dressed for a night on the town followed them and called out to the throng, voice straining with emotion.

"People! Listen, please, for God's sake! I am Dr. Albert King. The president is gravely injured. Everyone stand back and let us move him to a place where he can find the proper care!"

Slowly, moaning like a wounded animal, the crowd drew back and split apart, forming a path for the procession to pass through. Two other grim civilians, possibly physicians, fell in line with Dr. King and led the soldiers carrying the president past ranks of stricken faces. Mary Lincoln, almost childlike in her stature, walked behind the soldiers carrying her husband, looking dazed.

And going where? They didn't seem to have the first idea. Their party turned first toward the nearby Star Saloon, then seemed to reconsider, veering off across Tenth Street. A man with a lantern in hand emerged from the Peterson boardinghouse, a three-story redbrick structure directly opposite Ford's, and called out to the burdened bluecoats, "Bring him in here! Bring him in here!"

Dr. King picked up his pace, the soldiers trying to do likewise without jostling their commander in chief. They reached the sidewalk, climbed a curving flight of concrete steps to reach the open entry to the boardinghouse, then disappeared inside. The tall door slammed behind them with a sound uncomfortably like a gunshot.

Ryder let his legs unwind, slid down the lamppost, and dropped the last three feet. He almost tumbled, trembling legs protesting, then regained his balance and followed the crowd's flow across the street toward Peterson's. His mind was racing, trying to decide what he should do. Stay there and wait for news? Go home and wait to read about it in the

Daily Morning Chronicle? Was leaving a betrayal of the president, somehow, although Lincoln would never hear of it and didn't even know Ryder existed? He'd been ousted from the Marshals Service, owed the government no duty whatsoever, yet the thought of leaving still felt like desertion.

Ryder looked back across Tenth Street toward the Star Saloon, a two-story building next door to the looming bulk of Ford's Theatre. He knew the owner, Peter Taltavull, from visits to the barroom in his former professional capacity and as a private patron. They were cordial, although not close friends; Taltavull was an ex-marine who'd played a French horn in the Marine Corps band for twenty-odd years before retiring to serve thirsty Washington residents. A counterfeiting case had taken Ryder to the Star, about a year ago, but Taltavull had not been involved.

A drink or three would suit him well, right now, but others obviously had the same idea. The crowd outside of Peterson's was growing by the minute, but was also losing people from its fringes to the Star Saloon. Ryder decided that he'd rather have fresh air, if he was standing in a crush of bodies, than to squeeze himself inside a barroom rank with sweat and stale tobacco smoke.

Call it a vigil, then, and he would stick until young Dr. King or one of his associates came out with an announcement. Ryder's fleeting glimpse of Lincoln had not been encouraging. Head wounds were always serious, and penetration of the skull meant probing into Lincoln's brain if King or someone else wanted to get the bullet out. If it had fragmented while piercing bone, he guessed the president must be as good as dead.

Goddamn it!

Ward Hill Lamon had been guarding Lincoln for the past four years, and chose this day, of all days, to leave

Washington? Ryder had felt contempt for Lamon after he was fired, that morning; now, it blossomed into full-blown rage. Surely, he must have left *someone* in charge to keep the president from harm, but whoever inherited the job had clearly failed.

That was a name Ryder would like to ferret out and pay the worthless slug a visit. Not the best idea he'd ever had, perhaps, but at the moment it felt right. It wasn't murder that he had in mind, but something in the nature of a thrashing that would leave its mark and teach the sluggard that a failure in responsibility had consequences.

As for Lincoln's would-be killer, it was on the street already that he had escaped from Ford's. An actor, it was said, one John Wilkes Booth. Soldiers and members of the Metropolitan Police Department had fanned out in search of him, while drunken lynch mobs did the same. No matter which side caught him, Ryder wouldn't bet á nickel on his chances of survival through the night.

A half hour into the vigil, two familiar figures arrived by carriage outside the Peterson house. Ryder recognized them instantly as Edwin Stanton, Secretary of War, and Gideon Welles, Secretary of the Navy. Both bearded and grim-faced like biblical prophets, surrounded by more boys in blue, the pair vanished into the rooming house, leaving half their armed retinue on guard outside.

Was Lincoln still alive, inside there? If not, as Ryder understood it, power would devolve upon Vice President Andrew Johnson, former military governor of occupied Tennessee, picked as Lincoln's running mate in 1864 to demonstrate the president's belief that Rebel states were still part of the Union, whether they liked it or not. His ascension to office would rile the Republican Congress, but tawdry politics seemed insignificant tonight, with Lincoln lying on his deathbed only yards away.

A ripple started at the far edge of the crowd assembled outside Peterson's, anger and sorrow, spreading word of some new outrage. Ryder heard a name amidst the muttering and cursing.

"Seward! *Seward!*"

Ryder grabbed a fellow passing by and asked, "What's happened?"

"Secretary Seward was attacked at home," the stranger answered, almost breathless. "Cut to pieces, what they're saying. May be dead already, with his family."

Ryder released him, watched him disappear into the crowd. William Henry Seward, Secretary of State and next in line for the presidency after Johnson, had been thrown from a carriage nine days earlier, suffering a concussion, broken jaw, and fractured arm. He'd been laid up at home on Madison Place, facing Lafayette Park. Word of the new attack told Ryder that the Lincoln shooting hadn't been some solitary madman's work, but rather part of a conspiracy.

The list of suspects would be endless. Anyone who lived below the Mason-Dixon Line, for starters, then add all the copperheads who'd called themselves "Peace Democrats," while scheming to support the South and slavery. And truth be told, there were some people in the president's own party who would have to fake grief at his passing. Rumor had it that Edwin Stanton was one of them, often at odds with Lincoln over the handling of ex-Confederates and terms for readmission of their states into the Union.

Ryder had begun to reconsider visiting the Star Saloon when someone jostled him in passing, bawling out, "Goddamn King Abraham, and Seward, too!" The loudmouth's passage caused an eddy in the crowd, others recoiling from his bulk and roaring voice. A few quick strides brought Ryder up behind him, clutching at his shoulder, turning him around, breath redolent of alcohol.

"I didn't catch that, friend," he told the grinning drunk.

"I *said*, god*damn* King Abraham and Sew—"

The first punch broke his nose, a satisfying crunch, and Ryder just had time to strike once more, before the squaller dropped unconscious to the pavement. Several bystanders cheered, one slapping Ryder on the back, but most of them retreated from him as he turned back toward the rooming house where Lincoln was sequestered, dead or dying.

As the night wore on, with no word out of Peterson's, more news arrived by word of mouth from other parts of Washington. Search parties hunting John Wilkes Booth had so far failed to locate him. Now there were fears he might have slipped the net, escaping into Maryland or possibly Virginia. Either way, there'd be no dearth of Rebels happy to conceal him and assist in his escape. The hunt was widening, a full-scale military operation now, but no one could predict success with any certainty.

The good news had to do with William Seward. Although stabbed repeatedly by a demented stranger—who had also gravely injured two of Seward's sons, his butler, and a messenger who had arrived coincidentally while the attack was under way—the secretary was expected to survive and to resume his duties, once he had recovered fully. As for the would-be assassin, unidentified as yet, he'd managed to escape on foot, armed with a dagger and a pistol that had failed him by misfiring during the assault.

The night passed in an ebb and flow of rumors. Rebel spies were circulating through the city, planting explosive charges set for synchronized detonation at dawn, noon, whenever. Quantrill's guerrillas, last heard from in Kentucky, were racing toward Washington, hell-bent on topping their civilian massacre at Lawrence, Kansas, back in August 1863. A force of Rebel regulars, defying Lee's surrender order, was advancing on the capital to raze it, or to hold its people hostage.

None of those arrived, in fact, but Ryder recognized more local luminaries rushing into Peterson's throughout the night. Secretary of the Interior John Usher, with his top aide, William Otto, joined their fellow cabinet members inside the boardinghouse. So did Attorney General James Speed and Postmaster General William Dennison. Hugh McCulloch, Secretary of the Treasury, arrived with chief assistant Maunsell Field. The senate's leadership was represented by Charles Sumner of Massachusetts. John Hay, the president's private secretary, arrived with the wounded chief's son, Captain Robert Lincoln. He was outranked, in turn, by Gen. Henry Halleck, Gen. Montgomery Meigs, Gen. John Blair Todd, and Gen. Elon Farnsworth in their best dress uniforms, bedecked with medals.

Other faces Ryder did not recognize, but heard names whispered almost reverently as they passed. Chief Justice Salmon Chase, of the Supreme Court. Richard Oglesby, the governor of Illinois. Rufus Andrews, named by Lincoln as surveyor for the Port of New York. Justice Chase stayed briefly, left, and then returned about an hour later. Secretary McCulloch departed at five o'clock, with gray light rising in the east, shaking his head at questions called out to him from the crowd.

Full sunrise came at half past five o'clock, with no explosions audible from any quarter of the capital. No troops in gray appeared, and daylight found no battle smoke rising on the Potomac. Outside Peterson's, some members of the waiting crowd departed to their homes or jobs, while others came to join the throng. It had become almost a living thing itself, some members of the grim assemblage mouthing prayers, while others joined in singing hymns. Ryder kept silent, but for a persistent rumbling from his empty stomach, hungry and embarrassed at the same time by his body's failure to accommodate the solemn situation.

At 7:34 A.M. by Ryder's pocket watch, Secretary Stanton emerged from the boardinghouse, facing the crowd. He waited for their murmuring to cease, then said, "The president is gone. His wounds proved mortal. Now he belongs to—"

A wail went up from the crowd, dozens of voices joining in and drowning out Stanton's last word. *Now he belongs to* what? Ryder wondered. It sounded like *ages*, but could have been *angels*.

No matter. He turned away, eyes burning, breathing past a hard, painful obstruction in his throat. Swallowing grief, he moved with urgent strides toward Pennsylvania Avenue, already certain what must happen next.

APRIL 15, 1865

The U.S. Treasury Building at 1500 Pennsylvania Avenue had opened for business in August 1839, while only partially complete. Designed by architect Robert Mills—whose monument to George Washington had been stalled, uncompleted, since 1854—the Treasury Building was a classic example of high Greek Revival architecture, boasting thirty columns carved from single blocks of granite, each thirty-six feet tall, across its east front colonnade. Completed in 1842, the building's 150 rooms had proved too small for its ever-growing staff by March 1855, when Congress approved the addition of a south wing, completed in 1861. Still, Treasury kept going, with a west wing begun in 1862, finished in 1864. Now, there was talk of a new north wing, but construction had not started yet.

Treasury would normally be closed to visitors on weekends, but this was no normal Saturday, and Ryder's errand was no normal visit. He didn't know exactly where to look for William Patrick Wood, whose Secret Service agency would not officially exist for three more months, but Treasury seemed the logical starting point. If Wood had not reported on this day of days, Ryder would find a guard, a clerk, a janitor—someone—who could direct him to Wood's office or his residence.

And Ryder wasn't going home until they'd spoken one more time.

From Pennsylvania Avenue, he climbed a flight of steps and passed beneath his destination's massive portico. Four soldiers armed with Burnside carbines barred his entry to the building, one of them—a corporal, with new stripes on his sleeves—demanding Ryder's name and business. They had no list of persons authorized to enter, but it hardly mattered, since they'd never heard of William Wood or anything related to the Secret Service. Ryder finally persuaded them to let him pass by mentioning Ward Lamon's name, after they frisked him thoroughly for weapons.

Treasury was cold and cavernous inside. His footsteps echoed through the lobby, with its vaulted ceiling, marble underfoot. He'd been expecting someone else to challenge him, direct him, *something*, but the place appeared to be deserted. Ryder had a fleeting, childish thought of running willy-nilly through the empty halls until he found the cash repository to stuff every pocket that he had with greenback currency. It passed, and he embarked on a concerted search to locate someone, anyone, who knew his way around the place.

Ten minutes later, Ryder found him. Entering the south wing, he was met by a young man of twenty years or so, with curly auburn hair, a pair of pince-nez spectacles clamped to his nose. His style of dress, together with the batch of papers in his arms, identified him as some kind of clerk or secretary. He was clearly startled at the sight of Ryder, frowning as he clutched his paper bundle tightly to his chest.

As if from force of habit, be inquired, "How may I help you, sir?"

"I'm looking for the Secret Service office," Ryder said. A gamble.

"Secret Service?"

"Mr. William Patrick Wood?"

"Hmm. Mr. Wood is . . . well, of course, I don't know *where* he is. But you can find his office in the west wing, back that way." A nod, in lieu of pointing, since his hands were full.

Another yawning corridor, with floors stacked overhead.

"How will I know it when I see it?" Ryder asked, growing impatient.

"Hmm. There ought to be a name plate on the door. If I am not mistaken, you should try the second floor."

"And if he isn't in?"

"Then I suppose he would be out, sir. Hmm?"

Ryder proceeded to the west wing, climbed a curving marble staircase, and resumed his search. Five minutes later, he was standing at a door that bore Wood's name, head bent and listening for any sign of movement from beyond it. Nothing, but he took a chance and knocked, regardless.

"Enter!" came the order from within.

Ryder turned the brass doorknob and stepped into an office that was smaller than he had expected, barely furnished with a desk and single chair. The man he'd come to see was standing at the only window, overlooking Pennsylvania Avenue. When Wood swiveled to face him, recognition sparking in his eyes, it seemed to Ryder that he'd aged a decade overnight.

"I'd say good morning, Mr. Ryder, but I hate to start a conversation with a lie."

"It's why I'm here, sir," Ryder said.

"And why is that, exactly?"

"Rebel bastards killed the president and tried for Secretary Seward. Let me help you hunt them down."

"As I've explained to you, I'll have no agency or personal authority until July. If you return then—"

"I believe you're doing something now, sir."

"Do you?"

"Yes, sir."

"You're not entirely wrong," Wood granted. "In conjunction with the U.S. Marshals Service, I'm coordinating efforts to locate the individuals responsible for these attacks."

"The Marshals Service has no use for me," Ryder reminded him.

"Their loss may be my gain," Wood said. "You would answer directly to me, not to Mr. Lamon."

"Sounds better."

"So, you'll join us, after all?"

"It's why I'm here, sir."

"I'm referring to the service, Mr. Ryder, not the manhunt. I need men to go the distance."

Ryder spent a long ten seconds thinking through it, then said, "Yes, sir."

"Good. Then I can tell you what we know so far. The president's assassin, as you've no doubt heard, was John Wilkes Booth."

"The actor, right."

"The actor *and* Confederate partisan. He hails from Maryland, you know. In 1859, after Harpers Ferry, he joined the Richmond Grays militia, to guard against abolitionists trying to rescue John Brown from the gallows. I dare say that he was disappointed when they didn't show. After the war broke out, he never missed a chance to criticize the Union or the president. St. Louis coppers held him for a while, in '63, for saying—and I quote—he 'wished the president and the whole damned government would go to hell.' They let him go, of course."

"Too bad."

"Freedom of speech. Today, we know that he's been close to Confederate agents, here and in Canada. He met with members of the Rebel secret service last October, on a trip to Montreal."

"And wasn't jailed when he returned?" asked Ryder.

"Understand, we're learning most of this through hindsight, from informants. At the time . . ." Wood spread his empty hands. "It's one more reason why we need the service you'll be joining, come July."

"There's more," said Ryder, confident that Wood had not shown all his cards.

"There is. We're fairly sure that Booth has fled back home, to Maryland. We believe his object is to hide out somewhere in the South, or else—more likely, I suspect—to flee the country altogether. If he ships for Europe, or to South America, consider him as good as gone."

"Send me to Maryland," said Ryder.

"First things first. We also have a clue of sorts to Secretary Seward's would-be killer. Near the scene of the attack, his bloody knife has been recovered from a gutter. Nothing points us to him yet, but I suspect that he, at least, is still somewhere in Washington or its immediate vicinity."

"You have a good description of him?"

"Here," Wood answered, passing him a printed sheet of paper from a stack atop his desk.

There'd been no time to have a portrait of the traitor done, but his description as compiled from witnesses to the attack was clear enough. Twenty to twenty-five years old, dark hair under a slouch hat, with a Deep South accent. He had posed as a messenger delivering medicine to Secretary Seward, then run amok when denied entrance to Seward's bedchamber. Six witnesses stood ready to identify him, once he was in custody.

"You have a weapon, I assume?"

"Yes, sir."

"We've no credentials yet, you understand, but this should serve for now." As Wood spoke, he removed a business card from his vest pocket, took a dip pen from the inkwell on his desk, wrote something on the backside of the card, and blotted it. Over Wood's neat signature, the message read:

Agent of the U.S. Secret Service

"I'll have something better for you in July, if you're still with us."

"Yes, sir," Ryder said and pocketed the card.

He left Wood's office thinking, *One job at a time.*

3

CHARLES COUNTY, MARYLAND
APRIL 26, 1865

★ I hate these damned mosquitoes!" Jimmy Lucas muttered, slapping at his neck. "They've got more of
my blood inside 'em than I have in my own veins."

"Forget about the bugs," said Ryder, huddled on the
skiff's front seat with Lucas poling. "Let's just get this
done."

Zekiah Swamp lay at the headwaters of the Wicomico
River, a tributary of Chesapeake Bay on Maryland's eastern
shore. It sprawled over 450 acres, and every square foot of
it lived up to the original Algonquin name of *Sacaya*, trans-
lated to English as "dense thicket." Aside from mosquitoes
and leeches, the marsh—Maryland's largest, running clear
across Charles County—also swarmed with snakes and
snapping turtles, skunks, beavers, and black bears. Ryder
hadn't seen an alligator yet, but kept his lever-action Henry
rifle ready, just in case.

With Lucas and the third man in their skiff, Bob Elder,

he was hunting John Wilkes Booth. Throughout the swamp surrounding them, a dozen other three-man teams were scouring the wetland for a glimpse of Lincoln's killer, each man hoping that he'd be the first to spot Booth or his partner, David Edgar Herold. In an inside pocket of his coat, Ryder carried a folded copy of the wanted poster Secretary Stanton had issued six days earlier. It offered fifty thousand dollars for capture of Booth, twenty-five thousand for Herold—his name misspelled in print as *Harold*—and for a third conspirator still at large, John Harrison Surratt.

The others—those who'd been identified, at least—were already in custody. Mary Surratt, John's mother, ran a boardinghouse in Washington that catered to Confederates. City police and members of the U.S. Army's Provost Marshal's detail knew son John as a Rebel courier and an associate of Booth. They'd visited Mary's place at two A.M. on April 15 and she'd put them off with lies, but two days later, one of Mary's servants told investigators of a meeting held beneath her roof the night Lincoln was shot, including Booth and others. On their second visit, April 17, the officers searched high and low, discovering photographs of Booth and Jefferson Davis, a pistol, percussion caps, and a bullet mold. While they were hauling Mary out, one Lewis Powell arrived, introducing himself as a workman on Mary's payroll. Confused, she denied knowing him, and he joined her in jail, soon identified as the man who had wreaked bloody havoc at Secretary Seward's home three nights earlier.

On April 20, another suspected conspirator, George Atzerodt, had been run to ground at a farm outside Germantown, Maryland, twenty-odd miles northwest of Washington. According to police, Booth had assigned Atzerodt to murder Vice President Johnson, and while Atzerodt had booked a room at Johnson's hotel, he then lost his nerve and fled, leaving a pistol and a Bowie knife beneath his pillow for police to find. Now, he was under lock and key with Powell and Mary Surratt, aboard the monitor USS *Saugus*, anchored at Washington's Navy Yard.

Booth, David Herold, and John Surratt, meanwhile, were all in the wind. But Ryder thought their lead was narrowing.

Today, authorities knew that Booth had crossed the Navy Yard Bridge into Maryland, on horseback, within thirty minutes of the shooting at Ford's Theatre. Herold made the same crossing, about an hour later, and rendezvoused with Booth before proceeding to Surrattsville, in Prince George's County. There, they'd retrieved stockpiled weapons and other supplies, then ridden to Bryantown, stopping at the home of a local physician, Dr. Samuel Mudd. Mudd, in turn, had splinted Booth's right leg—broken sometime during his escape—and fashioned him a pair of crutches. Booth and Herold had spent another day with Mudd, then hired a local man as their guide to the Rich Hill home of another Confederate sympathizer, Col. Samuel Cox. Fearing arrest himself, Cox spilled the fact that he had shown the fugitives a place to hide.

In Zekiah Swamp.

Cox swore the conspirators had moved on by April 24, crossing the Potomac River into Virginia with aid from a new guide, one Thomas Jones, but Ryder had his orders: leave no stone—or mossy, rotten log—unturned. Some thought that Cox was brave enough to lie for Booth and Herold even now, diverting searchers while they fled deeper into the South by some alternate route. Ryder disagreed, but he was under orders. More important, he thought there was a possibility—however slight—that one or both conspirators might still be hiding somewhere in the swamp, and he was not about to be the man who let them slip away through negligence.

Even without assassins in the underbrush, the hunt was perilous. Aside from copperheads—the reptile kind—and timber rattlesnakes, black bears and rabid skunks, the man-hunt had already cost multiple lives. A barge loaded with Union soldiers tracking Booth, the *Black Diamond,* had collided with the steamer *Massachusetts* on the Potomac, both sinking near Blackstone Island. Among the fifty dead were Union prisoners of war lately paroled in exchange for Confederate captives.

All that, without a shot fired, yet.

Ryder had given up on bagging Booth himself, a fantasy he'd briefly nurtured in the early hours of the manhunt. Now, it seemed that someone else would have the honor, if the actor didn't slip away entirely. Thinking of him safe and sound in Dixie Land infuriated Ryder, much less the idea of him sailing off to foreign shores. No other country had offi-cially allied itself with the Confederacy, but France had sympathized with the Rebels—and its troops had invaded Mexico in December 1861, capturing Mexico City in June 1863. Maximilian I—an Austrian archduke installed as emperor of Mexico by France's Napoleon III in April 1864— might well shelter Booth south of the Rio Grande, if he even knew where the assassin had concealed himself.

And could a lone, determined man then track Booth down and treat him to a taste of justice?

Possibly. Something to think about, at least.

A gunshot from the west snapped Ryder's head around and made him raise his Henry rifle. Seconds later, he picked out another skiff with searchers in it, heading his way. In the bow, a man he recognized as Emil Crowe was waving, calling out, "It's done!"

"*What's* done?" Ryder yelled back at him.

"They got the sumbitch, in Virginia. Shot him dead as dirt."

"Where in Virginia?" Ryder asked.

"On a tobacco farm, outside Port Royal."

"You're sure about this, Emil?"

"Positive. Had his initials tattooed on his hand, 'long with a scar somebody recognized, back of his neck."

"And Herold?"

"He's surrendered. No sign of Surratt, though. Thought is, now, he mighta run for Canada."

The news was mostly good, so why did Ryder feel a sudden letdown, hearing it? He couldn't answer that and wondered what it said about him. Would he rather still be hunting Booth than have him measured for a casket?

No. And yet . . .

He turned to Jimmy Lucas, on the pole, and said, "All right, let's head for home."

OLD ARSENAL PENITENTIARY, WASHINGTON, DC
JULY 7, 1865

It was a gray day for a hanging. Clouds were scudding over Greenleaf Point, the peninsula marking the confluence of the Anacostia and Potomac Rivers. Ryder stood with fifteen hundred spectators inside the prison courtyard, most dressed in their Sunday finery, although this was a Friday morning. Thirty-odd soldiers in uniform, all armed with muskets, stood along the wall behind the scaffold. On the gallows platform, fifteen attendants fumbled at binding and hooding the condemned, while four held black umbrellas up to shield their heads from spitting rain.

Ryder had no umbrella, just his flat-brimmed hat and overcoat to keep him dry. Beneath his coat, pinned to his vest, he wore the Secret Service badge he had received from William Wood on Wednesday, after Wood himself was sworn in by Secretary McCulloch at the Treasury Building. That badge, in turn, legitimized the pistol he was wearing, a Colt Army Model 1860 revolver holstered on the left, butt-forward, for a cross-hand draw.

He wouldn't be needing the pistol today.

Director Wood had passed on witnessing the execution of the four Lincoln conspirators condemned to hang, but Ryder felt he ought to see it through. He was the only Secret Service agent in attendance and would file a full report when it was finished, so he focused on the smallest details as the ritual proceeded.

Several hundred persons had been held for questioning after the president's assassination, all but eight released without charges. Nine alleged conspirators had been identified, with one of them—John Surratt—still at large. President Johnson had created a military commission on May 1 to try the remaining eight, and it convened for the first time eight days later. The trial lasted through June, concluding on the last day of that month with guilty verdicts for all eight of the accused. Four of the plotters—George Atzerodt, David Herold, Lewis Powell, and Mary Surratt—had been condemned to hang. Dr. Samuel Mudd's life was spared by a single vote, resulting in a term of life imprisonment. Also sentenced to life, Samuel Arnold and Michael O'Laughlen, both convicted of plotting with Booth to kidnap Lincoln a month before he was murdered.

The odd man out, Edman Spangler, had been employed at Ford's Theatre, preparing the president's box on April 14. A coworker recalled him saying, "Damn the president!"

while he was working on the box, and other witnesses reported seeing him converse with Booth when the actor entered through the theater's back door. One claimed that Spangler held Booth's horse while he was busy murdering the president, while others disagreed. The panel voted to convict him, but he got off with a relatively lenient six-year prison term.

Now it was time for the condemned to pay, in spite of protests that Mary Surratt should be spared on account of her sex. Lewis Powell, belatedly, insisted that Surratt was innocent of any part in the conspiracy, but no one trusted him. Judge Advocate General Joseph Holt had presented President Johnson with a clemency petition for Mary on July 5, but Johnson had refused to sign it, declaring that she had "kept the nest that hatched the egg" of treason.

By then, the details of Booth's death were known and had been published widely. Sgt. Boston Corbett was the triggerman who'd dropped him, after soldiers torched the barn where Booth was hiding out on Richard Garrett's farm. According to Corbett, Booth brandished a pistol as he hobbled from the barn, forcing Garrett to fire in self-defense. Lt. Col. Everton Conger, commanding that phase of the manhunt, disputed that story, reporting to Secretary Stanton that Corbett had fired "without order, pretext, or excuse." He arrested Corbett for disobeying an order to take Booth alive, but Stanton had dismissed the charge, granting Corbett $1,653 from the $50,000 price placed on Booth's head.

It hardly mattered to the actor-turned-assassin. Booth had survived for two hours, his spinal cord severed, whispering to one bystander, "Tell my mother I died for my country." His last recorded words—"Useless, useless"—fairly summarized his wasted life, in Ryder's mind.

Atop the scaffold, preparations for the execution were

complete. Each of the four condemned was hooded with a white sack like a pillow case. White strips of cloth, as if from shredded sheets, secured their arms behind their backs, and wrapped around their thighs, to keep their legs from thrashing when they dropped. Mary Surratt, off to the left, was dressed for her own funeral in a black long-sleeved, ankle-length dress. The others—Powell, Herold, and Atzerodt from left to right—were also dressed in black, except for light gray trousers worn by Herold.

The chosen hangman, Col. Christian Rath from Michigan, remained with the condemned as various assistants left the scaffold. Ministers appointed to provide whatever solace they could manage—two priests for Mary Surratt on her own—were gathered off to one side of the gallows, muttering the prayers dictated by their creeds. Mary Surratt, like Booth and Dr. Mudd, happened to be a Roman Catholic, a circumstance that had produced wild rumors of a Papist plot to kill the president. Ryder had heard the stories, but he couldn't figure out how Pope Pius IX in Rome would benefit from Lincoln's death. It smacked of the Know-Nothing bile that had sparked riots in the streets of Baltimore and Louisville, before the war, together with the burning of a church in Maine.

Ridiculous.

As far as Ryder was concerned, the president had died at Rebel hands. It would have pleased Ryder to see old Jeff Davis on the scaffold with the other four, but he was under lock and key at Fort Monroe, off the Virginia coast, awaiting trial for treason. If and when he was condemned, Ryder thought he might make time to attend that hanging, too.

A silence fell over the crowd, as Colonel Rath took his position by the lever that would drop all four conspirators at once. Off to the left, somewhere, a drum roll issued from the shadows near the prison wall, where Gen. Winfield Scott stood supervising the proceedings. At a nod from him, Rath yanked the lever and propelled four bodies into space.

A jolt brought them up short, Ryder imagining that he could hear their necks snap, more or less in unison. Death from a proper hanging was supposed to be immediate, but all four of the hooded bodies twitched and wriggled at their ropes' end, like blind tadpoles swimming helplessly against a tide too strong for them. At last, after a minute, maybe more, the trembling ceased and they hung still.

Some of the spectators were cheering and applauding now, but most of them were solemn, silent, as they watched the corpses swing. By twos and threes, then larger groups, they started filing toward the exit from the prison yard, anxious to leave now that they'd seen the spectacle. Worried, perhaps, that they had been contaminated through their close proximity to sudden death.

Ryder fell into step behind them, feeling no regret per se but canceling his plan to go directly on for lunch.

This job was finished, but he still had work to do.

TREASURY BUILDING, PENNSYLVANIA AVENUE

"How was the hanging?" William Wood inquired.

"About what I expected," Ryder said.

"Was justice done?"

"According to the court."

"Ah, yes. And are you ready for your next assignment?"

Ryder nodded, asking, "What's the job?"

"Our main concern is counterfeiting, as you know, but that falls within the broader purview of detecting persons perpetrating frauds against the government of the United

States. In that regard, we share shared jurisdiction with the Customs Service when it comes to smuggling."

"Smuggling?"

"Have you ever been to Texas, Agent Ryder?"

"Texas?" Ryder was starting to feel like a parrot.

"More specifically, to Galveston?"

"No, sir."

"Nor I," said Wood, "but I've been studying its history. It is a city on an island, also known as Galveston, after the Spanish nobleman who first settled there, Count Bernardo de Gálvez y Madrid. He was the sixty-first viceroy of New Spain, during the time of our own revolution against England. Two hundred years before his time, Cabeza de Vaca and his crew were shipwrecked there. They called it the Isle of Doom."

"Sounds inviting," said Ryder.

"So it was, despite that gloomy start. French pirates led by the Lafitte brothers planted a colony they called Campeche on Galveston Island in 1815, raiding merchant ships over the next six years. Mexico established a port on the island in 1825 and built a Customs house in 1830. Six years later, Galveston served as interim capital for the Republic of Texas, bankrolled with fifty thousand dollars from Canadian investors. Confederates captured the city in January 1863 and held it until Lee's surrender. Now, it's ours again, after a fashion."

"And there's smuggling."

"An epidemic of it, so I'm told. All manner of cargo and contraband passes through Galveston, coming from Mexico, Cuba, Jamaica, and God knows where else. Customs taxes what they can, but some estimates suggest that they're missing more than they catch."

"And we're supposed to shut it down?" asked Ryder.

"That may be a trifle optimistic," Wood replied. "But we're obliged to do our best."

"How many agents are you sending?"

"Only one, for now."

"Just a trifle optimistic?"

"Don't be too discouraged. Naturally, I would not expect you clean up a port the size of Galveston, all by yourself."

"So, what *would* you expect?"

"I have a more specific goal in mind for you. A more specific target, I should say."

"And that would be . . . ?"

"One Bryan Marley, known to some in Galveston as King of Smugglers."

Ryder frowned. "I never heard of him."

"No reason why you should have. Marley's a Louisiana native, thirty-five years old or thereabouts. He's been a smuggler for the past twelve years, at least, according to his Customs file.

"During the war, he was a blockade runner operating out of Galveston, bringing supplies to the Confederates. Since Appomattox, he's been back in business for himself."

"But not alone," Ryder surmised.

"By no means. He's an admiral of sorts, commands a small fleet of his own ranging across the Gulf of Mexico and into the Caribbean. We estimate he has a hundred sailors under his command, and that may be conservative."

"Can't say I like the odds."

"Your focus will be Marley. And his second in command, as well. A character called Otto Seitz. German extraction, served a year in the Texas State Penitentiary at Huntsville for manslaughter, circa 1859."

"A whole year?"

"I believe the circumstances were . . . ambiguous."

"Uh-huh. What kind of contraband does Marley handle?"

"Anything and everything that he can sell for profit," Wood replied. "He was part owner of the *Wildfire*, a slave ship seized by our navy off Florida's Key West in April 1860, with four hundred fifty Africans on board. Marley himself escaped indictment in that case, although one of his partners and the *Wildfire*'s captain were convicted in federal court."

"I assume he's not slaving, these days."

"One would hope not. From what Customs tells me, he leans more toward rum, certain tropical fruits . . . and, of course, there's the gold."

Ryder didn't catch himself in time, before he echoed, "Gold?"

"Not bullion. Coins and other items," Wood elaborated. "Gems, as well. Some of the items that have passed through Galveston of late suggest Marley or the people he's associated with have tapped into a pirate's trove."

"What, like Captain Kidd and Blackbeard?"

"Kidd and Blackbeard—or Edward Teach, as he was born—were wiped out during colonial times. The brothers that I mentioned earlier, Pierre and Jean Lafitte, are much more recent, and their progeny have shifted into smuggling for the most part, though they aren't above looting a ship from time to time. In this case, we—or *I*, at least—suspect that someone has uncovered treasure cached by those long dead and gone, moving the goods through Galveston and on from there."

Ryder thought he saw where this was going, but he had to ask. "So, what's the plan?"

Wood smiled and said, "I'd like you to become a smuggler."

"Oh?"

"Impersonate a smuggler, I should say. Our difficulty, when it comes to Bryan Marley, has been finding anyone to testify against him. The officials he's suborned are well established in the area, and they're adept at covering their tracks. The fences who receive his merchandise are wealthy and protected in their own right. As for Marley's gang itself, Customs persuaded one of them to squeal quite recently, but something happened to him."

"Something? Such as . . . ?"

"Sharks are common in the sea surrounding Galveston, apparently. This individual—"

"I get the picture," Ryder said.

"The job is not without its risks, of course."

"I gathered that."

"Marley is cautious, a survivor well established at his trade. Convincing him to take you on may be a challenge."

"Who am I supposed to be?"

"A drifter, disrespectful of the law. Create a simple history and memorize it. Keep details of your jail time vague enough that Marley won't be able to refute them easily."

"Get next to him, and then what?" Ryder asked. "Buy him a drink and ask him to confess?"

"To testify effectively, you must be witness to his criminal activities."

"And that means joining in," Ryder observed.

"To some extent, perhaps. Ideally, you should avoid participation in a felony."

"And if I'm part of Marley's operation, will a court accept my testimony afterward?"

"There is a precedent for infiltrating outlaw bands."

"The Pinkertons," said Ryder.

"Among others. New York City's Metropolitan Police

have had some fair results from working in this manner, also."

"How far is it from Washington to Galveston?"

"About twelve hundred miles, as the crow flies."

"And how am I supposed to get there?"

"Not by crow," Wood answered, smiling. "Are you prone to seasickness, by any chance?"

4

★ Gideon Ryder spent the day after his interview with William Wood preparing for his trip to Galveston. There wasn't much to do, in fact, since he had always lived in rented rooms and traveled light. He packed some clothes and shaving gear into a portmanteau, procured a leather case to hold his Henry rifle and its cleaning gear, then settled with his landlord on the rent. He did not pay to have the small and spartan room reserved for his return, since Ryder couldn't say exactly when—or if—he would be coming back.

Small loss.

He had no friends of any consequence to trouble with good-byes, though Dolly had seemed pleased to see him for a quick roll in the hay before he sailed. Or pleased to see his money, anyway.

The *Southern Belle* was waiting when he reached Baltimore's waterfront, on the Patapsco River. She was a stylish boat or ship; he never fully understood the difference between the two. Three hundred feet in length and painted white above the water line, the *Southern Belle* had three decks and sprouted a tall single smokestack amidships. Its wheelhouse stood atop the upper deck, forward, while its engines drove a single giant paddle-wheel astern. As he prepared to go aboard, mounting the gangplank, some of Ryder's fellow passengers were at the rails on their respective decks, waving and calling down to friends or family who'd come to see them off.

Steamboat traffic on Chesapeake Bay had been pioneered in 1840 by the Baltimore Steam Packet Company, also known as the Old Bay Line. Its vessels were dubbed "packets" for the parcels they transported under government mail contracts, although paying passengers were also welcome. In their two decades of operation prior to the War Between the States, Old Bay Line packets only traveled between Baltimore and Norfolk, Virginia, but their range was expanding in response to competition from the North. Ryder was sailing on a boat/ship of the Leary Line, launched out of New York City, serving ports from Baltimore on south to Norfolk, Wilmington, Charleston, Savannah, Jacksonville, Miami, and around the tip of Florida to Galveston, across the Gulf of Mexico.

Competition between steamboat lines had driven the price of a fare down to bedrock—three dollars for Ryder—but the frequent stops also meant more time at sea, if coastal waters qualified. Seven days and nights aboard the *Southern Belle*, which still beat traveling by train and coach through Dixie, where so many railroad lines had been destroyed by one side or the other in a bid to keep their enemies from moving soldiers and materiel. The trip from Washington to Texas might have taken him two weeks if he'd gone overland—or longer, if he'd traveled all the way on horseback.

Ryder's cabin, when he found it, was located on the second deck, roughly halfway between the bow and stern. It was his first time on a steamboat, and he found the throbbing rumble of the engines two levels beneath his feet a bit unsettling at first, as if the vessel had an epic case of indigestion and was on the verge of heaving up its latest meal. In fact, he understood there was a crew belowdecks, stoking giant boilers, building up the head of steam required to turn the paddle-wheel when they were finally untethered from the dock.

He thought their job must be a paid preview of Hell.

Before embarking, Ryder had considered the inherent risks of steamboat travel. He had read somewhere, likely the *Daily Morning Chronicle*, that during the forty years after the invention of the steamboat, some five hundred boats had gone down, killing four thousand passengers. In 1852, the federal government had cracked down with regulations on construction and maintenance of steam boilers, but accidents still happened. Only three months earlier, in fact, the Mississippi steamer *Sultana* had exploded near Memphis, Tennessee, killing more than fifteen hundred passengers, leaving hundreds more badly burned. Adding insult to injury, many of those lost were Union soldiers, recently freed from Confederate prison camps.

His cabin, so called, was more of a cubbyhole and made the rented room he'd left behind seem spacious by comparison. Its eighty-odd square feet contained a bunk that he could just about stretch out on, and a straight-backed wooden chair tucked into a desk-type dresser of sorts with drawers on one side and a mirror on top. A printed card on the bunk told Ryder that each deck had its own dining room, smoking lounge, and bathroom facilities. The latter were segregated by sex, with the women's facility forward, the men's located aft. Ventilation and a view of the outside world—or, presently, the backsides of his fellow passengers standing along the rail—was provided by a porthole the size of a dinner plate.

Ryder didn't bother to unpack, just yet. He set his portmanteau and rifle case atop the narrow bunk and made sure that his cabin door was locked before he left and moved along a corridor, known as a passageway on shipboard, toward a staircase sailors labeled a companionway. That took him up and out onto the upper deck, where he could scan the docks and almost see the point where the Patapsco River flowed into Chesapeake Bay. Beyond lay the Atlantic Ocean, and a long run down the Eastern Seaboard to the Gulf.

And then?

The rest, he thought, could wait until he had his feet on solid ground again, in Galveston. Or did an island qualify as solid ground?

He'd find out soon enough, in any case, and then his real work would begin.

Sailing from the harbor seemed to be a cause for celebration on the *Southern Belle*, though Ryder could not figure out exactly why. He understood the whistles sounding, as a warning to the other boats or ships nearby, but since the steamer came and went from Baltimore at weekly intervals, routine departure on another run did not impress him as a grand occasion for the cheers that echoed from its crowded decks and from spectators lined up at quayside.

Then again, perhaps he simply wasn't getting in the spirit of the thing.

For many of his fellow passengers, he guessed, the *Belle*'s departure signaled the beginning of a personal adventure.

Some of them were on vacation, heading off to visit relatives or friends or lovers. Others would be traveling on urgent business, anxious to cash in on profits promised by the end of war. A few were probably Republicans, embarking on a perilous endeavor as officials named by Washington to help administer the late Confederacy. What awaited them when they arrived was anybody's guess, but Ryder doubted that they would be welcomed to the South with open arms.

*Fire*arms, perhaps. But that was what the bluecoats stationed in the former Rebel states were for, to keep the peace.

Ryder supposed that no one else aboard the *Southern Belle* was traveling on business quite like his, a secret mission for the government—but then again, how would he know? President Johnson was following through on his late predecessor's plan for readmission of the former Rebel states on relatively easy terms, while his Republican opponents in Congress—lately dubbed "radicals" in the Democratic press—clamored for giving former slaves the vote and passing legislation granting them complete social equality with whites. Johnson was holding firm against that tide so far, but even his plan would demand that southern legislatures ratify a new Thirteenth Amendment to the U.S. Constitution, banning slavery. Lincoln had sought compensation for slave owners forced to release their human property, but members of his own party had killed that provision before passing the amendment through the House in April 1864, and through the Senate nine months later.

There was still, Ryder reflected, ample room for intrigue on both sides of the Mason-Dixon Line—and would be, he supposed, for years to come. The hatred spawned by civil war would not fade quickly, if at all, nor would the counterfeiters who had prospered during wartime suddenly give up their trade.

From his hasty education as a Secret Service agent, Ryder knew that a nationwide network of some sixteen hundred private, state-chartered banks were authorized to print paper money and did so, producing a staggering thirty thousand different varieties in all colors and sizes. In 1861, Congress had authorized the U.S. Treasury to print its own "demand notes," replaced a year later by currency widely dubbed "greenbacks." The vast array of paper money presently in circulation made America a happy hunting ground for counterfeiters, printing reams of "bogus," as the operators called it, every month.

While I'm off hunting smugglers. Just my luck, he thought.

Ryder was still uneasy with the plan outlined by William Wood. His former duties with the Marshals Service had been more or less straightforward: guarding federal judges who'd been threatened in performance of their duties, tracking fugitives who'd been identified by other officers but managed to elude them. He had never tried to infiltrate a gang of any kind, or even thought about it heretofore. Ryder had told his share of lies, but never had occasion to pretend that he was someone other than himself, much less a hunted criminal.

First time for everything.

The trick would be ensuring that it didn't prove to be his *last* time.

Going in, he had a physical description of his target, Bryan Marley, and a short list of red-light establishments he patronized in Galveston. Beyond that, Marley was suspected of assorted crimes ranging from theft and smuggling contraband to murder, but he'd never been indicted, much less tried and convicted. Bagging him depended on whatever evidence Ryder could collect, if any, and his own survival to present a case in court.

The *Southern Belle* took its time steaming out of Baltimore Harbor, into the Patapsco River. From there, Ryder
knew, it was 39 miles down to Chesapeake Bay, then another
173 miles to the boat's first stop at Norfolk. Call it 2,300
miles from start to finish, by the time they reached Galveston on the Gulf of Mexico, with the *Belle* making an average
18 miles per hour between stops.

The prospect of a week on board was daunting, but at
least he felt no stirring of seasickness yet. In fact, the grumbling in his stomach now reminded him that he'd skipped
breakfast to be early for the sailing, and he wondered how
long it would be before some kind of food was ready in the
dining hall. It wouldn't hurt to see if any serving times were
posted, then he could explore the boat for safety features,
means of disembarking in a hurry, any kind of firefighting
equipment. Just in case.

If something happened to the *Southern Belle*, he didn't
plan to be among those lost at sea. Enough danger awaited
Ryder at the far end of his journey without drowning or
becoming food for sharks. He wanted to survive, at least
until he went ashore at Galveston.

Beyond that, only time would tell.

Lunch service aboard the *Southern Belle* began at noon,
five hours after leaving port and six hours before the
steamer's stop at Norfolk. Ryder's stomach was protesting
volubly by then, which might have been embarrassing except
for all the talk and clatter in the dining hall, accompanied
by steady rumbling from the engine room below. There was
no system for assigning seats at any of the round tables
designed to serve four diners each, so Ryder took one in a
corner of the room, his back against the nearest wall—or

bulkhead, as they called it on a sailing vessel—with three empty seats around his table when he first arrived.

The dining hall began to fill up shortly after Ryder took his corner seat, couples and larger parties fanning out to empty tables, leaving Ryder on his own. He didn't mind the solitude—in fact, preferred to eat alone if possible—but soon the other seats were taken and his luck ran out. A portly fellow crossed to stand before his table, nodding to the empty chair directly opposite and asking, "May I?"

"Go ahead," Ryder replied.

The new arrival had a drummer's look about him: thinning hair slicked back, a waxed mustache and easy smile, ruddy gin blossoms on his cheeks and bulbous nose. He wore a broadcloth coat over a silver satin vest and white shirt with a black string tie. His hands, atop the table, looked like hair spiders. Underneath his jacket, on the left side near the armpit, a small pistol in some kind of a shoulder holster bulged against the fabric.

"Arnie Cagle. I'm in ladies' corsets," he announced and snorted laughter at his own bon mot. Ryder obliged him with a smile and introduced himself as George Revere, the alias he and Director Wood had finally agreed upon in Washington.

"You kin to Paul Revere?"

"Not that I ever heard."

"Now, when I say that I'm in ladies' corsets—"

"Let me guess. You sell them?"

"You got it right in one. Other foundation garments too, of course. Your basic camisoles and crinolines, garters and drawers, the latest—"

"May I join you gentlemen?"

Ryder glanced up to find a well-dressed woman of about his own age standing several paces from their table, studying the drummer with a look of mild amusement on her heart-shaped face. It was a good face, somewhere short of beautiful, but certainly attractive, underneath a small green feathered hat that rode atop a frothy pile of auburn hair. She wore a blue silk dress, high-necked, with wide pagoda sleeves, the hem of her wide paneled skirt grazing the carpet of the dining hall. Ryder had no idea if she was wearing anything from Cagle's stock beneath the dress but gave his mind freedom to speculate.

Cagle was first to rise, wearing an unctuous smile and saying, "Please, by all means, grace our lonely company."

Ryder kept quiet, trying not to roll his eyes.

Cagle stepped back to help the lady with her chair, adjusting it until she thanked him, granting leave for them to sit. "I'm Irene McGowan," she announced. "And you are . . . ?"

"Arnie Cagle," said the drummer.

"He's in ladies' corsets," Ryder interjected.

Cagle shot a glare at him, while Irene said, "We'll keep that to ourselves, shall we, mister . . . ?"

"Revere," he told her. "George Revere."

"No relation to Paul," Cagle added.

She blinked at Cagle. "Paul?"

"It's not important."

"I would not have pegged you for a George," she said.

"Oh, no?"

"Something a trifle more adventurous, I think. Perhaps Gerard, or Graham."

"Sorry. Just plain George."

"I wouldn't go that far, Mr. Revere."

Cagle frowned, seemed on the verge of making some remark, but he was interrupted by a waiter stopping to deliver menus. Irene asked about the soup du jour, but grimaced when she learned that it was turtle, opting for a lobster tail instead. "I draw the line at reptiles," she told Ryder, with a quirky smile.

He ordered T-bone steak with baked potato. Cagle put the waiter through an inquisition on the merits of the fried and roasted chicken, then decided on pork chops instead. They sat and talked about the *Southern Belle*'s accommodations and their several destinations while they waited for their food. Cagle was headed for Savannah, while Irene was going on around the Keys and Straits of Florida to visit kinfolk in Tampa.

She lit up with another smile when Ryder said that he was traveling to Galveston. "I hear it's very wicked there," she said.

"I couldn't tell you," he replied. "It's my first time."

"In Galveston, he means," said Cagle, smirking.

Irene blushed at that, but the arrival of their meals saved her from having to respond. Ryder picked up his knife, imagining how it would feel to let some air out of the corset salesman, but he cut a bite out of his steak, instead, and found it was delicious.

Small talk occupied them while they ate. Ryder let Cagle carry most of it, describing a variety of trades he had pursued before he settled down to women's intimates. Most of it had to do with clothes, though he'd spent the war designing military uniforms.

"Which side?" asked Ryder.

"The correct one," Cagle said and gave him an exaggerated wink.

"And what do you do for a living, George?" Irene inquired.

It was a chance to try his cover story on for size. "Import and export," he replied, leaving it vague.

"So, shipping," Cagle said.

"My part has more to do with acquisition," Ryder said, "and distribution."

"Such as?" Irene pressed him.

"Anything my customers desire. Jamaican rum's a popular commodity. Some other products from the islands. Now and then, a little something more exotic."

"And you've visited these places?"

"All a part of doing business."

"You must tell me more about them, when we have the time."

Leaving the dining hall when they were done, Ryder decided that the trip might be more interesting than he'd thought.

Ryder soon discovered that the *Southern Belle*'s arrival in a port produced the same reaction as its steaming out of Baltimore. The packet's whistle sounded well before it docked, drawing a crowd to meet it at the pier. Some came to welcome disembarking passengers, while others paid their fare and came aboard, bound for some other port. Cargo was hauled ashore and rapidly replaced with other items. Some folks simply came to gawk, while others stood and waited for their mail.

Norfolk wasn't much to look at, in his personal opinion, when they reached it in late afternoon. All Ryder knew about it was what he had read in newspapers, during the war. The Battle of Hampton Roads had been fought there, at sea, in March of 1862, between the ironclads USS *Monitor* and CSS *Virginia*, built from remnants of the old USS *Merrimack*. It came down to a standoff, with some 340 dead and about 120 wounded, but Gen. John Wool had captured the Rebel port two months later, holding it for the remainder of the war. It had been spared from any major damage, and appeared to be a thriving spot for commerce now.

Their second day at sea established Ryder's pattern for the trip. He had an early breakfast in the dining hall and had a walk around the deck, stopped by the boat's small library but couldn't find a book that suited him, then went to lunch at noon. Irene McGowan met him there, while Arnie Cagle chose another table, trying out his jokes on a new audience. This time, they shared their table with an aging couple on their way to Jacksonville, to see their third grandchild.

The *Belle*'s next stop—at Wilmington, North Carolina— came up in the afternoon, some twenty hours out of Norfolk. A major port for the Confederacy, on the Cape Fear River, Wilmington had been the capital of blockade runners after Norfolk's fall, holding out until February of 1865. When Gen. Braxton Bragg evacuated, driven out by Union troops, he'd burned large quantities of cotton and tobacco marked for sale in England. Even so, most of the action had occurred outside the city, leaving stately antebellum homes intact.

The packet's stops in one port or another soon became routine to Ryder. There was Charleston, scene of Fort Sumter's bombardment, and Savannah, captured by General Sherman as a Christmas present for President Lincoln in December 1864, where Arnie Cagle took his bulging sample case and disembarked. The weather started getting steamier as they continued down the coast to Florida, stopping again at Jacksonville, a seedy and dilapidated port where shirtless black men loaded ships under the watchful eyes of overseers, much as Ryder thought they must have done before they were emancipated. Eighteen hours farther down the coast, Miami was a tiny settlement, noteworthy only for its lighthouse at the southern tip of Key Biscayne.

Mostly, he concentrated on Irene McGowan, sharing

meals with her and, by their third day on the *Southern Belle*, accompanying her on walks around the packet's several decks. On the night they left Miami, Ryder had a feeling that she might invite him to her stateroom, but she left him standing at the door instead, after a chaste peck on the cheek. He chalked it up as progress of a sort, and went off to his narrow bed alone.

Proprieties.

It was too much, Ryder supposed, to think that she would risk her reputation on a man she barely knew, and whom she'd never see again after they parted at Tampa. So much for shipboard romance.

They were finishing breakfast, four days out, when the *Belle*'s steam whistle sounded their approach to Key West, dominated by Fort Zachary Taylor and a U.S. Navy base. Key West had stayed in Union hands throughout the war, despite Florida's secession, and Fort Jefferson—sixty-odd miles distant, on Garden Key in the Dry Tortugas—presently served as a federal prison, with Dr. Samuel Mudd numbered among its inmates.

The island wasn't large, less than eight square miles of land, but it was jammed with shops and houses lining narrow streets, its harbor filled with ships and boats of every size. Ryder went ashore with Irene, browsing at shops and market stalls, but limited his purchase to a bag of oranges. Four hours out of port, the *Southern Belle* entered the Straits of Florida, starting its swing into the Gulf of Mexico and up the long peninsula's west coast to reach Tampa, the best part of another day ahead.

Standing with Irene at the rail, sharing an orange, Ryder considered that they still had one more night on board, together. He had already decided not to press his luck, simply enjoy her company and not make anything more of it, feeling fairly virtuous for his restraint. At the same time, he wondered whether he had lost his touch with women other than the working ladies he had patronized in Washington.

In any case, considering the job at hand, this wouldn't be the time to start—

"Oh, look!" she said. "Another ship!"

It was a sleek, three-masted clipper, sails billowing as it tacked from westward, on a course that seemed designed to intercept the *Southern Belle*. Ryder could see the crewmen scurrying about on deck, doing whatever sailors did to maximize a vessel's speed.

"You don't suppose we'll hit it, do you?" asked Irene.

"Doubtful."

As if on cue, the *Belle* sounded its warning whistle, sharp and shrill.

"They're putting up a flag!" Irene exclaimed.

"It isn't just a flag," said Ryder. "That's a Jolly Roger."

"What?"

"It means they're pirates, and they plan to come aboard."

5

★ **R**yder led Irene McGowan to her cabin on the *Southern Belle*'s topmost deck, instructed her to lock the door, then hurried back downstairs to his own cabin amidships. There, he donned his pistol belt, double-checking the Colt's cylinder, then loaded fifteen .44-caliber rounds into his Henry rifle's tubular magazine. A quick pump on the lever-action put one cartridge in the chamber, permitting Ryder to load a sixteenth round before he left and locked his cabin.

When the Union Army had begun to issue Henry rifles, Confederates armed with muzzle-loading weapons had complained that the new guns could be loaded on Sunday and fired all week. That wasn't strictly true, of course, but its high rate of fire—up to forty-five shots per minute by some estimates, in true expert hands—had proved devastating against charging lines of graycoats.

Ryder had only used his Henry for target shooting so far,

but he knew that 200-grain bullets fired from its .44 rimfire cartridges left the rifle's muzzle traveling around eleven hundred feet per second. Too slow for big-game hunting or a long-range shot of any accuracy, but the slugs were hell on human targets out to fifty yards or so.

And Ryder didn't think the pirates would be that far from the *Southern Belle*.

The packet's whistle shrieked as Ryder made his way back to the main deck, jostling other passengers along the way. Panic was spreading, heightened by a crack of pistol fire across the water as the clipper closed to firing range. Some of the people Ryder passed drew back from him, seeing the rifle in his hands, but he ignored them. What they thought of him was meaningless. His sole priority was to prevent the raiders clambering aboard the *Southern Belle* and wreaking bloody havoc there.

They had a decent chance, he thought, assuming that the steamer's captain didn't quail and cut his speed in some misguided bid to save the boat. In that case, Ryder knew, it could mean fighting hand to hand along the rails, and from the flight of passengers he'd seen so far, it didn't seem that many were inclined to risk themselves in combat for the Leary Line.

What they'd forgotten was that once the pirates came on board, no one was safe.

The very thought of pirates raiding in the modern day and age struck Ryder as ridiculous, but it was happening, and it brought back to mind what William Wood had told him about Galveston. He had no reason to believe that these were Bryan Morley's men, but meeting them was an ironic introduction to his job in Galveston.

Now, all he had to do was stay alive for the remainder of the trip.

Which might prove difficult.

The clipper was already close beside the *Southern Belle* when Ryder reached the main deck, one of its burly crewmen leaping toward the packet, catching hold of its brass rail. He was a bearded thug, with a revolver tucked under his belt and a long knife clenched in his teeth, freeing both hands for climbing as he came aboard, snarling at nearby passengers to frighten them away.

Instead of fleeing, Ryder stepped up to the rail and slammed his Henry's brass butt plate into the scowling face, driving the blade back through its hairy cheeks with an impressive splash of blood. Squealing, the pirate lost his grip and tumbled backward, falling in between the clipper and the *Southern Belle,* where he was lost to sight.

Another burst of gunfire crackled from the clipper, sending Ryder down below the steamer's gunwale to avoid the bullets flying overhead. As he was ducking, Ryder glimpsed the name painted across the clipper's bow: *Revenant,* which, if he recalled correctly, was some kind of ghost or evil spirit.

Apt enough, under the circumstances.

Ryder wormed his way along the gunwale, moving forward, while his would-be killers wasted ammunition on the spot where they had seen him last. One of the fleeing passengers was cut down as he headed aft, thrashing around a deck suddenly slick with blood.

Ryder popped up, shouldered the Henry for a hasty shot, and winged one of the pistoleers who lined the clipper's starboard rail. The man let out a squawk and lurched away, his left arm dangling, while the others turned their guns toward Ryder and he ducked back under cover.

There'd been no opportunity for him to count the men aboard the *Revenant,* but guesswork pegged the number visible on deck near twenty-five or thirty. Not a large force, in comparison to passengers aboard the *Southern Belle,* but none of those showed any inclination yet to join Ryder in fending off attackers. He could understand the women running, some with kids, but he had hoped at least a handful of the men would stand and fight.

Where was the crew? Were there no arms aboard for such emergencies, when they were hauling U.S. mail?

Instead of waiting for a hero to appear, Ryder continued on his slow way toward the steamer's bow, staying below the gunwale as he crawled along on hands and knees. The deck was clear now, as other passengers had ducked into companionways or fled back to their cabins. He supposed they meant to hide out if the *Southern Belle* was overrun, a sign that fear had robbed them of their basic common sense.

If pirates took the steamer, they'd be going door to door in search of plunder, maybe killing as they went. He didn't like the women's chances of remaining unmolested, thinking some of them might be hauled off as hostages or worse. He didn't know of any slavery per se remaining in the world, but chivalry and pirates didn't go together in his mind, either. Ryder imagined females being used, then tossed over the side to rid the *Revenant's* rough crew of witnesses, wherever they were going next.

Unless he stopped them here and now.

The next time Ryder risked a look over the rail, the *Revenant* seemed to be losing speed, letting the *Southern Belle* pull out ahead. It made no sense, until he saw a clutch of half a dozen pirates at the clipper's stern, manhandling a pair of wooden beams they'd propped across its starboard rail. He took another moment, putting it together, then saw that they meant to jam the steamer's paddle-wheel if they could manage it.

He risked a rifle shot from where he was but missed, and the returning storm of pistol fire drove Ryder back below the gunwale. All that he could think of now was getting to the pilothouse, to warn the steamer's captain and avert what might be crippling damage to the *Southern Belle*.

But that meant leaving cover for a spring up narrow stairs, exposed in daylight to the shooters on the *Revenant*. Ryder supposed the run up to the bridge would take a minute, maybe two, in normal circumstances, but he couldn't outrun bullets on the best day that he'd ever had. Granted, the pirates hadn't shown much skill at marksmanship so far, but any hit at all—even an accidental one—could finish him.

Or, he could wait right where he was, until they jammed the paddle-wheel, then poured over the rail in strength.

No choice, really, at all.

Ryder was up and running in another heartbeat, half crouched, with his shoulders hunched in grim anticipation of a hot slug in the back. The pirates poured it on, but they were either hasty shots or poor ones, peppering the *Southern Belle*'s bulkhead but doing poorly with a moving target. Even so, as Ryder reached the stairs—or "ladder," as the sailors called it—rising to the wheelhouse, he was sure that he had stretched his luck beyond the breaking point.

Somehow, he made it to the bridge without taking a hit. The port side door was closed, but opened to his touch. Slipping inside, he ducked again as gunfire smashed the window to his left, glass flying everywhere.

Ryder had glimpsed the steamboat's captain from a distance, several times during their voyage, and had been impressed with both his size and his demeanor. Six foot four or five in height, and barrel-chested, graying hair and beard to match. He hardly looked the part of a commander now, as Ryder found him on one knee behind the steamer's large spoked steering wheel, cringing from bullets as they whistled overhead.

Seeing Ryder with his rifle on the bridge, the captain closed his eyes, clung to the wheel, and said, "All right, then. Shoot! You may as well."

Ryder crouched down beside him, saying, "Listen, Captain! I'm one of your passengers. You probably have pirates on the *Belle* by now, and they're about to jam the paddlewheel."

"We're finished, then," the captain told him, bitterly. "My crew's not worth a damn for fighting. In the old days—"

"Can you get more speed out of the engines?" Ryder interrupted him.

"Maybe a knot or two."

"What's that mean?"

"It's a measurement of—"

"Never mind. Do what you can. I'll try to hold them off." Retreating toward the open wheelhouse door, he paused and added, "If you get a chance, why don't you ram the bastards."

"Dangerous," the captain said.

"You think we're not in danger now?"

Gunfire was crackling from the *Revenant* as he emerged, the pistols' popping punctuated by a shotgun blast. From his position at the apex of the steamer's superstructure, Ryder had a clear view of the pirate clipper and its men still laboring to jam the larger vessel's paddle-wheel with wooden beams, her captain shouting orders at them from the bridge. Although exposed to gunfire from below, he paused to aim his Henry down the full length of the *Southern Belle* and triggered two quick shots in the direction of the wrecking crew.

One found its mark and dropped a pirate twitching to the deck. Without him, two more who'd been helping aim one of the long beams toward the steamer's paddle-wheel were thrown off balance, lost their grip, and watched it tip over the gunwale, gone.

Which just left one.

Unfortunately, shooters on the *Revenant* had Ryder spotted now, and they were pouring on the pistol fire. Their aim had not improved, but they came close enough to make him drop and crawl along the deck, working his slow way toward the stern. Beneath him, Ryder felt the steamboat shudder as it put on extra speed, but he had no idea if it would be enough.

And there *were* pirates on the paddle-wheeler now. He heard them calling back and forth to one another from the main deck, mostly cursing, while a woman screamed somewhere below him, toward the stern. It set his teeth on edge, but Ryder knew there were too many passengers aboard the *Southern Belle* for him to help them individually. His first priority was making sure the pirates didn't stop the *Belle* dead in the water, where it would be easy prey.

And that was proving difficult enough.

In fact, he thought, it might turn out to be impossible.

Throughout his tenure with the U.S. Marshals Service, Ryder had been called upon to fire his pistol only once. As luck would have it, that event had ended his career—and, indirectly, placed him in his current life-or-death predicament. He wasn't squeamish when it came to shooting, but he'd never pictured holding off an army, either.

Or, was this part of a navy?

Either way, quick action was required, or he was sunk.

When he had crawled approximately half the steamer's length, Ryder popped up again and risked another glance in the direction of the stern. All five remaining pirates there were grappling with the one remaining spar, trying to jam the churning paddle-wheel, but its ungainly length and weight was stalling them. Before their shipmates had another chance to spot him, Ryder raised the Henry rifle to his shoulder, sighting down its twenty-four-inch barrel toward the clipper's stern.

His first shot drilled one of the pirates closest to the rail, pitching him forward so his body fell across the beam, adding more weight as his supporting grip was lost. His next round hit the crewman bracing up the butt end of the spar and sent him tumbling to the deck. Before Ryder could fire again, the other three gave up and scampered off in search of cover, while the beam slid overboard.

One problem down, but now the pistoleers were after him again, slugs hammering the steamer's woodwork all around him. Ryder ducked into a nearby passageway that ran from port to starboard and descended to the middle deck from there, safe for the moment with the full bulk of the *Southern Belle* between the pirates and himself. As for the boarders from the *Revenant,* he'd have to hunt them down and deal with them as best he could.

And it appeared that he'd be doing it alone.

Ryder heard shouts, screams, crashing sounds as cabins were invaded, raiders kicking in the doors. He ran in that direction, through another passageway to reach the port side of the boat, nearer the *Revenant.* Halfway along, another figure blocked the daylight at the far end of the passageway— a burly, bearded man with a revolver in his hand, aimed straight at Ryder's face.

The shooter pulled his trigger, and the pistol's hammer fell with a resounding *snap.*

Misfire!

Ryder bellowed and charged him, swung the Henry's butt

into the big man's groin and heard the air evacuate his lungs as he hunched over, clutching at himself. Ryder's momentum carried both of them along the short remainder of the passageway and to the steamer's railing, where a final shove was all it took to roll the pirate overboard.

Shark bait? It didn't matter, just so long as he was gone.

Close to the *Revenant* again, Ryder took cover at the gunwale and began to rapid-fire across the rail, spraying the clipper's deck with lead. He hit one of the crewmen, likely not a fatal wound, and saw more of them dive for cover. From the bridge, one of the crew—maybe the man in charge—was shouting to be heard over the sharp reports of gunfire, calling to the members of his boarding party.

"Ahoy! Belay the boarding! All hands back to me!"

Ryder supposed he could have shot the man, captain or not, but let him keep on bawling orders as a couple of the men who'd come aboard the *Southern Belle* leaped back in the direction of the *Revenant*. One made it, rolling nimbly on the weather deck and springing to his feet among his shipmates, but the other timed his jump poorly, his face smacking the clipper's rail before he dropped into the water, quickly sinking out of sight.

The *Revenant* was veering off to westward now, frustrated crewmen loosing off a blaze of parting shots, but in another moment they were out of range, tacking southeastward toward the Keys, or maybe Cuba, farther on. Ryder was glad to watch them go, until he heard a growling sound behind him, and a woman's gasp.

Irene McGowan stood before him, trembling in the grasp of a straggler who'd missed his ride home. The pirate was bald, with skin like tanned leather, a thick blond mustache masking lips like a slash in his face. Those lips were drawn back in a snarl now, as he held a Bowie knife to Irene's throat.

"George, please!" she said.

"George, *please,*" the pirate mimicked her. Then, with a glance to sea, he growled, "The hell are they goin' without me?"

"Looks like you missed the boat," Ryder replied.

"Screw that. You're putting me ashore."

"Do I look like the captain?"

"You look like the guy who's gonna tell him what I need."

"Or, what?"

"Or you can see this little piece without a head. How's that?"

Instead of budging, Ryder raised the Henry to his shoulder, sighting on the pirate's face. "How do you see that working out for you?" he asked.

"I mean it, boy! If you don't think—"

The Henry spoke, and he was gone, a dead weight sprawling on the deck behind Irene. She screamed, and might have fallen to the deck if Ryder had not closed the gap between them, taking her into his arms. He felt her shivering against him, weeping as she spoke.

"My God, he . . . You . . . How did you . . . ?"

Lucky shot, he thought. But said, "You're safe now, let it go."

It wouldn't be that simple, he imagined, but the *Revenant* was nearly out of sight, soon to be lost among the Keys. All that remained aboard the *Southern Belle* was dealing with the wounded and the dead.

The captain—Angus Gleason, Ryder learned, from chatter overheard in passing—pulled himself together before coming down to deal with his excited, frightened passengers. A quick search of the steamer, carried out by crewmen who had disappeared during the fight, revealed no living pirates left on board. Three corpses were recovered, two male passengers and Ryder's kill, all stowed together in the *Southern Belle*'s cold room pending arrival at Tampa, some nineteen hours hence. Ryder helped wrap them in tarpaulin, bound with heavy twine, and made sure they were separated from the steamer's stock of meat and vegetables.

When that was done, life on the *Southern Belle* returned to normal, more or less. One of the passengers who'd died was traveling alone, no one to mourn him on the steamer, but the other one had been a married man. His widow shut herself inside her cabin, telling anyone who tried to talk her out that they could go to hell or she would see them in St. Pete. Among the other passengers, some five or six had minor injuries, small cuts and bruises suffered when the pirates came aboard. The captain's worry, now, appeared to be that they might sue the Leary Line, and he was circulating in a bid to charm them out of it.

Retreating to his cabin, Ryder cleaned the Henry and returned the rifle to its leather case. The busy work permitted him to ponder what had happened, wondering if he should take it as an omen for the job he'd been assigned in Galveston. That was a stretch, he realized, but when was the last time he'd even thought of pirates, prior to being given his assignment by Director Wood? Sometime in childhood, probably, never believing that they still existed in the flesh.

Maybe it was true, he thought, that wonders never cease.

But linking the attack to Bryan Marley, still some seven hundred miles and forty hours distant, with the stop-off at Tampa, was stretching things too far. Even supposing that he dealt with pirates roaming through the Keys, that didn't mean he knew about specific raids they staged on coastal shipping. And he obviously couldn't know that Ryder had been sent to find him, traveling under an alias.

Unless there was a spy at Treasury.

Ridiculous.

Even if Marley had a spy inside the Secret Service, newly formed in Washington, willing to tip him off, how would he get the news in time to mount a raid against the *Southern Belle*? And would he waste that kind of energy, trying to reach a single passenger among the several hundred traveling aboard the paddle-wheeler, without knowing who he was or even what he looked like?

No. The very thought was foolish.

His stomach growled, reminding him of how long it had been since breakfast. Ryder checked his pocket watch and saw he'd have to wait another hour until lunch was served, assuming that the dining hall opened on time.

At least the battle had not killed his appetite. In fact, the only thing he felt, aside from hunger, was relief at having come out of the scrape alive and well. Did that make him unusual, somehow? Should he be suffering from guilt? If so, for what?

A sudden muffled rapping on his cabin door brought Ryder's right hand to his holstered Army Colt. He rose, leaving his bunk, and crossed the narrow space, standing to one side of the door. No point in taking chances, just in case.

"Who is it?"

"George?"

Irene.

He opened up. She had changed clothes since Ryder saw her last, with pirate's blood spattered across the bodice of her dress, but still looked flustered. Glancing down, she saw the pistol on his belt and asked, "More trouble?"

"Nope. Just haven't packed it up. Are you okay?"

"I think so. Shaky, but he didn't hurt me. Thanks to you."

"My pleasure."

"While I was changing, it occurred to me," she said. "I never thanked you."

"You just did."

"No, I mean properly."

"Not necessary," Ryder told her. "Anybody would have done it."

"No one did. Just you. May I come in?"

"Come in?"

She blushed. "Rather than standing in the hall."

"Oh, sure." He stood aside to let her pass. "There's barely space to turn around."

"I'm sure it's big enough," she said, closing the door behind her. Then, a breathless tone, "Turn me around, if that's your pleasure, George."

"My pleasure?" Ryder felt the words catch in his throat.

"It's only fair," Irene replied. "I would be dead now, if it weren't for you."

"Well, I—"

She stepped in close to him and smothered Ryder's answer with a kiss, then whispered, as it broke, "The hero claims his prize."

Hero? Ryder would probably have laughed at that, in other circumstances, but her lips and hands distracted him. *Why not?* he asked himself.

And once again, before they started grappling with each other's clothes. *Why not?*

6

★ They tried to be discreet. Over the best part of their final day and night together on the *Southern Belle*, mealtimes aside, they stayed in Ryder's cabin or Irene's, dividing their time between bedrooms afloat, watching out for other passengers in transit as if they were spies engaged on some perilous mission behind hostile lines. In Ryder's case, that would soon be a fact, but for the moment he enjoyed the playful intrigue, slipping in and out of rooms, scuttling down passageways, pretending to meet accidentally in the dining hall.

It ended on arrival at Tampa, tucked away at the northern end of a bay that shared its name. It didn't look like much from shipboard, still recovering from multiple engagements in the recent war and rife with yellow fever, as Irene described it. Eight hundred people, more or less, trying to build the settlement back up to something like its antebellum size. When Ryder asked why she was bothering to go there in the first place, she'd described an ailing, widowed sister with two children to support, and he had let it go. There was no arguing with family.

They parted with a chaste handshake as Irene went ashore, the tone of her good-bye communicating a regret that Ryder shared. Once she was gone, though, he returned his focus to the task ahead of him, preparing for his debut on a stage where actors who forgot their lines could wind up dead.

It was another seven hundred miles to Galveston, his last day and a half aboard the *Southern Belle*. After their run-in with the pirates, Captain Gleason kept the steamer fairly close to shore, although it did not seem to Ryder that the wild coast they were passing offered much in terms of sanctuary if they were attacked a second time. Some of it looked like jungle, from the tales he'd read of Africa, but most of it was scrub land, spiky with palmettos. All of it seemed inhospitable to Ryder, causing him to wonder if the former Rebel state had any value other than its ports on the Atlantic side.

Their last stop, on the way to Galveston, was at Biloxi, Mississippi, where they put some mail ashore and took on half a dozen passengers. None went ashore, and Ryder couldn't blame them. Once again, as at Miami, the main feature of the settlement appeared to be its lighthouse, tall and painted white. The stevedores unloading other ships in port were white and black, the work crews strictly segregated, but all labored with the sluggishness of weary men who hated their jobs.

Ryder spent his last full day aboard the *Southern Belle* sleeping and eating. There was nothing more for him to do before he went ashore and tackled his assignment in a nest of smugglers, thieves, and cutthroats. Without knowing when or where he'd sleep next, what the food would be like, or how plentiful, it was the only way that he could think of to prepare.

He had his cover story memorized, such as it was. He'd have to play the rest of it by ear, waiting to see what happened, how accessible his targets proved to be. Marley and Seitz were criminals by trade, which meant they'd be suspicious, maybe quick to take offense, and dangerous if riled. They hadn't earned their present reputation by permitting their competitors to poach on territory marked off as their own.

One false step, Ryder understood, could be his last.

The swamp and jungle vegetation disappeared for good as Mississippi and Louisiana fell behind them, pushing on toward Texas. It looked more like desert then, beyond the beaches, and they saw horsemen occasionally, trooping up and down the shoreline as if on patrol. Ryder had been expecting cattle, but he guessed they kept the beef herds farther inland, where there was something to graze on besides cattails and scrubby brown grass.

Texas was tough. Ryder knew that without having been there before, from what he had read in the press. During the war, it had supplied the Rebel side with men, horses and cattle, until Union forces seized control of the Mississippi River in 1863. Even then, no Texas territory had been conquered by the bluecoats at war's end, and the conflict's last major battle had been fought at someplace called Palmito Ranch, at the farthest southern tip of Texas, a full month after General Lee surrendered at Appomattox. Ryder had a feeling that the Texans who had fought for slavery were not about to change their attitude and welcome Union troops into their state with open arms.

Not my problem, he decided, as the steamer's whistle

signaled their approach to port. He was an outlaw now, for all intents and purposes. He ought to fit right in with the unruly citizens of Galveston.

Ryder was packed and ready as the *Southern Belle* prepared to dock. He left his little cabin and its memories, carried his portmanteau and rifle case on deck, and got in line to disembark. There was no system to it, simply waiting for the hawser lines to be secured, the gangplank to be lowered. First-class passengers, he found, had no priority in line to go ashore, though chivalry persisted in allowing ladies extra elbow room.

Ryder was pleased to have his feet on solid ground again, the first time since Key West. He had not helped unload the bodies they'd deposited at Tampa, thinking that it might be out of character and that he'd done enough, adding a pirate to the butcher's bill. Now, as he put the *Southern Belle* behind him and became a land lubber once more, it came as a relief.

Whatever happened next, Ryder believed he was prepared.

At least, he'd better be.

The port was similar to all the others he had seen before it, ships tied up to piers, with work gangs loading and unloading cargo. Bales of cotton dominated items being loaded into holds for export, while incoming products, for the most part, were concealed in wooden crates and burlap bags. He saw already how a canny smuggler could disguise a load of contraband as anything from fruit to textiles, leather to machine parts, without tipping Customs to the game.

Especially if Customs had been bribed to look the other way.

Priorities.

The first thing Ryder had to do was send a telegram off to Director Wood in Washington, announcing his arrival on the scene. They'd worked that out ahead of time, avoiding any mention of the Secret Service or the Treasury Department, with the telegram to be delivered at Wood's home. No one who intercepted the short message should be able to divine that George Revere was working for the U.S. government, or that his business on the island was a bit of treachery. For safety's sake, only Director Wood himself knew Ryder's mission and his present whereabouts.

That could be good or bad, depending on how things played out in Galveston, and back in Washington. If anything unfortunate befell his boss, Ryder would find himself cut off from any aid. Conversely, even if he needed help and asked for it, the best that Wood could do was contact local law enforcement officers—who might be working hand in glove with Marley and his gang.

Ryder found a Western Union office near the docks and paid two dollars to dispatch his simple message, stating that he had arrived and was investigating "local opportunities." From there, he went in search of lodging and discovered that the city, with some ten thousand inhabitants, had no shortage of boardinghouses advertising weekly rates with small signs in their parlor windows. Ryder chose a neat two-story place, ten minutes from the waterfront on foot, and paid six dollars in advance for his first week.

Whatever else it might be, Galveston would never be described as cheap.

Ryder had noticed, on his short walk from the docks, that most men whom he passed along the street were wearing pistols. Some carried their guns concealed, barely, in shoulder rigs that bulged beneath their jackets. Many also carried knives of various descriptions, with Bowies and Arkansas toothpicks among the most popular. Pugnacious expressions completed the picture, suggesting a populace primed to fight at the drop of a hat.

The women, he noted, were different and seemed to be divided by class. The respectable sort appeared prim, even dour, and walked in groups of three or more if unaccompanied by men. The freer sort, including some he took for hookers with some free time on their hands, were more likely to sashay through the town alone—or, if in clusters, to be talkative, verging on boisterous.

Around the docks, he'd seen a fair number of black men working, once again in segregated parties. Others visible, along the waterfront, were Mexicans and some he thought were probably Italians, both groups mostly loading or unloading produce. He saw no Indians, but had not been expecting any, figuring that they should be out galloping across the plains somewhere, inland.

As far as smugglers went, for all he knew, half of the people working on the docks could be involved in sneaking contraband past Customs. Ryder harbored no illusions about stopping it, convinced that he would have his hands full with the Marley operation, on its own.

After he acquired his room, unpacked his things and locked the door behind him, Ryder went to see the rest of Galveston. Not all of it—the island sprawled over forty-six square miles—but enough to get a flavor of the place and learn his way around the parts that he supposed would matter to him. First, he visited the Customs house, built in 1830 and briefly pressed into service as the capital of Texas six years later, when Anglo Rebels threw off Mexican rule. The present version, all red brick and white Greek columns, had been finished right around the time that Texas had seceded from the Union. Now, with the wartime blockade a fading memory, it was a busy place, men coming and going with serious faces and money in hand.

This was the public face of Galveston, or one of them. It symbolized the kind of commerce states were proud of, business of the sort that built a civilized society with rules and regulations equally applied to all—at least, in theory. He noted that the faces trooping in and out were uniformly white, well fed, and more or less well groomed. A line was clearly drawn between the affluent and those who did their bidding on the waterfront, on fishing boats, or further inland, tilling fields.

The city had another face, as well, of greater interest to Ryder as he prowled its streets. There was another Galveston, deliberately overlooked by those who called the shots except when pleasure or another kind of commerce took then out of offices and homes to areas where the respectable were ill at ease.

The kind of place where he might find a smuggler's den to penetrate, and see what happened next.

There was no end of seedy bars, brothels, and gambling dens in Galveston. Most places Ryder visited combined the functions of all three, with liquor, women, and assorted games of chance beneath a single sagging roof. Most of the customers appeared to be seafaring men, though Ryder also saw a few who had the look of trail-worn cowboys, down at heels and wearing looks that said they wouldn't mind a fight. In fact, he witnessed brawls at two of the saloons he visited, with knives drawn in the second melee and at least one of the five or six combatants badly wounded. None of it appeared to faze the tipsy spectators, much less the hulking bouncers who moved in to pummel all concerned with fine impartiality.

It was a different world from Washington—which had its fair share of debauchery, as Ryder could attest from personal experience. In Galveston, the vice was on display like notions in a dry-goods store, for anyone to pick his poison. So far, other than some Customs agents at the waterfront, Ryder had seen no law enforcement officers in town, though logic told him there must be some, somewhere on the island. If so, it seemed that they were disinclined to interrupt the night's festivities, even when blood was spilled.

What did it take to get locked up in Galveston? If he was forced to test the boundaries, he would have liked to know the rules, but maybe that was something best learned as he went along.

One thing he learned, and quickly, was that even human frailty recognized a color line in Galveston. There were no posted signs, as far as he could see, but figured out by trial and error that the races did not mix where drinking, wagering, and whoring were concerned. The sole exception to that rule, in three of the establishments he briefly patronized, was the inclusion of black women on the menu for their upstairs cribs. Beyond that, Ryder got the feeling that if he entered a bar reserved for blacks or Mexicans, he might be lucky to come out alive. The same, he guessed, was true for any colored man who had a suicidal urge to drink with whites.

Since he was working and not celebrating, Ryder kept his drinking to a minimum while touring the saloons. He had to buy a beer, at least, to hang around and scan the crowds for someone matching the descriptions he'd received in Washington of Bryan Marley and his crony, Otto Seitz.

There were no photographs available of either man, but sketches and descriptions on a couple of old wanted posters were better than nothing. Marley was approximately six feet tall, around two hundred pounds, with handsome chiseled features under an unruly shock of dark brown hair, distinguished by a scar along the left side or his jaw. Seitz was a smaller man, five-eight or -nine, balding and bearded, with a nose that had been broken more than once. No other scars distinguished him, but he was said to have a tattoo of an eagle on his chest, if seen undressed.

No, thank you, Ryder thought. He'd stake his hopes on Marley's scar and Seitz's shiny scalp, if it was all the same.

Of course, he'd known it wouldn't be that easy when he got down to it. Once he started on his rounds, it seemed that every second man he saw was scarred in some way, many of them balding, and most had cultivated facial hair of some description. Even those without obvious weapons on display looked dangerous. Their boozy laughter sounded like the baying of a wild dog pack.

Ryder had spent enough time in saloons to know that bartenders and bouncers knew their customers. In Galveston, with ships arriving and departing all the time, the clientele would be more fluid, but quickest way to put himself at risk would be to show up out of nowhere, asking questions about someone well known on the island as a smuggler. That approach could land him gutted in an alley, and since Ryder did not plan to end his days in Galveston if he could help it, he'd decided on another course of action.

First, survey the territory and discover which saloons attracted customers most likely to engage in smuggling and related violations of the law, versus the normal sailors on a binge before they put to sea again. Once he had narrowed down the field, Ryder could introduce himself under his George Revere alias, planting the word that he was in that line of trade himself, open to any business opportunities.

that might arise. From there, with any luck, he would slip into Marley's orbit, find some menial position with his crew, and try to work his way up through the ranks.

Simple, until it came to execution. Ryder took for granted that his targets must have friends *and* enemies in Galveston, where one wrong move to either side would be enough to get him killed. Reconnaissance came first, watching and listening until he had a feel for how the island town did business. Beyond that, it would be a game of calculated risks.

And something else to think about, while he was sizing up the city: smugglers, by the very nature of their trade, could not spend all their time in port. They would be on the move, collecting contraband. It could be days, or even weeks, before he stumbled over Bryan Marley by pure luck. Ryder had thought of certain ways to cut that time, but first he had to do the necessary groundwork, build himself up with the locals as someone worthy of meeting Marley in the flesh.

All that, and somehow manage not to draw attention from the smuggler's adversaries, who might want to cut his throat just for the hell of it.

It was enough to drive a man to drink.

Ryder had set himself a goal of ten saloons, nursing a beer in each and leaving several barely touched to keep his wits about him, as he scrutinized the customers without being conspicuous. Each place had managed to adopt a flavor of its own, with several trying variations on a nautical motif, from nets and harpoons on the walls to one with gaping shark jaws mounted all around the main barroom like empty picture frames with fangs. One featured a suspicious-looking mermaid on the bar, under a dome of glass, perhaps twelve inches long and shriveled like a corpse left too long in the desert sun. It had a face of sorts, like none Ryder had seen before, and could have been a fish or some monstrosity coughed up by Davy Jones.

It made his skin crawl, either way.

One thing the barrooms had in common was a thick haze of tobacco smoke that clung to Ryder's clothes and nearly made his eyes tear up. He'd never caught the smoking habit, but abstention placed him in a small minority among the boozers he had seen so far in Galveston. Another common feature, gambling, was displayed in permutations ranging from the standard dice and faro games to something known as keno, where the players marked five numbers on a printed card, then waited while a barker spun a cage atop the bar, extracting numbered wooden balls. Another smoky den encouraged wagering on feats of strength, chiefly arm wrestling. In yet another, drinkers bet their money on a fight between a scorpion and a tarantula, penned up together in a cardboard box.

Ryder was on his ninth saloon, feeling the hour and the beer he'd drunk, when he spied Bryan Marley on the far side of the room. He wasn't sure at first, just registered a dark-haired man fitting the general description he'd received, and made his slow way through the press of bodies until he could get a closer look. The man—Marley, or someone else—was sitting with three others at a table, near the west end of the bar as oriented from the entrance, pouring shots of liquor from a dark unlabeled bottle, laughing at some story one of them had told.

From fifteen feet, risking a glance in their direction, Ryder glimpsed a scar along the tall man's jaw line, on the left. Better, but still not good enough. He waited, sipping stale, flat beer, until one of the others at the table tugged the scarred man's sleeve and called him Bryan, then leaned in to ask a question Ryder didn't catch.

A lucky turn—but what came next? Approaching Marley where he was, with friends around him, was a losing proposition. Hasty action would not aid his cause and was more likely to rebound against him. It was better, Ryder thought, to wait and watch, eavesdrop a bit if he could get away with it, and maybe follow Marley when he left the bar if that was feasible.

If not, at least he'd found a place where Marley liked to spend his time and money. Ryder couldn't say he was a regular, for sure, but once he had a starting place . . .

Behind him, at the table, Marley told the others he was leaving. Ryder left some money on the bar and made his own way toward the exit, careful not to look and see if any of the others rose with Marley. Outside, on the sagging sidewalk, Ryder drifted to his left and ducked into the deeper shadows of an alleyway that hid him while he watched the door for Marley to appear.

His man came out alone, looking around, and struck a match to light the stub of a cigar protruding from his mouth. When it was going to his satisfaction, Marley stood and smoked awhile, then turned away from Ryder, moving west along the sidewalk with a sailor's rolling gait. Ryder gave him a half block's lead, then left the alley and began to follow Marley on his way.

To where?

It hardly mattered. Any information he could gather on the man, at this point, would be useful. Best of all would be his home address. Beyond that, Ryder thought, he'd take whatever he could get.

They had covered three long blocks, with Ryder hanging

well back from his quarry, when it happened. Three men stepped out of an alley, blocking Marley's path, while yet another crossed the street to come around behind him, cutting off retreat. From the expressions on the faces he could see, revealed by lamplight, Ryder guessed they didn't qualify as friends.

He closed the gap, but cautiously, doing his best to keep from clattering along the wooden planks beneath his boots. From forty feet, he picked out terse, determined voices, though he couldn't make much sense of what they said. A challenge, maybe, or an accusation of some kind. Marley stood tall, facing the men in front of him, then glanced over his shoulder at the one standing behind him.

"Only four of you?" he asked them, sounding reasonably calm.

"We reckon it's enough," one of them answered, as he drew a wicked-looking knife.

7

⭐ **R**yder had stopped dead on the sidewalk when the men accosted Marley, hanging back in shadows where no lamplight fell. He had a choice to make, and quickly. Should he intervene or let the confrontation run its course? If Marley died before his eyes, was that the end of his assignment or a complication that diverted him toward other targets? On the moral side, could he stand by and watch a murder, even if the victim was himself a criminal?

Oddly, he found the latter prospect did not tweak his conscience much. There was a class of people, he had found, who lived outside the law and settled their disputes without involving courts and lawyers. Generally, when they killed or maimed each other, it had no more impact on so-called polite society than when he crushed a cockroach. They existed in a world apart, and only when their violence spilled into "better" neighborhoods were any but the most extreme of moralists alarmed.

No, Ryder thought, he *could* stand back and watch a killing, but he worried how it would affect Director Wood's opinion of him, and his service with the agency.

Having decided he must intervene, the question that remained was *how?* He had no time to ponder it and took the only avenue that instantly occurred to him, slumping his head and shoulders, making sure to drag his feet and mutter to himself distractedly as he moved forward, doing his best imitation of a drunkard.

They were bound to see him, three of Marley's adversaries facing the direction Ryder came from, but they did not seem to notice him at once. He overheard a bit more of their conversation as he lurched and staggered toward them, tilting like a sailor on a storm-tossed deck.

"You had your chance to quit," one of the ambush party said.

"I didn't feel like leaving," Marley answered.

"Well, you're—what'n hell is this, now?"

So they'd spotted him. Ryder lifted his head, eyes narrowed down to slits, wearing a loose, lopsided smile. "Evenin', gents," he slurred. "Nice night for it."

All of them were watching his approach now, Bryan Marley likely wondering if the distraction could be useful, maybe even his salvation.

"Just a sot," the man nearest to Ryder told his three companions. "I'll get rid of him."

Ryder met him halfway, stumbling on his last step so the thug would either have to catch him or jump back and let him fall. Instinctively, the burly man reached out to grasp Ryder with knobby-knuckled hands, his face a mask of pure contempt.

Ryder let his momentum carry him, driving his right

forearm into the stranger's mug. He felt the nose crack, heard the shout of pain, then brought his right knee up into his target's groin with crushing force. The shout became a wheeze, his interceptor doubling over, dropping to his knees, and vomiting across the wooden planks. To keep him there, Ryder hauled back and kicked him in the face.

Marley was lashing out by then, himself, punching the nearest of his enemies with force enough to stagger him. The other two leaped in immediately, flashing knives, but Marley managed to avoid their blades, hopping away from them and off the sidewalk, to the unpaved street. One of them followed him, still swiping at him with his long knife, while the other turned toward Ryder.

"Don't know who you are," he said, advancing, "but I'm gonna gut you like a tarpon."

Ryder scuttled backward, gave himself some room, and drew his Colt Army. "I'd think about that twice, if I were you," he said.

The bruiser thought about it for a second, made his choice, and cocked his arm as if to throw the knife. Before he had a chance to follow through, Ryder lunged forward, pistol-whipping him across the face. It staggered his opponent, drawing blood, and Ryder struck again immediately, kicking at his enemy's right knee, buckling the leg. As he collapsed, Ryder stepped in and brought a boot down on his knife hand, crushing it, then bent down to relieve him of the dagger.

Marley was dodging, feinting with his last standing assailant, parrying the brawler's quick thrusts with a knife he'd drawn from somewhere underneath his coat. Steel clanged as blades collided, both men ducking, circling, as if they were used to fighting for their lives. The strange part, from the look on Marley's face, was that he seemed to be enjoying it.

Until the odds shifted against him, anyway.

The slugger he'd knocked down a moment earlier was rising, groggy but determined not to miss the action's finish. Ryder moved around the dancing duelists, closing in to meet the odd man out. Distracted, turning toward the interloper he had never seen before tonight, the ruffian stooped to retrieve his fallen knife.

And it was Ryder's turn to try a throw, although he'd never practiced it. Holding his borrowed dagger by the blade, he put his weight behind the pitch with no idea which end would hit his target, if it struck at all. In fact, the pommel smacked into his adversary's forehead with sufficient force to pitch him over backward, sprawling empty handed in the street.

An anguished cry behind him suddenly demanded Ryder's full attention. Turning, he found Marley in a clinch with his would-be assassin, both men standing rigid for a moment in the lamplight. Marley pushed away a moment later, gave his dirk a sideways flick to clear its blade of blood, and watched the man he'd stabbed collapse facedown.

"Well, now," he said to Ryder. "I suppose you'd better tell me who you are, or maybe use that Colt."

"You want to talk about it here? Right now?" Ryder inquired.

Marley considered it, surveyed the scattered bodies of his enemies, and said, "All right. Put up the gun and come with me."

Ryder holstered his Colt and fell in step beside the man he'd traveled some twenty-three hundred miles to find. Marley seemed perfectly relaxed, now that the skirmish was behind him, but he kept an eye on Ryder all the same.

"George Revere," said Ryder, when they'd covered half a block and turned a corner, with their fallen adversaries out of sight. "And you are . . . ?"

"Bryan Marley. You aren't drunk at all, I take it?"

"Thought I'd have a better chance to get in close," said Ryder, "if they didn't take me seriously."

"Right. And why'd you bother?"

"As opposed to watching you get killed, you mean?"

"Or turning back and going on about your business. It's what I'd have done."

"You have a funny way of saying thank you, Mr. Marley."

"Make it 'Bryan,' since you saved my skin. Same question: why?"

"I might have watched you fight with one, or even two. The four of them, I guess it just seemed wrong to me."

"Felt wrong enough to risk your life?"

"Maybe I didn't think it through."

"We haven't met before," said Marley. Not a question.

"No."

"You don't sound much like Galveston."

"I move around a lot," said Ryder.

"Doing what, if you don't mind my asking?"

"This and that. I move commodities from here to there."

"Commodities. What kind?"

"Whatever's in demand. Man has to make a living."

"True. I've done a bit of that myself," Marley replied.

"And made some enemies along the way, I guess."

"Competitors. Some take it worse than others when you top them on a deal."

"Apparently."

"So, thank you."

"Welcome."

"Since we both agree you're sober, could you stand a drink?"

"I wouldn't mind."

"You ever been to Awful Annie's?"

"Haven't had the pleasure," Ryder said.

"Some might not call it pleasure," Marley told him, "but the Menefees won't find us there."

"The Menefees?"

"Our sparring partners. There are more than four of 'em."

"I see."

"The good news is, they won't know who you are if you're just new in town."

"My lucky day."

"The bad news is, the ones we didn't kill will recognize you next time."

"Ah."

"You might consider getting out of town."

"I just got in today."

"Like what you've seen so far?" asked Marley.

"I've seen worse."

"Moving commodities."

"You never know where you'll end up."

"Ain't that the truth."

"This place we're going—"

"Awful Annie's."

"Right. Is it much farther?"

"Two blocks, give or take."

"It's a saloon?"

"They sell a bit of everything."

"That's handy."

"Can be, if you know the management."

"And you do."

"Pretty well. It's like my second home."

Ryder refrained from asking where his first home was. Too much, too soon.

"And here we are," said Marley, as they neared a

three-story ramshackle building with a tavern on its ground floor, music from a trumpet and piano blaring past its bat-wing doors into the street. There was no sign announcing Awful Annie's, maybe something that you had to know before approaching the anonymous establishment.

Marley pushed through the swinging doors and Ryder followed him inside.

Another crowded, smoky room. As *awful* went, it didn't seem much worse than any other place Ryder had visited so far in Galveston. In fact, he might have said the painted women circulating through the room, some perched on knees or hanging over gamblers' shoulders, were younger and marginally more attractive than those who'd been work-ing the saloon where he first spotted Bryan Marley.

He was trailing Marley toward the bar when someone shouted, "There's the boy himself!" and shouldered through the crush to intercept them. Balding and bearded, flat-nosed. Ryder couldn't see his chest, but he assumed that this was Otto Seitz.

Marley confirmed it when he spoke, saying, "I see you're nice and comfortable, Otto. I could've used your help tonight. More trouble with the Menefees."

Seitz glowered. "You're okay, though?"

"Thanks to George, here," Marley said, cocking a thumb over his shoulder.

Seitz appeared to notice Ryder for the first time, narrow-ing his eyes. "George, is it? Got another name to go with that?"

"Revere," Ryder replied. "No kin to Paul."

"Huh?"

"Never mind."

Seitz shifted his attention back to Marley. "So, what happened?"

"Hunsaker and Sloan were waiting for me outside Jenny's, with a couple others. Thought they might filet me."

"But you beat 'em."

"*We* did," Marley said, tipping a nod toward Ryder. "If he hadn't happened by, you just might be in charge."

Seitz turned his gimlet gaze on Ryder once again. "Awright, so he's a Good Samaritan. Now he can—"

"Stay right here and have a drink or three," said Marley, interrupting his lieutenant. "Right, Otto?"

Before Seitz had a chance to answer, someone shouted Marley's name out in a brassy voice and Ryder saw a woman of astounding girth approaching them, plowing ahead and jostling anyone who blocked her path without a semblance of apology. She must have weighed three hundred pounds, confined after a fashion by a larger version of the outfits worn by other women prowling the saloon. Her face was painted garishly, with bright rouge on her cheeks and kohl smudging her eyelids under reddish hair piled high and spiked with feathers.

"Annie," Marley said as she embraced him.

Riddle solved.

"You've been a stranger lately," Awful Annie chided, as they disengaged.

"Been keeping busy," Marley said, by way of an excuse.

"And raising Cain, from what I hear?"

"Who from?" asked Marley.

"Oh, the usual."

"Uh-huh."

She looked past Marley now, toward Ryder, asking, "Who's your handsome friend?"

"Annie, meet George Revere. He pulled my fat out of the fire tonight."

"My girls tell me there ain't an ounce o' fat on you," the lady of the house replied. "Though I have yet to find out for myself." She winked at Marley, then reached out for Ryder. "Welcome, George. I hope you'll make yourself at home."

Ryder was reaching for her hand when she enfolded him with stout arms, crushing him against her more than ample breasts. The hug was brief but powerful, leaving him close to breathless when she pushed away.

"You'll want the usual, I guess?" she said to Marley.

"Maybe just a quiet corner, first," he told her.

"Quiet's hard to come by, but you want to use the room in back, it's free."

"Appreciate it, Annie."

Marley led the way, Seitz making sure he got between his boss and Ryder, giving no sign that he meant to shed the sour face. Before they reached the back room, three more men had fallen into step with them, all peering curiously at the stranger in their midst.

Annie was right about the room. It offered privacy, once Marley shut the door, but music from the main barroom was only muffled by its walls, and Ryder heard a bedstead creaking rhythmically above them, from the second floor.

Another job well done.

When they were settled at a table, whiskey all around, Marley finished off the introductions. Joining him and Seitz were Tommy Rafferty, Ed Parsons, and Joe Wallander. Ryder repeated each new name in turn while shaking callused hands and memorized their rugged faces. Once they'd heard their boss's story, each of them seemed fairly well disposed toward him for helping Marley out of a tight spot.

Except for Otto Seitz. Ryder had worked out for himself

that Marley's second in command would need a better reason to relax his vigilance than Ryder saving Marley's life. He would be one to watch with special care, a wild card in the game they were about to play.

Ryder bolted down a shot of rotgut, trying hard to keep a grimace off his face, as Marley turned to him and said, "So, George. You want a job?"

Ryder tried to keep it casual, pouring another dram of whiskey. "Doing what?

"Are you particular?" asked Marley.

"Not especially."

"I didn't think so. Way you fight and wear that Colt, I figure you've been in your share of scrapes."

"I've been around," Ryder confirmed.

"You wanted anywhere?" asked Seitz.

"That's not polite, Otto," said Marley. "Everyone we know's been wanted somewhere, one time or another."

"Yeah, but if somebody's trackin' him—"

"I'd say he's come to the right place. Where better to get lost than Galveston?"

"If you say so," Seitz groused.

"I do." To Ryder, then: "So, how about it, George?"

"I always need more money," Ryder answered. "Sure. Why not."

"Let's drink to that, and then I've got a little something special for you."

Ryder didn't ask, downing the liquor he had poured himself and letting Marley fill his glass again, before he passed the bottle on to Seitz and it began to make its way around the table. Marley raised his glass and toasted, "Here's to George, for being in the right place at the right time."

Other whiskey voices croaked, "To George," but Otto

Seitz stayed silent, tossing back his shot, eyes fixed on Ryder till it hit his throat and made him wince, despite himself.

Ryder took a moment to recover, making sure he wouldn't wheeze when speaking. "Now, about that job . . ."

"Tomorrow's soon enough," Marley advised him. "Have you got someplace to stay?"

"I booked into a boardinghouse."

"You may not make it back tonight," said Marley, smiling. "Come along and get your present."

She was somewhere in her later teens, a slim brunette, still fresh enough to get along without a pound of war paint on her heart-shaped face. Her name was Nell, and when she smiled Ryder was pleased to find she still had all her teeth.

When Marley introduced them, Nell clasped Ryder's hand in both of hers and stroked his palm while giving him a sultry smile. "Long fingers," she observed.

Ryder could feel the color rising in his cheeks as he replied, "I never thought about it."

"Nell," said Marley, "try and give my friend here something special."

"Everything I got is special," she retorted. "You should know that, Bryan."

"True enough. You two have fun."

That said, Marley retreated toward the bar's back room, while Nell kept hold of Ryder's hand in one of hers and led him toward the stairs. Before they started climbing to the second floor, she paused and rose on tiptoes, whispering into his left ear, "I can't wait to feel those nice long fingers up inside of me."

Ryder had trouble walking up the stairs then, but he made it, trailing Nell along the second-story hallway to the third door on their right. She opened it without a knock and pulled him in behind her, taking care to lock the door when it was closed again.

"Some of the drunks go wandering around," she told him. "We don't want to be disturbed, do we?"

"No, ma'am."

"Oh, it's 'ma'am,' is it? I remind you of your teacher back in school?"

"Not so you'd notice."

"Not your mommy?"

"Definitely not."

"I'm glad to hear it."

Nell's working outfit was a kind of corset that laced up in front, together with a frilly knee-length skirt, dark hose, and high-heeled patent leather boots that added inches to her height. She tugged at one end of the bow securing her corset at the bust line, then glanced down at the lopsided knot and frowned.

"You want to help me out with this?" she asked.

"I wouldn't mind."

"A gentleman."

"I try to be."

"But not *too* gentle, hmm? I guarantee you, it's more fun that way."

When Marley had released the others, Otto cornered him, asking, "What do you know about this guy?"

"I told you. I was cornered and he waded in. I likely wouldn't be here if he hadn't helped me out."

"Convenient, ain't it," Seitz suggested.

"Meaning what?"

"Just when you're in a tight spot, there he is."

"I'm tired," said Marley. "If you've got a point, get to it."

"I just think it's stretching a . . . a . . . damn! A whatchacallit."

"A coincidence?"

"That's it."

Marley appeared to take him seriously, frowning as he asked, "So, you think—what? He works for Menefee?"

"The hell would I know?"

"Because otherwise, it's nothing *but* coincidence, him happening along just when he did."

"Bryan—"

"You heard me say I stuck Bill Hunsaker tonight. He's dead, Otto. You think Jack Menefee would sacrifice his best foot soldier so I'd buy some character a drink?"

"It ain't a drink! You offered him a *job*."

"That's right. I did."

"And I don't think—"

"Remind me who's in charge, Otto."

Seitz swallowed down the first retort that came to mind and said, "You are."

"Because I wasn't sure there, for a second."

"All I'm sayin' is—"

"Enough!" Seitz recognized the tone that brooked no contradiction. Kept his mouth shut tight as Marley finished. "George is with us. If he does his job, so be it. If he doesn't . . . well . . . I'll see you in the morning, Otto."

"Right."

When Marley left, Seitz sat alone in the back room of Awful Annie's, brooding. He could understand the boss feeling a sense of gratitude toward someone who had helped him when his back was up against the wall, but how did that translate to asking someone he had never met before to join their operation? What was Marley thinking, anyhow?

This George Revere was new in town, had never been to

Galveston if you believed his story, and they welcomed him aboard as if they'd all known him for years? It stuck in Otto's craw. Not simple jealousy, he told himself. It was a matter of security for what they'd built up over time, and for the pending operations they were working on.

He went back to the main barroom, made sure Marley was gone, then whistled up Joe Wallander. The big Swede ambled over, with the normal blank expression on his face below a shock of hair so blond that it was almost white. He was a mountain of a man, so muscular it always looked as if he wore his shirts a size too small.

"Step in here for a minute," Otto said and led him back into the private room.

Wallander rarely showed a spark of curiosity, and this was no exception to the rule. He took a seat and poured himself another shot of red-eye without offering to do the same for Seitz, then sipped it, waiting.

"Any thoughts about the new guy?" Seitz inquired.

Wallander shrugged. "He seems all right."

"Judging by what?"

"He gave the boss a hand."

"Did he?"

"You heard what Bryan said."

"Yeah, yeah. But did he *really* help?"

Wallander's pallid eyebrows edged closer together as he frowned. "Hold on. You saying Bryan made it up?"

Seitz shook his head. "I'm sayin' maybe it was too god-damn convenient that this character none of us ever met before just *happens* by and jumps into the middle of a knife fight, buncha total strangers, when the odds are four to one."

"Good thing he did, for Bryan's sake."

"But what if it's a put-up job?"

"What makes you think that?"

"Just a feeling, so far. But I need to check it out."

"Okay."

Wallander rose as if to leave, but Otto caught him by the sleeve. "Hold on. You're helpin' me."

"Do what?"

"Keep track of him. See where he goes and who he talks to."

"Bryan likes him, Otto."

"Makes it easier for him to take advantage."

"And I've got my own work needing to be done."

"This'll pay a bonus. Shadow him tonight, and we can talk about the rest later."

"That's easy. He's upstairs with Nell."

"She never keeps a customer all night. Just find out where he's stayin'. Can you do that much?"

"For twenty in advance."

"Jesus, you Swedes!"

Once Wallander had left with Seitz's money in his pocket, Otto gave some thought to what should happen next. If he looked close enough, he might find something that would sink the new man, or he might not. All that mattered in the long run was the basic rule that Marley had laid down: the new boy had to prove himself before he was accepted as a full-fledged member of the team.

And if he failed?

By that time he would know too much to simply let him walk away.

It would be Otto's mission to ensure that George Revere fell short—and once he started falling, see him tumble all the way to Hell.

8

★ **R**yder walked back through more or less deserted streets at half past one o'clock, to reach his rooming house. Between the street fight, meeting Marley's crew, the alcohol they had consumed, and energetic little Nell, he felt wrung out and capable of sleeping through tomorrow, maybe even the day after.

Not a choice that circumstance was offering.

In parting, Bryan Marley had been vague about their meeting time tomorrow—or *today*, that was—and the arrangements for their get-together. Ryder didn't know if he was meant to rendezvous with Marley and the others back at Awful Annie's or, if so, when he should put in an appearance there. He'd made a start, but that was all. Whatever happened next, he had to gauge the situation as it was developing and keep a sharp eye out for booby traps along the way.

When he had covered roughly half the distance to his rooming house, a scuffling sound behind him interrupted

Ryder's pensive thoughts. Already cloaked in shadow, walking down the east side of a residential street with no lamps burning, Ryder stopped and turned to face the block he'd just traversed. He seemed to be the only person out and moving on the street, but proving that required him to go back and search the darkness for potential hiding spots, a fruitless exercise.

Who might be trailing him? The easy answer would be one of Bryan Marley's crew, whether the boss had ordered it himself or someone from the ranks had chosen to pursue the mission on his own. Nothing Marley had said or done before they parted hinted at suspicion, but he *was* a criminal who'd managed to outwit the law for better than a decade, even while his smuggling activities were recognized. From that record alone, Ryder presumed he was a cautious man who hedged his bets and only took a chance when he believed the odds were in his favor.

Standing in the dark with one hand on his Colt, Ryder breathed slowly, silently, and listened to the night. The sound he'd heard was not repeated, leading him to wonder if he had imagined it. More likely, it had been something pedestrian: a cat seizing a rodent for a midnight snack, or something at a distance, misinterpreted as being close at hand. Despite that rationale, he stood and waited for a full two minutes, staring into shadows his vision could not penetrate, until his eyes began to burn from lack of blinking.

Nothing there, he thought and finally moved on. But for the last five blocks he walked more carefully, took care to make no shuffling noises of his own that might come back to haunt him as an echo. Far off, toward the waterfront, he heard drunkards carousing, scraps of tinny music carried on the breeze. As far as anyone pursuing him, the night was dead and sterile.

He paused once more, outside the rooming house, then took care when he entered, not to rouse the owner or her other guests in residence. A couple of the stairs creaked as he climbed them, but another moment put him in his room and at its window facing on the street. He left the lamp alone and scanned the block as far as he could see, one final check, but he caught no one lurking in the neighborhood.

Stretched out on his bed, the Colt beside him on a chair he had positioned for convenience, Ryder replayed the night's events once more, skipping the interlude with Nell, and found his progress satisfactory so far. It could have taken days to simply locate Marley, but a stroke of luck had placed Ryder inside the smuggler's orbit without any of the convoluted schemes he had considered on the trip from Washington.

Easy? Not yet.

He had contrived an introduction and secured a little trust, but nothing more. Marley's lieutenant, Otto Seitz, had not been welcoming and might turn out to be a problem, but for now, at least he'd found a starting point. Where Ryder went from there depended on his adversaries and his own initiative, his willingness to play the role that was assigned to him.

He had no doubt it would mean wading into dirty work, but that was inescapable. You couldn't penetrate a gang of criminals without becoming one of them. The trick, he thought, was setting limits, drawing lines, and then deciding which were relatively safe to cross in an emergency.

Safe for himself, and for the job at hand.

Still pondering that riddle, Ryder drifted into sleep.

The price of Ryder's room included breakfast. On his first morning in Galveston that wound up being two fried eggs, a biscuit topped with sausage gravy, and a steaming cup of coffee that might well have been the best he'd ever drunk. The food was good and plentiful, preparing him to face the day ahead although he still had no clear notion as to what it held in store for him.

His first surprise occurred when Ryder left the boardinghouse, a little after nine o'clock. A boy was loitering outside, pacing along the curb with hands stuffed in his trouser pockets. Ryder guessed that he was probably eleven, maybe twelve years old, with wild dark hair, a face that needed washing, and a slender frame that hinted at a paltry diet. Spotting Ryder, he stopped pacing and stood close beside the small gate in the rooming house's picket fence.

"Would you be Mr. George Revere?" he asked, as Ryder cleared the gate.

"I would. I am."

The kid's eyes dropped to Ryder's belt, the pistol holstered there, then snapped back to his face. "I got a message for you, from the boss."

"Who's that?" Ryder inquired.

The boy looked back at him as if he'd lost his senses. "Mr. Marley. Who else would it be?"

"Just checking. What's the message?"

"Meet the boss at Awful Annie's. Sundown."

"Nothing else?"

"Not that he tells the likes o' me."

Duty performed, the youth left Ryder, sauntering along the sidewalk in the general direction of the waterfront. He had a certain air about him, strutting like a bad man in the making now that he had taken care of business and was on his own once more.

Ryder dismissed the boy from mind and focused on the more important question—namely, how had Marley tracked him to the boardinghouse when Ryder had not given him the address? He recalled the sound he'd heard the night before, while walking back from Awful Annie's, realizing that he likely had been followed after all.

Good news and bad news mixed together there. The *good* was that he'd done nothing while walking home that should arouse suspicion from whoever shadowed him. The *bad* was that he had not actually caught the watcher, hadn't even glimpsed him, even when a careless scuffing footstep had betrayed the spy.

Ryder decided to brush up on his survival skills. When he had been a U.S. marshal, there'd been times when he was called upon to follow suspects, but he'd never worried much about a felon trailing him. His present job was altogether different, requiring a new level of alertness if he wanted to survive.

Beginning now.

He owed Director Wood another telegram, reporting progress on his mission, and he didn't want a follower from Bryan Marley's crew tagging along to watch him send it. Knowledge that a message had been sent was one short step from learning what it said. A telegram could be diverted, stolen, or the clerk who sent it could be bribed, maybe intimidated, into giving up its contents. Ryder planned to keep his message cryptic, but the very act of visiting the Western Union office might arouse suspicion that he didn't need right now.

Plus, watching for a shadow on his way would be good practice.

And if he discovered one? What then?

That only took a moment to decide. He was supposed to be a criminal, which meant that he would not appreciate a stranger dogging him around the streets of Galveston. He had a role to play, which would include expressing disapproval of such actions in a forceful way.

Of course, the way he handled it—if there was anything to handle—would depend on who was trailing him. If it turned out to be a youngster like his morning messenger, a swift kick in the pants might be sufficient to discourage him. For someone else, like one of Marley's men he'd met the night before, dissuasion would required more energy. More force.

He didn't want a feud with Marley's crew, particularly when he'd just made their acquaintance, but it wouldn't hurt his reputation to be seen as someone with a taste for privacy, who took offense at being placed under surveillance. He might even turn it further to his own advantage, claiming that he thought the shadow was a copper snooping into his affairs.

That prospect put a smile on Ryder's face as he moved off along the street.

It was risky using Western Union at the docks, where Ryder knew he might be spotted by some member of the Marley gang he had not met so far, but he had no alternative. Before proceeding to the waterfront, he spent the best part of an hour roaming aimlessly past shops and offices, ducking down alleyways, watching for anyone who might be trailing him, and came up empty. He spotted no one in the process and could only hope that he'd invested time and energy enough to lose a shadow if there had been one he'd failed to spot.

The Western Union clerk on morning duty was a sickly looking man with sunken cheeks and a mustache that made his mouth appear off-center on his face, somehow. One of his eyes was lower than the other, too, as if his face had once been cut in half and reassembled out of kilter, carelessly. Ryder supposed that was the reason why he didn't smile at customers or hazard any small talk while he took their messages and pocketed their money.

During his maneuvers to avoid pursuit, Ryder had sketched the content of his telegram to Washington. Again, the address for delivery would be Director Wood's home in the capital, and after due consideration, Ryder had reduced the message to its simplest form:

CONTACT ACHIEVED

He signed it *GR*, which could stand for George Revere, and paid the sallow clerk to send it on.

Which left the best part of a day to kill, with no plan for exactly how to spend the time. The one thing Ryder *couldn't* do was loiter around Awful Annie's through the afternoon, assuming that the place was even open during daylight hours. At best, he would seem overeager; at the worst, somebody might suspect that he was prying into gang affairs. In either case, it made a bad beginning to whatever Bryan Marley had in mind for him.

To fill time, Ryder strolled along the waterfront, watching the work gangs loading and unloading ships. If he was seen and questioned later, he could chalk it up to normal curiosity, a smuggler taking stock of operations in an unfamiliar port of call. In fact, he witnessed nothing that aroused his personal suspicion, but the sheer volume of cargo passing in and out of Galveston would tax an honest team of Customs agents to discover any hidden contraband. If they were paid to turn a blind eye on the docks, the possibilities were limitless.

Ryder observed no evidence of payoffs going on, but he had not expected to. If Marley knew his business, he would deal with crooked officers in private, letting one or two distribute money to the rest, without a public assignation to embarrass anyone. And since Ryder had been dispatched to deal with Marley, not investigate the local Customs house, his only interest in local officers lay in avoiding them. If he discovered evidence of bribery, he would report it back to Washington and let somebody else follow that trail.

At noon he stopped for lunch at a restaurant that advertised Acadian cooking, soon identified as a selection of dishes prepared by descendants of French settlers in Louisiana, now transplanted to Texas. He wound up eating jambalaya and a filé gumbo, both of which conspired to set his mouth and throat on fire. As luck would have it, the establishment kept adequate supplies of beer on ice to soothe a scalded palate, and when Ryder left the place an hour later he felt game for anything.

More time to kill, and he employed it at the now familiar game of watching out for anyone who might be trailing him, pretending to examine wares displayed in windows of the shops he passed, using reflections in the glass to check for anyone suspicious in the neighborhood. As afternoon wore on, he gave it up, secure in knowing that the gang members he'd met last night, at least, were not pursuing him. If someone else had taken up the job, it hardly mattered, since they'd catch him doing nothing that was worth reporting back to Marley.

Finally, after a stop for coffee at a small sidewalk café and a detour to one of Galveston's convenient, if unpleasant, public privies, Ryder made his slow way back toward Awful Annie's through the purple shades of dusk.

Otto Seitz was covering the door when Ryder got to the saloon. At sight of him, the bald man grimaced as if he had tasted something sour. "Didn't think you'd make it," he told Ryder.

"Disappointed?"

One side of the smuggler's mouth ticked upward for a beat, before he said, "Back room. The rest are here already."

Ryder led the way, Seitz trailing. Bryan Marley had a dozen men gathered around him in the room they'd occupied last night, most of them smoking. Several, thought Ryder, would have benefited from a bath. Marley shook hands with Ryder, introducing him to those he hadn't met before, while Seitz hung back a bit and practiced glaring from the sidelines.

"Big doings?" Ryder asked, after he'd made the rounds.

"Settling old scores," Marley replied. "Jack Menefee's boys have been stepping on our toes for months. Tonight, we put an end to it."

"These are the ones who tried for you last night?"

"None other. We'll be having the last word this evening."

"Ready for that?" asked Seitz, off to his left.

"O' course he is," Marley replied, before Ryder could speak. "He brought his pistol, didn't he?"

The Colt Army felt heavier, for some reason, once Marley called attention to it. Ryder glanced around the crowded room and saw that all the others present had some kind of weapon tucked into their belts or close at hand. Most carried six-guns, half of them packing knives as well. Three double-barreled shotguns lay at one end of the table where their chief was sketching plans on butcher's paper.

"So, we're here," said Marley, as he drew an X to stand for Awful Annie's on a street he'd represented with a narrow double line. "And this is Gerta's place."

Named for another woman, Ryder noted, which appeared to be a trend in Galveston. Maybe it set a drinking, whoring mood somehow, but that appeared to be superfluous. As far as he could tell, men carried all the weight in Galveston. Except, perhaps, in Awful Annie's case.

"We'll split up when we leave here," Marley told his troops. "Half of you come with me, down Pearl Street. Otto takes the rest on Gem. We'll have them boxed in, front and back. My signal, we bust in and finish it for good."

A question came to Ryder's mind. "All of the people in this Gerta's place belong to Menefee?" he asked.

"There's likely to be other customers," Marley replied.

"Is that a problem, Georgie?" Otto interjected.

"Not for me," said Ryder, "but it strikes me that your sheriff, or whatever kind of law you've got here, might not like us putting ordinary people in the cross fire."

"*Ordinary* people," Seitz repeated, fairly sneering it.

"He's got a point," Marley admitted. "We've got fairly good relations with the coppers and I want to keep it that way. When we go in, spot your marks. We know Jack's plug-uglies by sight. Don't mix 'em up with yokels. And no shooting women."

"What if one of *them* tries shooting *us*?" asked Tommy Rafferty.

"Nobody's saying that you can't defend yourself," Marley replied. "Just do your best. And Jack belongs to me. Any more questions?"

"What about old Gerta?" Seitz inquired.

"Gerta can look out for herself. Let's go."

Marley and Seitz each took a shotgun, Joe Wallander

picking up the third. As they were crowding toward the exit, Otto said, "I'll take the new boy."

"Never mind," Marley replied. "He'll come with me."

On the map Marley had drawn, ten or eleven inches separated Awful Annie's from their target, but in fact, Gerta's saloon was closer to a quarter mile away. Their party, fifteen men in all, split up as soon as they were on the street. Ryder and half a dozen others followed Bryan Marley north on Pearl, while Seitz and his team vanished down an alley on their way to Gem Street and the rear approach.

Ryder was anxious as they moved along the mostly darkened street, wondering how he would acquit himself once battle had been joined. It was a murder party, plain and simple, not the kind of thing that was expected from an agent serving Uncle Sam. But what choice did he have? If he had begged off, any hope of staying close to Marley would have instantly evaporated—and the gang might well have turned on him as a potential witness to their scheme. Why leave him breathing if he wasn't on their side?

Now he was into it, faced with the quandary of how to pull it off and still avoid a charge of homicide that would contaminate whatever evidence he managed to collect and, incidentally, destroy his new career. The best that he could think of was to wait and see what happened once they got to Gerta's place. Protect himself and play the hand that he was dealt.

Gerta's saloon resembled Awful Annie's from the street, three stories tall with clapboard walls and no sign to proclaim its owner's name. Two drunks, unsteady on their feet, were exiting as Marley and his crew approached the swinging doors. One glimpse of all the guns appeared to sober them, and they were running full tilt by the time they reached the next corner, then vanished from sight.

"You think they'll bring the law?" asked Ryder.

"Screw the law," growled Marley, as he pushed in through the flapping doors.

A black pianist with a derby on his head stopped playing as he entered. Conversation dwindled down to nothing in another second, faces at the bar and at a dozen tables turning toward the door in unison. Some of the patrons blanched, cringing, while others scowled and tensed for action. Ryder saw hands slipping out of sight, reaching for weapons.

"We come looking for Jack Menefee and anyone who serves him," Marley told the room at large, raising his voice to make it heard upstairs. "Whoever doesn't fill that bill should get the hell out while you can."

Approximately half of Gerta's customers immediately bolted for the street, past Marley and his men, one of them jostling Ryder as he stood with one hand resting on the curved butt of his Colt. Upstairs, a door banged open on the second-story landing and a tall man with a plume of red hair standing straight up on his head appeared, clad only in long underwear, holding a pistol in each hand.

"Who wants Jack Menefee?" he called down into the saloon.

Marley stepped forward, answering, "You know me, Jack. It's no good playing dumb."

"I wondered when you'd come to see me, Bryan," Menefee replied—then dropped into a crouch behind the landing's rail, his pistols angling in between the balusters. Marley was quicker, squeezing off a shotgun blast, and then all hell broke loose.

Ryder was ducking, dodging, as the room echoed with gunfire, bullets whistling overhead and all around him.

Somewhere on the upper floor, a woman screamed, the sound cut short as if someone had cut it with an ax. Ryder felt a slug pluck at his sleeve before he reached the nearest table, tipped it over on its side, and hunched behind it. Flimsy cover in the middle of a lead storm, but it beat standing exposed with guns firing on every side.

He didn't hear the second party enter from the rear, until Seitz bellowed out some version of a Rebel yell and joined the battle with a vengeance. Ryder raised his head in time to see a blast from Otto's shotgun lift the barman off his feet and send him tumbling through the air, a lifeless straw man. Marley stood amidst the chaos, empty scattergun discarded, Colt in hand, firing methodically at fleeing enemies. Upstairs, Jack Menefee was on his back, one foot protruding through the rail, blood dripping underneath it to the bar below.

Behind Marley, a shambling figure rose up from the floor, one hand clutching a bloody, wounded side. It was the other hand that Ryder focused on, a long curved blade protruding from it, drawn back for a lethal strike. He fired instinctively, no thought behind it, dropping the backstabber with a bullet through his chest. The shot, so near at hand, made Marley flinch and turn. He saw the fallen adversary, glanced at Ryder then, and flashed a dazzling smile before he went back to the fight.

It didn't last much longer. With their chief down, caught up in the cross fire, Menefee's surviving men seized any opportunity to save themselves. Ryder saw two of them reach windows, one escaping in a headlong dive through glass, the other hastened by a bullet in the buttocks as he rolled over the windowsill. No one bothered to chase them, or to finish off the wounded groaning at their feet. Police whistles were shrilling somewhere in the dark, outside, and it was time to go.

Running with Marley, back down Pearl Street, Ryder felt his heart pounding against his ribs. They didn't slow until they'd covered half a dozen blocks and ducked into a side street, huddling there to catch their breath.

"That's twice you've saved my skin," said Marley, from the shadows.

"Seemed the thing to do," Ryder replied. Thinking, *You're no good to me dead.*

At least, not yet.

9

★ **B**ack at Awful Annie's the proprietress broke out champagne to celebrate the raid on Menefee and company, calling her girls downstairs to circulate among the victors if they weren't already serving other paying customers upstairs. Ryder had only tasted champagne once before, at a long-ago wedding reception, and discovered— for the second time—that fizzing bubbles in a glass of wine did nothing to enhance the pleasure he derived from drinking it.

Their triumph over the opposing gang, although complete in Bryan Marley's estimation, had a price attached to it. One of their own—the big Swede, Wallander—had been shot dead and carried off by three of Seitz's raiders for disposal in some place and way that was supposed to keep police from linking anybody else to the attack on Gerta's place. Two other members of the gang had suffered minor wounds and had gone off to see a doctor Marley paid to deal with such emergencies clandestinely. Both hoped to make it back and swill their share of booze before the party finally shut down.

Soon after their return to the saloon, Marley was called upon to eulogize their fallen comrade. While declaring at the onset that he had no gift for "speechifying," he proceeded nonetheless, with glass in hand, to offer the memorial.

"You all knew Joe," he said, while the combatants muttered their assent. "He never feared a man or anything, as far as I could tell. He put his whole heart into anything he did, and that was more than most manage to do. We'll miss him, but he went the way he would have wanted, fighting toe to toe with them that hated him and putting some of them away before they cut him down. God bless 'im, if the Devil hasn't got him yet!"

A cheer went up at that, and there were more drinks all around. Ryder hung back, tried keeping to himself without being standoffish in a way that might offend, sharing the laughs at jokes about how this or that member of Jack Menefee's crew had bled when they were shot or stabbed. It was the kind of talk he'd heard after horse races, sometimes after boxing matches, although spectators at prizefights were more likely to review the action than the battered pugilists themselves. He doubted whether many soldiers in the wake of battle sat around and crowed about their knack for killing, but then again, the draftees from the recent war had not been in the game for sport or profit.

The cops arrived some forty minutes later, after alcohol and Annie's girls had dampened down the first wave of excitement spawned by mortal combat. There were thirteen of them, with a captain in the lead, all looking nervous as they entered Awful Annie's, hands held close to holstered pistols. They were dressed in blue serge uniforms, vaguely resembling Yankee soldiers, but with peaked caps on their heads and badges made of polished brass. As they formed a ragged skirmish line, their captain asked, "Which one of you is Bryan Marley?"

Marley sauntered forward, smiling. "Don't you recognize me, Tom?"

"It's Captain Quinn to you," the officer replied. "We've just been 'round to Gerta's, where you left one fine helluva mess."

"How's that?"

"Jack Menefee and his boyos. Remember them?"

"The name's familiar, but I couldn't put a face on it," said Marley.

"Not tonight, especially," the captain answered back, "since someone blew it off for him. We've got nine dead so far, and three more on the way without much question."

"Lord have mercy! What's this city coming to?"

"As if you didn't know. All innocent as babes, I guess?"

"I wouldn't go that far," Marley replied. "But if you're trying to accuse us of some wrongdoing tonight, the fact is we've been here all evening."

"And you can vouch for one another, I suppose," the captain fairly sneered.

"We can. Along with Annie and her ladies."

"Ladies." Spitting out the word as if it had a rancid taste.

"I don't suppose you've come with any evidence against us?" Marley challenged.

"Funny thing about that. Dead men aren't too talkative, and those you left alive all have that whatchacallit. Bullshit when they can't remember nothin' that they saw or heard."

"Amnesia," Ryder offered, from the sidelines.

The captain spun to face him. Asked, "And who are you, exactly?"

"George Revere."

"A new frog in the pond, is it?"

"Just helping with your memory," said Ryder.

"Don't you worry, boyo. I'll remember *you*, all right." He turned back toward the others. "I'll remember *all* of you, and see you pay for this night's work, if nothing else."

"We paid you lot already," someone chimed in from the back.

"Who said that!" Fuming in his rage, the captain studied ranks of passive faces, then, through clenched teeth, told them all, "Don't think we're finished yet!"

"Drop in and see us any time," Marley encouraged him. "The more, the merrier."

Rude laughter saw the coppers on their way, then Marley was beside him, voice low-pitched. "I'm going to relax upstairs a while. In case I miss you later, come around the docks at noon tomorrow. We've got cargo coming in."

"I'll see you there," Ryder replied.

Smart-aleck bastard. Who's he think he is?"

"What's that?" asked Tommy Rafferty.

"The new boy," Otto Seitz replied. "See how he's kissing ass with Bryan?"

"*Saved* his ass a couple times, I'd say."

"Who asked you?"

"You did," Rafferty reminded him and drank another shot of whiskey.

"Christ, am I the only one who sees it?"

"Sees what, Otto?"

"How he comes out of nowhere and worms his way into our business."

"Same way that anybody get to be a part of it. Bryan invites 'em in, is how."

"You think so, do you?"

"What's your story, then? You reckon that he came from Menefee? After tonight?"

"The only thing I know for sure is that there's somethin' wrong about him."

"Know what I think?"

"Do I wanna know?"

"I think you're jealous."

Seitz felt a sudden flush of anger heating up his cheeks. "The hell you mean by that?"

"You see him gettin' close to Bryan, and you think he's after your spot."

"That ain't gonna happen."

"But you're in a sweat about it, anyhow."

"A lot you know."

"I know I need to get a poke. You seen Lavinia around?"

Seitz turned away from Rafferty, disgusted by his inability to see the obvious. It was ridiculous to him, a total stranger being welcomed in to join a killing raid, of all things, when they barely knew the man. No, scratch that. None of them, in fact, knew George Revere at all. He was a cipher who had come from God knew where, appearing just when Marley needed him, as if by magic, and *voila*! The next thing Otto knew, Revere had joined their inner circle somehow and had saved Bryan *again*, shooting a man this time.

The thing Seitz couldn't figure out was *why*. What did he want?

There was the obvious, of course, if Otto took him at his word. Some kind of minor outlaw looking for a gang to join and maybe work his way up through the ranks. Nothing disqualified his story, on the face of it, though he'd been reticent about providing details. Some would call that only natural, if he was on the run, but Seitz still couldn't swallow it. He *wouldn't* swallow it.

Jealous? To hell with that!

He had the business to look out for, even if their leader wasn't doing what he'd call a bang-up job of dealing with security. No bummer off the street was going to invade and undermine their operation, not if Seitz had anything to say about it.

And he would. Oh, yes indeed.

Bryan had asked Revere to join them at the docks tomorrow, helping with a shipment that was scheduled to arrive. Call that another test, and Otto would be watching, primed to land on Georgie Boy with both feet at the first sign of a shady move. Both feet and then some, you could bet your life on that.

Lavinia appeared in front of him, a trifle tipsy, just the slightest bit unsteady on her feet. "Somebody said Tommy was lookin' for me," she told Seitz. "Know where he is?"

"Ain't seen him," Otto said. "But since you're free, why don't we head upstairs?"

"You think I'm free, you don't know much," she said.

"I know enough," Otto assured her. "You just wait and see."

Walking back from Awful Annie's to his boardinghouse, the second night in Galveston, Ryder was sure that he had someone trailing him. Make that at least two someones, since they muttered back and forth from time to time, not making any serious attempt at stealth. Two pairs of shoes plodding behind him, or it might be more, the way they echoed in the dead streets trying to catch up with Ryder.

Who this time? he wondered, as he ducked into an alley-way. All darkness, he had learned, was not created equal, and he wanted maximum concealment now, hoping that it would save his life.

Jack Menefee was dead or dying when they'd left him on the second-story balcony at Gerta's place, but Ryder guessed that other members of his gang could have been absent from the battle zone. If so, replacement of their fallen leader was inevitable, and it wouldn't take survivors long to lay the blame at Bryan Marley's doorstep—which, it seemed, meant Awful Annie's. And their next step would be . . . what? They might not be prepared for a reprisal in force, so soon after the beating they'd taken. But picking off a single member of the gang might help assuage their fury for the moment.

Ryder didn't know if he had been the first to leave the celebration of their victory. He'd spent a sweet, intense half hour with Nell upstairs and had not bothered counting heads as he was leaving the saloon. It would have served no purpose anyway, since any number of the crew might be engaged in similar activities with Annie's girls, behind closed doors.

The muffled voices had drawn closer now, approaching Ryder's hiding place. He had a choice to make, and quickly. Should he flee along the alley, seek another route back to the boardinghouse, or spring an ambush of his own and find out who was dogging him?

Another possibility, he thought, was Otto Seitz or some-one he'd put up to it. Marley's lieutenant had no use for Ryder and he took no pains to hide the feeling, even after Ryder saved his boss's life a second time. Did Seitz possess some pre-science, despite his brutish aspect, that had let him see through Ryder's pose as rootless felon George Revere?

Or were the midnight trackers simply muggers, of the

kind he might expect to find in Washington, New York, or any other major city in this lawless age? He knew that Galveston must have its share of cutthroats prowling after dark. Indeed, he'd met a few already, and might be considered one himself.

Ryder was running out of time. The shuffling feet had closed to half a block from his position, maybe less. If he was going to escape, he had to do it now. The darkness should conceal him if he left immediately and avoided making any noise. He had a fair chance to escape if they were simple muggers, but if Seitz had sent them, they could simply go on to the boardinghouse and head him off.

To hell with it, he thought and drew his Colt Army.

Nerves jangling, Ryder waited in the shadows at the alley's mouth until his trackers closed the gap to six or seven feet. He stepped into the open then, his pistol leveled, putting on a cheery tone to welcome them.

"Good evening, gents," he said, then registered their uniforms, the badges on their chests, and felt his stomach drop.

The two policemen gaped at Ryder for a heartbeat, then went for their guns, secured in military-style flap holsters. Ryder could have killed them then—or fired to wound them, maybe at their kneecaps—but he drew the line at shooting lawmen. Thinking quickly while they fumbled with their holsters, be sprang forward, swinging with his Colt to left and right, the weapon's eight-inch barrel making solid thunking sounds on impact with their skulls.

The cop to Ryder's left went down immediately, grunting softly as the Colt stunned him. His partner turned to meet the backhand swing Ryder directed at his temple, taking it across the forehead, stumbling as he went down on his backside. Ryder followed through, another swing to put him out, sprawled on the sidewalk with his gun still holstered.

Turning to the other, Ryder found him stretched out on his side, moaning, eyes closed.

Now what?

The first thing that he thought of, on impulse, was to snatch their badges, reaching quickly down to pluck each from its place on a blue coat and put them in his pocket. Let the two go home with headaches and concoct a story for their captain when they couldn't find their tin stars in the morning.

Would the pair of them be safe where they were lying, until they regained their senses?

Not my problem, Ryder thought and struck off toward his boardinghouse.

L isten, I know you trust him, but—"

"You don't. I hear you, Otto. What you can't explain is *why*?"

"I just—"

"Tonight makes twice he's saved my bacon, and this time he killed a man to do it."

"*May* have killed one."

"No. I saw the body. He was dead as dirt. Ike Murphy."

"Still . . ."

"Still nothing. First you thought he might be working on the sly for Menefee, and that turned out to be a load of bunkum. What's your story now?"

"I haven't got a story, but—"

"But what?"

"There's somethin' *wrong* about him, Bryan. I can smell it on him. You know I can always smell a rat."

"It sounds to me like you're nursing a grudge against this guy for no good reason."

"Oh, you'll hear my reasons when I've dug them up."

"Uh-huh. Meanwhile, don't go off half-cocked. And keep your boys away from him."

"I won't do anything without your say-so, Bryan. You know that."

"I know you'd better not." Then Marley smiled and placed a hand on Otto's shoulder, saying, "Just relax for once. Try to enjoy a bit of life."

"Who's got the time?" Seitz asked. "We have that load coming tomorrow, and I wouldn't be surprised if somebody took up the slack for Menefee. On top of that—"

"G'night, Otto. I'm going home. Stay here and worry to your heart's content if you've a mind to."

"Bryan—"

"But remember what I said. Hands off!"

"Hands off," Seitz solemnly affirmed. Thinking, *My hands, at least. For now.*

But when he had the evidence he needed, that would be another story. How to find it was the problem, or to recognize it once he had the proof in hand. And having made that recognition he would strike decisively, no begging Marley for the go-ahead. Given a choice between securing permission or forgiveness, Seitz would gamble on forgiveness nine times out of ten.

And this time, Otto realized, he could be gambling with his life.

George Revere—or whatever his name was—had impressed the boss. Okay. That part was understandable. You help a man out of tight corner, he's going to be grateful. Help him twice, and kill one of his enemies while you were doing it, you rose dramatically within his estimation. Knocking him back to normal size, and further down from there, would take some thought and effort.

Otto needed something dirty. Not a woman thing, or opium. Something that would diminish George Revere in Marley's eyes, make him expendable.

No, more than that. Something to be disposed of without hesitation, eagerly.

Or he could do the job himself, then turn around and blame it on some other gang in Galveston. Maybe just leave it unexplained, plead innocence when Marley questioned him and stick to that no matter what. The city was a rough place, dangerous, and Bryan's new best friend had shown a knack for making enemies.

Might be a way to go, if he was desperate. But first, Otto preferred to find out what was truly wrong with George Revere. Sniff out the rot that marked him as a danger to their gang and serve it up to Marley on a silver platter. Make it so that Bryan would be champing at the bit to kill Revere himself.

Otto would miss out on the fun that way, but vindication was its own reward. As much as he loved Marley—as a brother, mind you, not like a couple of Marys—Seitz admitted to himself that he would like to see his old friend taken down a peg or two. Leave him in charge, of course, but help him understand that others had a way of seeing things he might find helpful, worthy of considering.

Better a moment of embarrassment than being brought low by a stranger he had trusted on an impulse. Otto did not seek a change in leadership for their effective team, but if he thought about it now, who better to succeed his old friend than himself?

It would require a vote, simple majority if no one challenged him. And why would anyone dispute Otto's succession if he personally had revealed a traitor in their ranks? Of course, it would be tragic if he couldn't stop that traitor from eliminating Bryan Marley before Otto's bullets cut him down.

Something to think about, he told himself. And smiled.

Back in his rented room, Ryder considered what he'd done to the policemen. If they had been sent for him particularly, by the captain he had irritated, Ryder thought that he—or rather, George Revere—could be in trouble. On the other hand, if they'd been watching out for anyone from Marley's gang, there was a fair chance that they wouldn't know his name or his address in Galveston. A third alternative, and the least likely, would apply if they'd been simply watching out for anyone to roust and picked on Ryder by coincidence. In that case, Ryder thought, he would be free and clear.

But there were still the badges—no. 59 and no. 107—lying on the nightstand next to Ryder's narrow bed. It seemed unlikely to him that the city would employ that many officers, allowing for sequential issuance of numbers, but it ultimately made no difference. At least two cops would be intent on punishing the man who'd knocked them out and walked off with their tin, if they could manage to identify him. They'd be furious, might even put the order out to gun him down on sight, which would do nothing to help Ryder with the job at hand.

He had not counted on assistance from the local law, but neither had he figured on them hunting him. Ryder would treat it as another complication, keep his head down, and attempt to persevere. Meanwhile, he had another job ahead of him with Marley, shifting cargo on the docks at noon, which ought to rule out gunplay.

Maybe.

After two nights on the island, Ryder knew that he could take nothing for granted. No one from the crew that he had joined was trustworthy beyond completion of the basic tasks assigned to them, and any who suspected that he worked for law enforcement would dispose of him without a second thought, given the chance. Their competition, on the other hand, might kill him simply for consorting with the Marley crew. As for the local coppers, he'd been warned to view them as corrupt and likely brutal, not an element to trifle with.

His mission still remained a relatively simple one: catch Marley and the others smuggling contraband, avoiding payment of the legal duties, and deliver his report to William Wood in Washington. When it was time to make arrests, he had been told that reinforcements would be waiting, ready to assist since one man could not be expected to corral a gang. Ryder expected Yankee soldiers, if the city force could not be trusted, but he'd have to wait and see how things progressed. If Wood had any influence over the Texans— doubtful, on the face of it—Ryder might still find ways to work with some of them.

At least the ones he hadn't knocked unconscious.

Before lying down to sleep, he cleaned the Colt Army, reloaded it, and checked the barrel to be sure he hadn't knocked it out of true when he'd applied it to a pair of bony skulls. Finding no damage to the weapon, confident it would perform upon demand when needed, he stretched out atop his blankets, still wearing his shirt and trousers.

If someone decided to surprise him in the middle of the night, or at the crack of dawn, Ryder intended to be ready for them. If attacked, he would defend himself by any means available. The Henry rifle lying on the floor next to his bed was fully loaded, with a live round in the chamber, giving him a decent chance of fighting clear should someone try to storm the room.

And if the raiders were police?

He pushed that prospect out of mind and settled back to sleep, shifting his thoughts to Tampa and Irene McGowan, wondering if she had found her family and settled in with them. Ryder had no reason to think they'd ever meet again, but thinking of her settled him a bit. And later, in his dreams, when she got mixed up with Nell at Awful Annie's, Ryder had no reason to complain.

10

★ **S** tede Pickering enjoyed the feel of salt spray in his face, running across blue water with wind in his sails and the whole world in front of him, his for the taking. It was freedom, nothing more or less, the legacy his forebears had passed down to him through generations of dependence on themselves and no one else. As for the law, it was an inconvenience he avoided when he could, or met head on and shattered by pure brute force.

Another feeling he enjoyed.

The clipper had made good time from Tampico, with a stop at Corpus Christi, and was bound for Galveston. The gold Stede carried in the clipper's hold—some seven hundred pounds of it, concealed in crates of textiles—would be worth a little over thirteen thousand dollars on the open market, but the price he got in fact would be reduced by one-third at the dock, since the receivers had to cover costs of storing and distributing the contraband. The gems, pried out of rings and necklaces and such, sorted by type and quality, would bring another two, perhaps three thousand dollars.

Then, there was the ganja, grown and processed in Jamaica, where the clipper stopped at monthly intervals to fill its hold. Stede normally preferred a mug of rum when he was trying to relax, but he had tried the ganja once. A merchant's duty to his customers, learning his products inside out. It gave a pleasant lift, without the rage that sometimes settled over him when he was drinking heavily, but Stede still liked the potent kick of alcohol. Most of his ganja customers, before the war, had been plantation owners looking for a way to pacify their slaves—or so they'd said. He didn't know who used it now and frankly didn't care. The thousand pounds he carried should be worth four hundred dollars to him, more or less.

All told, when he had paid his crew and covered various expenses, Stede should have about five thousand dollars in his pocket. Not a princely sum, but it was more than most seafaring men would earn in eight or ten years' time. And once he'd spent it, celebrating his good fortune, he would start all over with another load. His cache of gold and gems was not exhausted yet, and by the time it was he meant to be retired, a member of the leisured class, perhaps inhabiting a private island of his own.

One place he wouldn't want to live was Galveston. Its crowded wharf and streets were like a glimpse of Hell to someone who had known and learned to love the freedom of the open sea. When Stede put into port and tried to walk through Galveston, he couldn't make a block without some stranger bumping into him and snarling as if *he* had been the clumsy one. He had thumped a few over the years, had been arrested once and forced to pay a fine for what they called battery, laughing up his sleeve the whole time at the things he'd done, which they would never know about.

The clipper was Stede's favorite ship, at least for now. He'd have to scuttle it someday, most likely sometime in the next few months, but there would always be another. For the moment, he enjoyed its speed and all he had accomplished as its captain. In Tampico, he had changed its name, the paint still bright and crisp across its bow.

Banshee.

He liked the sound of it, the images that it evoked. Stede was a superstitious man, like most sailors, although not religious in the normal sense. He'd witnessed savage rituals in Haiti, what they called *vodou,* and in Cuba, where Catholic saints were mixed into black magic for something called *Santería.* Stede had seen people possessed and behaving like animals, slathered with blood in the name of religion, and didn't know whether their prayers would be answered by gods or by demons.

Not that any of it mattered to him, either way.

Stede named his ships for ghosts because they were elusive, flitting here and there across the sea in answer to the winds and to their captain's will. And ghosts were frightening to most people, which often helped Stede in his chosen occupation as a predator. He changed the names from time to time, if they became well known, and made various superficial alterations to the vessels, thereby helping to prolong their useful life.

Banshee.

It had a nice ring to it.

And he had been growing bored with *Revenant.*

* * *

The waterfront was busy by the time Ryder arrived, ten minutes early for his meeting with the Marley crew. Upon arrival he had ascertained that work gangs labored more or less around the clock in Galveston, unloading cargo and replacing it with merchandise bound for other cities, some halfway around the world. Watching the segregated groups of stevedores, hearing the shouted orders from their foremen, Ryder wondered how much different the process was from antebellum days, when all the grunt work had been done by slaves.

That was illegal now, of course, at least in theory. A thirteenth amendment to the U.S. Constitution had been passed in Congress and ratified by twenty-three states, but still stood four states short of final ratification. Four of the eleven Rebel states had ratified the ban on slavery, which still left seven holding out, dragging their feet, Texas among them. It appeared that some Confederates still didn't realize they'd lost the war. An irritating fact, but not Ryder's concern just now.

He spotted Bryan Marley, standing near a hot tamale stand with Otto Seitz and several others Ryder recognized from their adventure of the night before. A pair of horse-drawn wagons sat to one side of the group, waiting to haul whatever merchandise they were expecting. Ryder made his way to join them, noting the change of expression on Otto's face as he picked Ryder out of the crowd. Seitz said something to Marley, speaking from one side of his mouth, and Marley turned to watch Ryder approaching.

"George," he said, "I'm glad you made it."

"It was touch and go," Ryder replied.

"How's that?"

"I had a spot of trouble on the way back to my boarding-house last night." He palmed the badges from his pocket, handing them to Marley.

"So, what's this?" asked Marley, clearly puzzled.

"Cops," Ryder explained. "They tried to jump me, but I beat them to it."

"Beat them how?" Seitz interjected, frowning.

"They're alive," said Ryder. "Or they were, with head-aches, when I left them. I can't say what might have hap-pened to them lying there, if someone hostile came along."

"You took their badges . . . why?" asked Marley.

Ryder shrugged. "Why not?"

"Coppers don't like being embarrassed," Seitz advised.

"Too bad. They had worse than embarrassment in mind for me, I'd say. With these"—he nodded toward the badges Marley held—"you can identify them."

"What's the point of that?" Seitz asked.

Ryder allowed himself another shrug. "It seems to me you must be paying off some of the law in town. If these two are collecting from you, Bryan here deserves to know he didn't get his money's worth."

Marley was nodding. "That's good thinking, George," he said and put the badges in his pocket. "I'll hang on to these and see who they belong to. If they're on our list, they'll need a talking to."

"Your call," said Ryder, with a pointed glance at Otto as he added, "You're the boss."

Seitz couldn't very well object to that, but he was obviously fuming as he turned his full attention toward the Gulf of Mexico. "This should be it," he said, to no one in particular.

Scanning the water, Ryder saw a clipper gliding into port, its crewmen scrambling like monkeys in the rigging, trimming sails. The ship sparked something in his memory, but Ryder told himself that clippers shared a common slender form and deep draft, built for speed, with sails aplenty to take full advantage of the slightest wind. There was no reason why this clipper should not bear a close resemblance to another that he'd seen, not long ago.

Five minutes later, Ryder saw the clipper's name—*Banshee*—painted across its bow, red letters on a white background. The paint looked bright and fresh, not weathered as it would have been by months at sea.

Coincidence, he told himself, but felt a niggling sense of apprehension in his stomach as the clipper docked and Marley's men rushed forward to secure its mooring lines. He waited for the gangplank to be lowered and the *Banshee*'s captain to descend, greeted by Marley on the wharf, with Otto Seitz beside him. Only when the bearded, grinning captain reached the pier was Ryder's first impression finally confirmed.

He'd seen that face before, all right. Not smiling; shouting orders in the midst of battle.

Fresh paint might disguise the clipper's old name, but he recognized the skipper of the *Revenant*.

B ryan Marley met the *Banshee*'s captain and his first mate at the bottom of the gangplank, shaking hands with both. Seitz hung at Marley's elbow, clearly wanting to be part of it, while Ryder hung back in the ranks of Marley's men collected on the pier.

"It's good to see you, Stede," Marley addressed the captain, then turned to his mate and nodded. "Randy."

"Same as ever," said the first mate, grinning at a joke he obviously told at every given opportunity.

"You know Otto and all the boys," Marley continued, nodding toward his crew.

"Not *all* of 'em," the captain—Stede—replied. "I see a new face over there."

Marley followed the sailor's gaze to Ryder. "Ah, you're right," he said. "George, come on over here and meet a friend of mine."

Ryder advanced to stand at Marley's side, letting him make the introductions.

"George Revere, Stede Pickering. He's captain of the *Banshee*." Grinning, Marley added, "Though I do believe she had another name last time I saw her."

"Names don't mean much to me," said Pickering. "But I remember faces, and I'd say yours looks familiar."

"Oh?" The best Ryder could do was act surprised.

"I've seen you someplace," Pickering insisted. "Can't quite put my finger on it, but I figger it'll come to me."

Trying to look confused, Ryder replied, "I'm pretty sure I would remember meeting you."

"Ah, well, I never said I *met* you, laddy. What I said is that I've *seen* you. There's a difference you know."

"That's true enough," Ryder agreed. "I can't imagine where that would've been."

"I'll work it out, don't worry." With a grimace, Pickering inquired, "You ain't a copper, are you?"

Ryder forced a laugh and said, "Not even close."

"He thumped a couple, though," said Marley. "Just last night, in fact. And brought me these to show for it."

He took the badges from his pocket, letting Pickering examine them. The captain's frown inverted, turned into a gold-toothed smile. "They'll have to spin a tale today, I reckon, showin' up without 'em."

"So," said Marley, pocketing the badges as he got around to business. "Have you got the goods?"

"Indeed I have, and then some," Pickering confirmed. "Your lads ready to help off-load?"

"That's why they're here," Marley confirmed.

"Well, come aboard then, and we'll get 'em started workin' for a living."

"Don't say that," Marley advised him. "It's what they've been trying to avoid."

Pickering laughed at that and answered, "Ain't we all?"

The gangplank groaned beneath their weight as Marley led his team aboard the *Banshee*. Ryder eyed the crewmen lined up on the clipper's deck, around the open hold, but Pickering remained the only one he recognized. As they approached the hold, Stede Pickering ran down the list of cargo they'd be carrying ashore.

"I've got the usual pistoles and doubloons," he said. "Say seven hundred pounds in all, whether you want to pass it on as is or melt it down."

"At eighteen ninety-three per ounce," Marley replied, "that's—"

"Thirteen thousand two hundred and fifty-one dollars, retail on the open market. Since we're not exactly *on* the open market, I'll be asking nine."

Marley considered that, then nodded. "Done," he said. "The rest?"

"A fair number of gems, including diamonds, rubies, emeralds, with some topaz and sapphires. As for carats, I would estimate . . . well, how does one million strike you?"

"Nearly three pounds," Marley answered, when he'd done the calculation in his head. "How much?"

"Two thousand even," Pickering replied.

"All right. And what about the ganja?"

"Say another seven hundred pounds. I'd like to get four hundred for it."

"Fair enough. I've got a couple wagons standing by."

"What's ganja?" Ryder asked Ed Parsons, standing to his left.

Parsons responded with a crooked smile. "It's like tobacco, with an extra kick to it. You oughta try it, Georgie."

"Hmmm."

"You owe it to yourself to live a little," Parsons said.

"I'll think about it," Ryder said.

"Ask little Nell about that ganja, next time you go up to see her in her crib," Parsons suggested, chuckling as he moved off toward the *Banshee*'s open cargo hatch.

Ryder watched him go and put the ganja out of mind. He had been sent to document smuggling of gold and gems, a mission now completed once he traced the *Banshee*'s cargo to wherever Marley planned to stash it. Somewhere within Galveston, he calculated, for convenience. One thing the town had in abundance was warehouses, and a big-time smuggler without storage space available would soon be out of work.

"Awright," Stede Pickering called out to Marley's men. "You came to work, so get your backs into it!"

Otto Seitz refrained from heavy work whenever possible. He might not be the boss in fact, but being second in command still had its privileges. He got to supervise when there was sweaty work to do, and only joined in on the bloody bits when he craved some excitement. Now, he hung back while a hand-cranked pulley system started raising nets out of the *Banshee*'s cargo hold, each net supporting wooden pallets, which in turn held crated merchandise.

Seitz found Stede Pickering against the starboard rail, smoking a pipe that looked like ivory or scrimshaw, with some kind of nautical motif etched on its bowl. Joining the captain, careful not to crowd him, Otto got right down to business. "So, you think you've seen our Georgie boy somewhere before?"

"I'd wager on it," Pickering replied. "Faces stick in my head."

"I'm guessing that he hasn't been a member of your crew."

"No guessing there," said Pickering. "I'd have to be a total idjit to forget a man I've sailed with, wouldn't I?"

Ignoring that, Seitz said, "You would have seen him in a port then. Somewhere you put in for cargo or supplies."

"Well, you can bet I didn't see him floatin' on a raft at sea. Although . . ." The captain puffed a little cloud of smoke and squinted through it, toward the Gulf of Mexico.

"Although . . . ?"

Pickering shrugged. "Nothin'. Likely, I'll work it out after we sail. The ocean helps me think."

"But in the meantime . . ."

"This boy worries you, I take it," Pickering suggested.

"I'm just curious about him," Otto said. "Guy shows up out of nowhere at the perfect time. Next thing you know, he's friends with everybody."

"Not with *you*," said Pickering.

"I like to know my friends a little better. Find out where they come from, what they did there, this and that."

"I've got a gold doubloon that says you don't know ever'thing about the boys you call your friends, much less this George Revere. We've all got secrets, Mr. Seitz."

"I know enough about the others," Otto said. "But this one, he's a cipher to me."

"And you don't like mysteries."

"Not when they might come back to bite me."

"Alas, I've told you all I can, at least for now. I've definitely seen him somewhere. If it comes to me before we sail, I'll pass it on."

"I'd rather that you didn't tell the boss we talked about this," Otto said.

"A little secret is it?"

"I don't want to worry him, in case it turns out being nothing."

"Leave his mind at ease, you mean."

"If possible."

"And maybe deal with it yourself."

"May not be necessary."

"But you *hope* it will be."

"Did I say—"

"You didn't have to say it, laddy. It's as plain as plain can be."

"Well, anyway. If you can think of anything about him, I'd appreciate it."

"And you'd show me that appreciation . . . how?"

"What do you want?"

"Not sure yet, but I'll think on it."

Marley called out to Seitz just then, hailing him from the cargo hatch. He left Pickering at the rail, smoking, uncertain whether he had said too much or if the captain would run straight to Marley with the details of their conversation. Moving toward the hold, he realized that Pickering had not responded to his plea for confidentiality, but Otto didn't want to double back and press his luck, making an issue of it. If Pickering *did* squeal, then Otto supposed that he could weather any minor squall it caused, considering the time he spent with Marley.

"Sorry to interrupt your little chat," said Marley when they stood together, watching two stout crewmen crank the windlass hoisting cargo into daylight.

"No problem," Seitz replied.

"Something I ought to know about?"

"Just jawing," Otto told him. "Nothing special."

"Well, in that case, maybe you could fetch the wagons up and start to get them loaded."

"Absolutely," Otto said, hearing the edge in Marley's tone. Frowning, he went to do as he'd been told.

Off-loading cargo from the *Banshee* took the best part of four hours. First came wooden crates with TEXTILES stenciled on the top and sides, each heavier than Ryder thought mere bolts of woven cloth should be. He took it that the gold coins and assorted gems were hidden in the boxes, adding weight, and while he kept an eye out for a Customs agent, none appeared to check the *Banshee*'s manifest. It made him wonder whether they'd been paid to stay away, or if the sheer volume of cargo moving through the port of Galveston made checking every ship impossible.

He'd make no judgment on the Customs men in his report, Ryder decided, if he didn't catch them with their hands out or collaborating in some other way with Marley's gang. Meanwhile, he helped unload the clipper, lugging crates from deck to pier, along the gangplank, and securing them in Marley's waiting wagons. On his first pass, Ryder caught the horses watching him, placid as he increased the burden they would have to haul away.

He counted eighteen crates before they started taking off the ganja, bagged in burlap, each sack weighing thirty pounds or so. The plants carried a smell of fresh-mown grass

about them, as he hoisted each across his shoulder and proceeded down the gangplank toward the second wagon.
Ryder guessed you'd have to chew or smoke it to receive the
kick Parsons had mentioned. In their present form, sacked
up, the plants succeeded only at inspiring him to sneeze.

When they were nearly finished, Ryder saw a couple of
policemen coming down the wharf, both armed with pistols
and with billy clubs, one of them twirling his club on a leather
thong that looped around his wrist. Neither of them resembled those Ryder had left unconscious on the street last
night, and both were wearing badges in their proper place.

Hoisting a sack of ganja to its place inside the second
wagon, Ryder watched the coppers draw Marley aside, followed by Otto Seitz. The four of them conversed, briefly,
none glancing Ryder's way before a roll of currency changed
hands. It was his first glimpse of a bribe in progress, and
while Ryder could not read the numbers on their badges, he
had memorized the faces of both officers before they ambled
off the dock and out of sight.

One more round-trip onto the *Banshee*'s weather deck,
and they were done, both wagons loaded. Ryder loitered on
the pier and watched as Marley paid the captain, then shook
hands with him and turned away. Seitz lingered for a
moment longer, said something to Pickering, and then followed his boss to join the others.

"Okay," said Marley. "Now we only have to stow the merchandise. Ed, you and Harry drive the wagons. Take a couple
of the boys along to help unload them at the warehouse."

Parsons turned to Ryder, nudged him with an elbow to
the ribs, and told him, "You're with me."

Ryder responded with a nod and mounted to the wagon's
high seat, letting Parsons take the reins. Behind them, Harry
Morgan and another member of the team, Bob Jacobs, rode

the second wagon trailing them. Ryder let Parsons navigate, watching for street signs as they rolled through town and counting blocks between those that appeared to have no names. It took them twenty minutes at a walking pace to reach a warehouse labeled TIDEWATER STORAGE in faded blue paint on a parched white background. Two men he didn't recognize were waiting by the open double doors, and Parsons greeted them by name—Johnny and Lee—before he drove the wagon through to the interior.

Inside, the warehouse seemed more spacious than it looked from streetside. Roughly half of it was filled with crated merchandise, stacked up in chest-high rows that ran the full length of the building. Ryder had no chance to examine any labels, but assumed that most of them were tagged to keep a casual observer from suspecting what might lie within. If so, it seemed that Bryan Marley had a sizable supply of contraband to move.

Parsons maneuvered to the far end of the warehouse, stopped his team with ample room to turn around when they were done, then hopped down from the driver's seat. Ryder joined him and focused on the task at hand, already thinking forward to the next free time he'd have, and what he'd tell Director Wood in his next cryptic telegram.

So far, he had received no answers from the capital and had not banked on any. If and when Wood moved against the Marley gang, Ryder supposed that it would take him by surprise. He only hoped that there would be warning enough to let him come out of the final scrape alive.

11

★ After going through the same half-hour routine to lose observers, Ryder made his way back to the Western Union office, where he wrote Director Wood another telegram. This one simply stated two words:

CARGO RECEIVED

Then Ryder revised the telegram to include for the first time the address of his boardinghouse. He did not expect an answer from the capital, but wanted Wood to know where he'd been staying if the play went wrong somehow.

And why?

He couldn't answer that specifically. Perhaps as a lifeline to the world outside of Galveston, although he knew it likely wouldn't do him any good. If Marley saw through his deception, Ryder guessed that he would simply disappear—or else be found some morning in a gutter, with his throat cut or a bullet in his head.

Or maybe both.

With that depressing thought in mind, he went to find a barbershop that offered baths. His afternoon of labor on the wharf and at Tidewater Storage had left him feeling grimy and fatigued. The place he found rented tubs for a dime per half hour and Ryder went for the works, adding a shave and haircut to make it an even six bits. He enjoyed the hot water, just soaking and thinking, but kept his Colt close on a plain wooden chair.

Just in case.

From the barbershop, he went in search of supper, settling on a restaurant that specialized in seafood. Ryder ordered something called a crawfish pie, with fresh bread on the side and strong black coffee. He was pleasantly surprised by the concoction he received—a kind of stew baked in a pie crust—and was quick to clean his plate.

Too quick, in fact, for his appointed meeting with the gang at Awful Annie's after nightfall. That afternoon, Ryder had asked whether they ever tried a different place, and Parsons had replied, "Why would we? Annie's got whatever anybody needs." That observation had reminded Ryder that he first saw Bryan Marley in a different saloon, before the ambush that he'd interrupted, and he wondered whether that had been significant in some way that eluded him.

Only one way to answer that, he thought and set off for the first saloon after he paid his tab and left the restaurant.

It took a bit of searching, since he'd found Marley by chance the first time, on an aimless tour of Galveston's bars. He had paid no special attention to its location, and the seamy streets looked different in any case, by daylight.

Finally, to save time, Ryder walked back to his boarding-house and launched his search from there, retracing his steps from two nights back as best he could. It took the best part of an hour, even then, for him to find the place where he had first found Marley drinking with a group of men Ryder had never seen again, among the smuggler's crew.

A quick look past the bat-wing doors confirmed no sign of Marley on the premises this afternoon. Inside the tavern, after he had checked its darker corners for a second time, Ryder proceeded to the bar and ordered beer. The mug arrived, he laid a silver dollar on the bar, and told the bartender, "I'm looking for a friend of mine who comes in here sometimes."

Eyeing the coin, ten times the price of Ryder's beer, the barkeep asked him, "Got a name, this friend a your'n?"

"It's Marley. Bryan Marley."

Fingers edging toward the silver dollar, the bartender said, "He drinks in here awright, from time to time. Ain't seen him in a couple days."

"Just one more thing."

"Wha's that?"

"Are any of his friends around today? Somebody who could tell me where to find him?"

Lazy eyes perused the crowd of customers. "Nobody here I ever seen him drinkin' with," the barkeep said. "Some of 'em won't be comin' back, I guess."

"Why's that?"

The silver dollar disappeared into the barkeep's pocket as he said, "They went'n got killed off last night. Lucky it didn't happen here. You gonna drink that beer, or what?"

Ryder emptied the mug in four great swallows, turning for the exit as he waited for the alcohol to hit him, either clear his head or drown the idea that was taking form inside it.

Murdered friends. A number of them killed the same night he had followed Bryan Marley into Gerta's for a showdown with Jack Menefee. Ryder did not remember Menefee himself among the men Marley was drinking with, the first time Ryder stumbled onto him in Galveston, but were the others members of the gang he'd fought at Gerta's place? No matter how he racked his memory, Ryder couldn't recall.

All right. Say Marley *did* have friends inside the rival camp. So what? Some of the gang had tried to kill him moments after others—if they did belong to Menefee—were sitting down and sharing drinks with him. Did it mean anything? And if so, what?

Ryder pushed through the swinging doors and stepped onto the sidewalk, pausing there to check his pocket watch. A slow walk down to Awful Annie's should be just about—

To Ryder's left, a window of the tavern shattered as a pistol shot rang out. He glimpsed the muzzle flash, across the street, then dived for cover, reaching for his Colt.

You missed, *pendejo!*"

"I can see that, damn it!" Harley Baker raised his pistol for a second shot, wishing that Tijerina would shut up and let him think.

"*Mira!* He's crawling to *el callejón.*"

The alley, Baker guessed he meant. "I *see* him. Shut your trap and lemme do this."

"*Dispárale, cabron!*"

The pistol jumped in Baker's fist, its smoke obscuring his target in the dusky street. He knew it was a wasted shot before the Mexican beside him yelped, "*Chinga!* You missed again, *estúpido!*"

"If you say one more goddamn word—"

But Tijerina didn't wait around to hear his threat. Instead, the slender pistolero bolted from the doorway that had sheltered them, running across the street to chase their target down the alley where he'd disappeared. Baker was slower off the mark—no great surprise, since he had eighty pounds on Tijerina, easily—and by the time he'd reached the alley's mouth, both of the other men had disappeared into its shadows.

Bad idea, he thought, but had to follow them regardless. He'd been paid to do a job, and failure carried penalties beyond refunding the advance. More to the point, he'd made the deal himself. If he let Tijerina bag their target on his own, how would it look? First thing he knew, the Mexican would want a bigger share, or he might strike off on his own.

Baker scuttled through the alley, virtually blind, mouthing a string of silent curses as he scattered rocks and trash in front of him, making a racket that would wake the dead. This was supposed to be an easy job, just trail the stranger for a bit and pick him off first time they had a clean shot at him. Baker had considered going for him at the barbershop, but that meant killing witnesses as well, and nobody was paying him for that. His rule—one fee, one body—was as simple as it got.

Ahead of him, a pistol cracked, its flash some thirty yards away. Baker, already winded from his short run, held a steady plodding pace as he approached the spot. He wasn't fool enough to blunder forward and expose himself to hostile fire before he knew exactly what was happening. That was the quickest way to die in Baker's line of work, and he intended to survive the night no matter who else bit the dust while he was at it.

One Alfredo Tijerina, maybe, if he got a notion he could claim the whole prize for himself.

They were friends after a fashion, barely, but the money mattered most. And when you got right down to cases, Baker figured he was just another Mexican.

Four shots remained in Baker's Colt Model 1861 Navy revolver, and he had a second pistol—a .436-caliber Dean and Adams double-action all the way from England—tucked under his belt as a reserve. If all else failed, the handle of a Bowie knife protruded from the top of his right boot, for close work in a clench. Whatever he discovered when he reached the alley's farther end, Baker imagined he was ready for it.

But it turned out he was wrong.

Nothing was waiting for him when he cleared the alley. No corpse on the ground, not even bloodstains to suggest that anyone was hit. No sign of Tijerina or the target, either, which confounded Baker, since he didn't know which way to turn.

Damn it! He couldn't match Alfredo's speed, and now he'd lost his quarry in the darkened maze of streets. Without a stroke of luck—

Two shots echoed from somewhere to his left, the sharp sounds overlapping. Tijerina only had one pistol, so that meant their mark was shooting back.

Trailing the echoes, Harley Baker caught his breath and broke into a shambling run.

Ryder knew he was running out of time and luck. The first two shots had missed him, but he couldn't count on hasty marksmanship to spare him if the chase dragged on. He had no destination yet in mind, but knew he couldn't run to Awful Annie's and the Marley gang if there was any chance at all of Marley setting up the ambush.

Why?

He couldn't say and had no time to ponder the dilemma. Maybe Seitz had swayed him, though there'd been no evidence of that during the afternoon. Had Pickering the pirate finally remembered seeing Ryder on the *Southern Belle*, battling his men? And what would that prove, other than determination to defend himself? There was no reason for the buccaneer to brand Ryder a traitor or informer, but he *might* have noted the coincidence of Ryder turning up in Galveston so soon after their skirmish in the Keys. Was that enough to land a target on his back?

Maybe. He might find out, if he could stay alive and capture the would-be assassin without killing him. No easy task on darkened, winding streets when he was busy running for his life.

Ryder had made it to the nearest alleyway, ducked in, and picked up speed, stumbling and lurching over cast-off garbage hidden by the shadows. Every noise he made betrayed him, but he didn't want to make his last stand in the alley, nothing in the way of cover for him if the narrow passageway became a shooting gallery. If he could make it to the other end . . .

Footsteps scuffled and scraped behind him, someone else contending with the alley's litter. Muttered curses—was that Spanish?—also helped him gauge the progress his pursuer made, while Ryder tried as best he could to watch his step and minimize his noise.

Not well enough, apparently. A shot rang out behind him, loud as thunder in the alley's narrow confines, and he heard the bullet ricochet off brickwork to his right. He ducked, a stupid reflex since the slug was already long gone, and quickly found that running in a crouch accomplished nothing but to slow him down.

He could return fire, but the muzzle flash would show his adversary where to aim unless he hit his mark by pure dumb luck, and Ryder thought the risk outweighed the possible reward. Killing the shooter, even if he managed it, would solve one problem while the other—finding out who'd sent him—still remained.

The alley's western mouth was twenty feet ahead of him, a slightly lighter patch of darkness to his straining eyes. He tried to hug the nearest wall while moving forward, fearful that the gunman on his heels would catch a glimpse of him in silhouette and hit him on the run.

One final dash and he was clear, ducked to his left and stopped some ten feet from the alley's entrance. Dropping to one knee, raising his Colt Army. Ryder braced it with both hands, since his right was trembling from the frantic sprint, pulse hammering against his ribs and in his ears. It nearly deafened him, but he could still hear someone drawing closer, stumbling, grumbling to himself.

"Chinga tu madre! Dónde estás, cabron?"

The footsteps slowed, then stopped completely, just inside the alley's shadowed mouth. Ryder imagined his intended killer poised there, trying to decide if it was safe to move. Was it a trap? Would a delay permit his target to escape?

"Mierda!"

The man made up his mind, emerged, crouching and scuttling sideways like a crab. He must have seen or sensed where Ryder was, swinging his pistol into line. They fired together, Ryder wincing at the muzzle flash that nearly blinded him, hearing the bullet whisper past his left ear in the night. His shot was better, smacking into flesh, dropping the gunman on his backside with a solid thump. From there, groaning, the shooter toppled slowly over backward, arms outflung, his six-gun tumbling from his hand.

Ryder edged forward, not convinced the man was dead—hoping, in fact, that he was still alive and fit to answer questions if they could communicate. Ryder could recognize the Spanish language, but he didn't speak it. If the shooter couldn't talk to him in English, or if he was too far gone to answer any questions, Ryder would be left in limbo with his quandary.

Watching the wounded gunman's hands, Ryder moved closer, knelt beside him, bending down to ask him, "Can you hear me?"

Goddamn it!"

That was English, but the words had not come from the supine pistolero's blood-flecked lips. Somebody else was coming down the alley, wheezing with exertion, heavy footsteps drawing nearer by the second.

Two assassins, then. At least.

Ryder eased backward from the dying man, who'd sprawled across the entrance to the alley on his right. He had no way of knowing if the second gunman had already glimpsed him, but if so, the stalker wasn't wasting ammunition on a risky shot. Waiting to close the gap, perhaps, and find out what had happened to his partner while he lagged behind.

The wounded Mexican gave out a final rattling gasp and died. Ryder felt nothing but relief over the killing, edged out by a mounting apprehension as the other pistolero shambled closer. From the sounds he heard, Ryder concluded there was only one man in the alley, but that didn't rule out others circling around the block to flank him from the north or south—maybe from both directions, if the hunting party had sufficient numbers.

Stay or run?

He had a choice to make, and quickly. If he waited for the second shooter to reveal himself he would surrender the decision, maybe find himself boxed in with no means of escape.

Splitting the difference, Ryder retreated to the far side of the street and ducked into the recessed doorway of a shop directly opposite the alley's mouth. The nearest street lamp was a block away, and he was confident no one could spot him where he stood, without a dangerously close inspection. Covering the alley with his Colt Army, he waited for the second shooter to emerge, while shooting glances up and down the street in search of any more.

It took a while—Ryder was starting to imagine that a beat cop might arrive before the gunman showed himself—but finally a hulking figure lurched out of the alley, swinging first one way and then the other with his pistol, seeking targets. Finding none, he knelt beside the fallen Mexican and shook him roughly, hissing, "Hey, amigo! Can you hear me?"

"I don't think so," Ryder answered from the shadows, still invisible, watching the big man over pistol sights.

The shooter jumped, tried scrambling to his feet, but slipped and lost his balance, nearly tipping over on his side. He caught himself, left hand outstretched to brace him, while he triggered two quick shots in Ryder's general direction. Ryder gave one back and heard his adversary grunt as it struck home somewhere within his bulky torso.

"Agh!"

"It's finished," Ryder told him. "Drop the piece!"

Instead, the wounded shooter struggled to his feet, back braced against the nearest wall, and raised his pistol, obviously trying to home in on Ryder's voice. He sent another bullet high and wide, thumbed back his weapon's hammer for another shot, but Ryder beat him to it, aiming low as he squeezed off another round.

The big man fell then, as his wounded left leg buckled under him. Ryder hurried across the street to snatch the pistol from his hand and toss it out of reach, frisking the shooter in a hasty search for any hidden weapons. Finding none, he rocked back on his heels and used his Colt to prod the fallen enemy.

"Who are you?"

"Go to hell."

He saw blood pumping from the shooter's punctured thigh, a darker stain spreading across his rumpled shirt. That blood was nearly black, an inky flood.

"Maybe I'll see you there," said Ryder. "Looks like you'll be going first."

"The hell do you know?"

"I can see you've got a bullet in your liver," Ryder said. "Call it a toss-up if you die from that or bleed out through your leg. I'd give you ten or fifteen minutes, either way."

"Doctor?"

"I'm new in town. Don't know one. Sorry."

"Bet you are."

"Tell me who put you up to this. I'll make it right."

"For . . . who?"

Before he had a chance to answer that, the big man gasped, his eyes rolled back, and he was gone.

Ryder considered trying to conceal the bodies, then decided it would be a waste of time and energy. The gunfire should have drawn police by now, although he heard none of their whistles in the distance yet. Whether they'd missed it somehow or were sneaking up to have a cautious look around before they showed themselves, Ryder was anxious to be gone.

He left the corpses where they'd fallen, hurrying along the street until he'd put three blocks between himself and his would-be assassins. He was overdue at Awful Annie's now, uncertain whether he should go ahead or skip the gathering and see what happened next.

If Marley was behind the botched attempt to kill him, Ryder might be walking into a death trap at Annie's saloon. On the other hand, if Otto Seitz had planned the ambush on his own, without Marley's approval or authority, he might expose himself with an expression of surprise at seeing Ryder still alive. Something to drive a wedge between the King of Smugglers and his second in command, perhaps, if it worked out.

Or was it worth the risk? Should Ryder simply make himself scarce and wait for Director Wood to drop a net on Marley's gang? How long would that take, if in fact it happened at all?

Without communication from the capital, Ryder had no idea if Wood was acting on the information he'd received so far, or if the telegrams had even reached his hands. Assuming that they had, it still remained for Wood to find the men and other resources he needed to conduct a raid in Galveston, where local lawmen—some of them, at least—took cash to let the smugglers operate with evident impunity.

If Wood was able to corral the Marley gang, could he trust any local jail to hold them? Was an honest judge available in Galveston—or anywhere in war-torn, Yankee-hating Texas—to preside over their trial? Could jurors be empaneled who would dare convict them on the evidence, at risk of possible retaliation? If convicted, would they be released with payment of a fine and warned to sin no more?

It was too much to think about just now, but Ryder had decided one thing, anyway. He would proceed to Awful Annie's as agreed and make-believe that nothing in the least unusual had happened to him on his way there. Wait and see if anyone reacted to him turning up, alive and well, when they had wished him dead.

And then, what? Let them try again, with better planning next time?

The half-mile walk to Awful Annie's was a nerve-racking experience. He kept expecting gunshots from the shadows, watching darkened windows for the flicker of a curtain to betray a sniper, half expecting enemies to rush at him from alleys or from recessed doorways. When he made it, uncontested, Ryder lingered for a moment at the entrance to the bar and bawdy house, steeling his nerve, then pushed his way inside.

"You're late, George," Bryan Marley said by way of greeting. "Come and have a drink."

Ryder crossed to the bar, telling the King of Smugglers, "Sorry. I'm still getting used to how the streets run every which way here in Galveston."

"It takes a while," Ryder agreed, filling a whiskey glass and sliding it toward Ryder. "Now you're here, I thought you'd want to know I found the coppers who were after you last night."

"And?"

"I gave their badges to a sergeant who's a friend of ours. He'll say he found them at a pawnshop, but the owner can't identify whoever left them there. The two you thumped have been suspended for a week, no pay."

"They won't be happy," Ryder said.

"Won't matter," Marley told him. "When they come back off suspension they'll be walking a beat around Broadway and Avenue L." Noting Ryder's lack of comprehension, Marley added, "It's all black around that neighborhood. They'll have a grand old time."

"And won't be carrying a grudge?"

"To hell with 'em. They come around harassing us again, they'll wish they'd let it go with bruises."

"Sorry if I caused you any trouble," Ryder said.

"All in a day's work," Marley said.

Scanning the faces of the crew assembled in the barroom, Ryder said, "I guess I'm not the only one who's late."

"Otto, you mean?" Marley was nodding as he spoke. "He had some business to take care of, but he'll be along directly. I think he's warming up to you a little."

"Oh?"

"You may have noticed that he's wary around strangers."

Ryder sipped his whiskey. Said, "I got that."

"But this afternoon, after you left with Ed and Harry, Otto said he thought you'd do all right."

"High praise."

"From him it is, believe me."

"Well."

"Get on his good side and you couldn't have a better friend. But if he has it in for you, watch out."

Feeling the burn of whiskey in his throat, Ryder replied, "Thanks. I'll remember that."

12

★ **O**tto Seitz was tired of waiting for his pistoleros to return. He pictured Harry Baker and the Mexican—Alfredo Something—stopping off somewhere along the way to wet their whistle, losing track of time while he sat there in the small, smoky cantina, sipping tepid beer. It's what he got for hiring sluggards, and he had a good mind not to pay what they had coming for the finished job, if they were too damned lazy to show up on time and claim their money.

Five more minutes, he decided. *After that, forget it.*

What could Baker do if he came in an hour late and Seitz was gone? Complain to the police? Sue Otto for defaulting on their contract? Any mention of their deal would put his fat neck in a noose, and Seitz didn't believe the gunman was that stupid.

On the other hand, the Mex seemed like a hothead, too damned cocky for his own good around white men. He might be the sort to hound Seitz, prodding him for payment even when the terms of their agreement had been violated, but it wouldn't get him anywhere. Except, maybe, a shallow grave.

Seitz wasn't taking lip from any Mexican *bandido*, nor a sweaty pig whose only talent seemed to be backshooting. Two could play that game. Arrange a meeting for a settlement, and when the pair of them arrived, pay them in lead. Otto was confident his sawed-off scattergun could do the trick, relieve him of a problem while it saved him money, and the rest of Marley's crew would never know a thing about it.

Perfect, then.

Time's up, he thought and drained his beer. Leaving the tavern, Otto spent a final moment on the sidewalk, peering north and south along the street, in case Baker and his amigo were approaching even now. Nobody visible from where he stood resembled them, and Otto spat into the street before he turned away, starting his trek toward Awful Annie's.

This was something he would never share with Bryan Marley. Seitz had acted for the benefit of all concerned, whether the boss saw it or not. He had mistrusted George Revere from their first meeting, thought there must be something false about him at the core, no matter how often he had contrived to rescue Marley from the jaws of doom. It wasn't simply knowing they would never be the best of friends; his animosity toward Marley's new good friend ran much deeper than that. Otto wasn't entirely sure he could explain it, even to himself, but he still harbored a conviction that eliminating Georgie Boy had been the proper thing to do.

And now, it seemed he'd managed to achieve his goal for half price, after all.

He had originally offered twenty dollars for the killing, ten paid in advance. He likely could have argued Harry down a bit, but since the fat man didn't care about collecting the remainder of his fee, it all came out the same.

Except to Harry and the Mex, if they came after him for more.

Otto heard the music blaring out of Awful Annie's from a block away, discordant as ever. Sometimes he had difficulty knowing if the bar's name was derived from its proprietress, its liquor, or its entertainment. Still, Annie's had come to be a kind of home away from home for Bryan Marley and his men when they were not engaged in forays to the wrong side of the law.

Tomorrow, for example.

But tonight—for Seitz, at least—a celebration was in order. Granted, he couldn't let it slip that he was tickled by the fate of George Revere, much less that he'd arranged it. No one else would know that they had lost the new boy yet, and Otto didn't mind keeping the secret. Let it come out in its own good time. Meanwhile, he'd tip a glass to Georgie Boy and to a job well done.

Marley would thank him someday, if he ever learned the truth. Or maybe it was better if he just kept Bryan in the dark. Let him believe that friends of dead Jack Menefee had managed to retaliate somehow, or that the coppers George had waylaid on his walk home from the bar last night had come back to avenge themselves.

It was all the same to Seitz, whatever, once the irritant had been removed.

Smiling, Otto pushed in through the swinging doors and felt his grin go rigid, turned into a grimace at the sight of George Revere standing before him at the bar, shoulder to shoulder with the boss. The two of them were drinking, talking amiably, with the others gathered round them. It was like awakening from pleasant dreams into a living nightmare, biting into fresh ripe fruit and finding maggots.

Still alive.

And what should Seitz discern from that? Had Harry and the Mex simply absconded with his cash? Or had Revere gotten the best of them somehow?

He obviously wouldn't learn a damned thing standing in the doorway, gaping like a fool, nor could he brace Revere and pose the question to him. Otto saw that he could only make the best of it, pretend nothing had happened—if, in fact, it had.

Seitz pictured Harry Baker and Alfredo Something laughing at him, laying out his money for tequila, and he hoped they *were* alive.

He would enjoy hunting them down and killing them himself.

Ryder saw Seitz hesitate as he came through the bat-wing doors, smile flicking off for just a second, then returning. Was he startled to see Ryder standing in the flesh before him, or was that simply the expression of distaste he usually showed to George Revere? Ryder could read it either way, but by the time Seitz reached the bar his face and attitude were back to normal.

"Otto, you get that business taken care of?" Marley asked him.

"Done," Seitz answered. "Then, I thought I saw a few of Jack's old boys prowling around, so I came out the long way."

"Did they spot you?"

"Guess not. Here I stand."

"I thought they might've learned their lesson," Marley

said. "Maybe we need to put the rest of them away." He brooded over that, draining his shot glass and refilling it, then said, "But first, we've got this other job to do."

Seitz cleared his throat, shooting a sidelong glance at Ryder as he asked, "You sure we oughta talk about that now?"

"Why not?" Marley replied.

"Well . . ."

"Otto, I've told you. George is one of us now."

"Fine. Okay."

Ryder kept silent during that exchange, trying to keep his face expressionless while reading theirs. Was it an act on Marley's part? On Otto's? Both? Could he trust Marley's claim to see him as a trusted member of the gang? Or had he come around to Seitz's way of thinking, setting up a trap to snare the traitor?

Ryder saw no other way to play it than proceeding on the course he'd chosen, taking Marley's comments at face value while he kept his guard up against any ambush laid by Seitz or both of them together.

"So, the other boys already know about this," Marley told him. "You'll be going on a little cruise?"

"I will?"

"Not by yourself, o' course. Otto's in charge, taking a dozen of the boys."

"You won't be coming?" Ryder asked him.

Marley shook his head, pouring another shot of liquor. "I've got business to take care of here in Galveston. More than I thought, if Menefee's ragtag and bobtail haven't figured out who's boss."

So he'd be working under Seitz directly, without Marley serving as a buffer. Ryder didn't like the sound of that, but couldn't very well refuse.

"Where are we going?" he inquired.

"You know Timbalier Island?" Marley asked him.

"Sorry. Never heard of it."

"It's off the coast of Terrebonne Parish," Seitz chimed in. His tone was almost normal, as if speaking to another human being. "That's Louisiana, southeast of New Orleans."

Ryder tried to picture it, imagining a map. "That's what, two hundred miles?" he asked.

"Two-fifty be more like it," Seitz replied. "You get seasick?"

"Not yet." He thought about the *Southern Belle*, churning along. "How long is that likely to take?"

Seitz answered with a question of his own. "You have someplace better to be?"

"Just curious," said Ryder, meeting Otto's gaze and holding it until the smuggler blinked. The answer came from Marley when he'd drained his latest shot. "Say thirteen hours out and thirteen back, depending on the wind."

"So, not a steamer then."

"A clipper," Marley said. "You helped unload it earlier today."

The *Banshee*. Formerly the *Revenant*.

"Ah," Ryder said and reached out for his whiskey glass, relieved to see no tremor in his hand.

"Stede thinks he's seen you somewhere," Seitz recalled.

Ryder allowed himself a shrug. Said, "Everybody makes mistakes."

"Uh-huh."

"What are we doing on this island?" Ryder asked, directing it to Marley.

"Digging up a buried treasure," Marley answered, smiling. "Did you ever want to be a pirate when you were a kid?"

"I never thought about it," Ryder answered, honestly.

"Well, here's your chance. You know that pirates used to

move their loot through Galveston, long time before the war?"

Ryder recalled Director Wood's short lecture on the French Lafitte brothers. "That sounds vaguely familiar," he acknowledged.

"Well, it didn't all come through," Marley explained. "Back in the day—say forty, fifty years ago—they made a deal with Washington to fight against the British, in return for all the booty they could steal. O' course, once Andy Jackson beat the redcoats at New Orleans, someone changed the rules. You know how that goes. One day, everybody's friends. The next"—he brought a hand down on the bar, as it were a hatchet's blade—"the law is hanging pirates right and left, grabbing their gold for Uncle Sam."

"No great surprise," said Ryder.

"Right. Except, they missed a few. More than a few, in fact. The ones they hung kept quiet to the end, about the fortunes they had stashed away. Those who survived, well, they laid low awhile, then went back to the only trade they knew. Over the years, they raised a new brood in Jamaica, Cuba, other places. Passing down the memory of where their fathers buried gold and jewels and who knows what all they collected through the years."

"Like what the *Banshee* brought today."

"Like that," Marley agreed. "Except the ganja. That's a new thing, more or less. The darkies like it, and it's catching on with certain others I could name."

"So," Ryder inquired, "when do we leave?"

"You've got an early start," said Marley. "Under sail by eight A.M."

"I'd better catch some sleep, then," Ryder said.

"Not yet, you don't," a soft voice said, beside him. Turning to his left, he saw Nell's upturned, smiling face. "Before you go, there's something that you need to see. Upstairs."

Y ou're special, George," Nell said, when they had finished for the second time.

"I'll bet you say that to all of your gentlemen callers," Ryder replied.

"O' course I do. But with you, I mean it."

"Might kind of you, but I believe you've worn me out."

"We aim to please," she told him, smiling sleepily.

"You hit the mark," Ryder assured her, as he slowly started getting dressed. He left two dollars on the dresser, well above the going rate.

"Come back and see me?"

"If I can," he answered, from the door.

"Say 'when,' not 'if,'" she chided him.

"That's what I meant."

"G'night, George."

"Good night, Nell."

He looked around for Seitz and Marley on his way downstairs, but spotted neither one. They had a way of disappearing once he went upstairs, a circumstance that troubled Ryder more tonight than in the recent past. He wasn't keen on the idea of sailing off with Pickering and Seitz to search for pirates' gold, but there was no way to refuse the order without goading Marley into suspicion along with his chief lieutenant.

Or did Marley suspect him already? Was that the purpose of sending Ryder off with Seitz and Pickering, while Marley stayed on shore? If so, and Ryder shipped out on the *Banshee* as commanded, he would be as good as dead. His only hope, if Seitz and Pickering both had it in for him, would be their fear of riling up the boss.

Another thought: was Pickering afraid of Marley? Would he hesitate to kill Ryder for fear of angering a customer?

No ready answer came to mind for that question. Ryder could only forge ahead, unless he planned to quit the Secret Service there and then—a move that still would not protect him if he stayed in Galveston. The prospect of escaping from the city on his own, making his long way back to Washington, confessing failure to Director Wood on his first mission for the agency disgusted him.

So be it. He would sail tomorrow on the *Banshee*, with his fingers crossed for luck and his Colt fully loaded. If their treasure hunt took a turn for the worse, at least he'd take a few pirates down with him.

And Seitz. Kill him first, if it came down to that. Blast the smug look right off of his face.

But first, he had to leave another message for Director Wood. His last, perhaps, leaving a trail for Wood to follow if he disappeared.

That meant another long, meandering excursion to the Western Union office, Ryder watching out along the way for any gunmen anxious to try their hands where the first pair had failed. Along the way, he wondered if he would have benefited from relating the attack to Marley, maybe looking for a flicker in his eyes to see if he had been informed of it beforehand, but the opportunity was gone. He might not see the boss tomorrow—off on "other business"—and it would seem bizarre for him to wait twelve hours before mentioning the ambush.

Skip it.

Western Union's night clerk was a tall, broad-shouldered man who liked his liquor, if the broken capillaries on his nose and ruddy cheeks were any indicator. Add them to the fumes that he exhaled, and Ryder marked it up as a sure thing. He guessed there was a paucity of supervision on the late shift, wondering how many telegrams were garbled in transmission.

As a hedge, he guessed the spelling of Timbalier Island, kept it short, and waited while the clerk tapped on his key to send the message off. Once its receipt had been confirmed, Ryder began the long walk back through mostly empty streets to reach his boardinghouse.

The street that Ryder sought was dark and silent when he reached it. Galveston had few street lamps on residential avenues, and none at all on this one. He would have to run the shadow gauntlet—or, more accurately, make his way along at a slow walking pace, drawing no unwelcome attention to himself while covering the two blocks to his destination.

And he had a choice to make, before that final trek began.

One way to do it would be walking down the middle of the street, avoiding all the darkest shadows where an ambush might be laid for him. That method would ensure that no one cut his throat, while leaving him exposed to gunfire from all sides. The other way—picking a side and staying in the very shadows where an enemy was likely to be hidden—left him open to direct attack throughout his two-block stroll.

He chose the shadows and prepared himself, drawing his Colt Army. From a trouser pocket, Ryder also removed a French Châtellerault switchblade knife, snapping open its six-inch blade with a touch to the button protruding from its stag horn handle. With the pistol cocked in his right hand, the long knife in his left, Ryder began the walk that would deliver him, with any luck, to his front door.

Each step he took bore Ryder closer to security, or its illusion. As he realized full well, there was a chance his enemies could be inside the boardinghouse, even inside his rented room, hoping to strike at closer quarters than the first pair that had failed. If they surprised and cornered him inside, his chances of survival would be nil, but it was far too late to look for other lodgings, and he didn't plan to spend the night roaming the streets of Galveston.

Halfway to his destination, Ryder heard a scuffling in some shrubbery to his right and swung the Colt in that direction, index finger tightening around its trigger. Just as he prepared to fire, a gray cat burst out of the bushes there with something in its jaws, perhaps one of the city's countless rats. He watched the hunter vanish with its prey, waited another moment for his pounding heart to find a normal rhythm, then proceeded on his way.

The biggest danger to him, once he'd reached the boardinghouse, was climbing to its porch and going on inside. From where he stood, Ryder saw no one seated in the pair of rocking chairs positioned on the building's covered porch, but there were shadows farther back that might conceal a crouching gunman, maybe even two. Steeling himself, perspiring even though the night was cool, he walked up to the porch, mounted its wooden steps, and waited for the ax to fall.

Nothing. No shots, no rush of adversaries to assault him.

For an awkward, deadly moment, Ryder had to put his Colt back in its holster while he found his key and opened the front door. Once he had stepped inside and latched the door behind him, he replaced the key and drew the gun again, proceeding to the nearby stairs with both hands full. If someone waited on the second floor to spring at him, he might go down, but not before his enemy had tasted lead and sharpened steel.

The stairs creaked under Ryder's weight; no help for that. It let the landlord know when boarders came and went, if it was any of his business, and it would announce him to an ambush party if they'd slipped into the house ahead of him. In that case, would the owner and the other tenants still be living now? Would killing Ryder, after one attempt had failed, be worth a wholesale massacre?

He reached the landing without incident, paused there, then moved along the short hall toward his room. The floor creaked, too, its squeaky music following his progress, maybe waking up the whole damned house if anyone beneath its roof was still alive. So far, he'd found no bodies, seen no bloodstains, smelled no gun smoke. It was early, though, for letting down his guard.

Standing outside his door, he had to use the *other* key. This time, he closed the switchblade knife, returned it to his pocket, and unlocked the door to his small room. Followed his Colt inside and spent a moment feeling empty space around him, before he was game enough to close and lock the door, lower the hammer on his piece, and holster it. Relaxing took a good deal longer, once he'd taken off his gunbelt, placed it on his nightstand, and sat down upon the bed.

Whoever hoped to kill him had already missed their chance tonight—not once, but twice. They still might storm the boardinghouse, or even try to burn it down, but Ryder couldn't guard the place all night. He had a rendezvous to keep with Seitz and Pickering tomorrow morning, sailing off to dig for pirate treasure on an island he had never heard of. Never in his wildest fantasy had he believed that such a thing was possible in 1865, much less that duty with the Secret Service would involve such antiquated hijinks.

If he hadn't shot that damned senator's son, if William Wood had simply let him climb inside a bottle after he'd been cashiered from the U.S. Marshals Service, Ryder thought he could be drunk right now and loving it, without a thought of whether he would be alive tomorrow—maybe forced to walk the plank somewhere over the Gulf of Mexico.

He shifted, lay back on the bed, still fully dressed, and closed his eyes. Although nearly exhausted, Ryder was not sleepy in the normal sense. His mind was racing, churning up successive questions that he couldn't answer, posing problems that he couldn't solve. Frustration kept his nerves on edge. His right hand twitched with memory of carrying the Colt Army.

Tomorrow, when he shipped out on the *Banshee* under Captain Pickering, it was entirely possible that he might disappear without a trace. A small voice in his head added, *But not without a fight*, small consolation in the present circumstances.

Make that none at all.

He didn't want to die at twenty-four years old but realized that his control over what happened next was minimal to nonexistent. He could cut and run, desert his post, try getting out of Galveston tonight. But otherwise, his sole choice was to sail at eight o'clock and see whatever Fate might hold in store for him.

He would go armed, of course, with knife, pistol, and extra loaded cylinders. The Henry rifle would, regrettably, remain behind. Too difficult for Ryder to explain it, when he had no reason to believe that they were going on a hunting expedition. Call it eighteen shots and no idea how many men would be aboard the clipper when they sailed from Galveston.

It was a deadly game, maybe a last-ditch play, and Ryder had already passed the point where it was safe for him to fold. He was all-in, even before the final hand was dealt.

Sleep caught him unawares and drew him down into the dark, where hungry things waited to tear him limb from limb.

13

★ **R**yder had an early breakfast—fried eggs, ham, and grits, with "Texas toast." The latter proved to be a kind of thick-sliced bread, toasted as advertised, slathered with spicy apple butter. It would have to get him through the day, for all he knew, and on into the night. If there was any food aboard the *Banshee*, it was likely to be jerky, hardtack, or some other recipe designed to crack a seaman's molars.

On his way out of the boardinghouse, he checked his pockets, verifying that he'd brought two spare cylinders for his Colt Army. The pistol was a muzzle-loading cap-and-ball revolver, each of the cylinder's six chambers being loaded individually with a paper cartridge consisting of a pre-measured black powder load and a lead ball, wrapped in flammable nitrated paper, pressed home with the pivoting loading lever attached beneath the Colt's barrel. All that, and you still had to place a percussion cap onto the raised nipple at the rear of each chamber. Slow reloading in combat could often be fatal, hence the common practice of loading extra cylinders in advance and switching them out in seconds, rather than minutes.

None of which would help if Ryder somehow got disarmed.

As far as he could tell, nobody trailed him to the waterfront. Why would they, when the gang knew where he was going and when he'd arrive? The only purpose for a shadow would be picking Ryder off if he attempted to escape, and he'd abandoned any thought of that last night.

Ryder was fifteen minutes early for the *Banshee*'s sailing, welcomed by a number of Marley's crew waiting to go aboard. On deck, he saw Stede Pickering and Otto Seitz together, in the midst of conversation until Otto saw him on the pier. For once, he didn't scowl, but he said something to the clipper's captain that made Pickering glance down toward Ryder, offer Seitz a shrug, then turn away.

Did that mean they were laying for him? Was he reading too much into an expression and a gesture? Ryder knew his best bet—no, his *only* bet—was to remain on guard throughout the voyage, keep his wits about him, and be ready as he could be if a trap was sprung.

"C'mon aboard!" Seitz called down to the men collected on the dock. Ryder went up the *Banshee*'s gangplank with a dozen others whom he knew from Awful Annie's and the raid against Jack Menefee, taking his place on deck amidst a group that showed no trace of military discipline.

Pickering's men hauled in the gangplank and cast off the mooring lines, not trusting it to landlubbers. Easing out of the harbor took some time, appointed sailors hurrying aloft without a second thought for altitude or what would happen to them if they tumbled from the rigging to the deck below. When they were under way, sails billowing, the captain made his way down from the bridge to speak with Marley's men.

As he approached them, Ryder noted that he had a pepper-box revolver tucked under his wide belt, and a knife the size of a short sword on his right hip. He wore a wide-brimmed floppy had to shade his eyes, and a red kerchief knotted around his neck. Soft leather boots reached almost to his knees, with dull toe caps that looked like tarnished brass.

"You lot won't know the arse end of a ship from for'ard," Pickering declared without preamble. "You're what we call ballast on the *Banshee*, but you'll have a mite of work to do ashore, when we get to Timbalier Island. In the meantime, stay out of the way and cause no bother. Any questions?"

There were none, apparently, the message being fairly simple. Ryder thought the pirate chief was staring at him during that brief monologue, but hoped it might be his imagination working overtime. If not . . . well, it was already too late for him to change the course of whatever might happen next.

They had a thirteen-hour run ahead of them, by Marley's estimate, assuming that the winds cooperated and their sails stayed full. The deck rolled gently under Ryder's feet—at least, so far—and thankfully had no effect on his digestion. When Bob Jacobs hit the starboard rail and spewed his breakfast out into the Gulf, it gave Ryder a fleeting opportunity to feel superior.

He wandered aft, alone, dodging the *Banshee*'s busy crewmen as they went about their duties, and stood watching Galveston recede into the hazy distance. Wondering if it would be the last time he saw land.

* * *

Standing on the *Banshee*'s fantail, Otto Seitz watched George Revere leaning against the starboard rail, no doubt feeling the salt spray in his face and thinking—what? That was the question Seitz would love to answer, but he wasn't sure he'd get the chance.

Last night, he'd slipped away from Awful Annie's when the others started drifting off upstairs to do their business with the working girls. He needed to find Harley Baker and his pal, Alfredo Tijerina, to find out exactly why in hell they hadn't done the job he'd paid them for. He'd checked the places where they normally hung out—a sad cantina called Diablo's and a whorehouse known as Zona Rosa—where the owners didn't care for white men unless they were spending money. More cash out of pocket, then, to learn that neither one of his two pistoleros had turned up at either place during the afternoon or evening.

After that, his time and money wasted, Seitz had walked to Revere's boardinghouse, then tried to follow the path he would probably take to reach Annie's. The bad news: there were half a dozen routes that fit the bill, depending on preliminary destinations, anyplace he might have stopped along the way to have a meal or meet with someone else. Seitz would have given up, disgusted, if the high note of a copper's whistle hadn't lured him off course and down an alley that he would have passed without a second glance.

Police were standing over Baker and the Mex when Seitz arrived. He hung back in the shadows, watching as they picked the dead men's pockets, taking anything of value for themselves. There went *his* money, spent in good faith to put George Revere away, once and for all. But what had happened to his shooters?

Back at Awful Annie's, there had been no mention of an ambush. If his target was the one who'd killed Baker and Tijerina, then Revere must have some reason not to mention it, the way he'd told Marley about his beating of the coppers who had followed him. He was suspicious, then, uncertain who had put the gunmen on his trail, worried that Marley might have been behind it.

Or, he hadn't done the job himself, at all.

Seitz guessed there was a chance—although a very minor one—that someone else had come along and killed his shooters. Stupid as they were, they might have jumped the wrong man in the dark and paid the price for it. He wouldn't put it past them to mess up a simple plan, and while it made no difference to Seitz whether they lived or died, it galled him that they'd let him down.

If you want a thing done right, do it yourself.

Which was exactly what he meant to do, this time.

Seitz didn't care for boats—could feel his stomach grumbling already, just a few short miles from land—but he was chewing on a fat plug of tobacco, hoping it would calm his gut and nerves. His move against Revere would wait until they'd reached Timbalier Island and the heavy work was done, the *Banshee* loaded with their cargo for the trip back home to Galveston. Then he would do what must be done, and use their thirteen hours on the water afterward to plan how he would break it to the boss.

Call it an accident? That wouldn't fly, since he had made no secret of his feelings toward Revere. Besides, even if he had sworn the other members of his crew to secrecy, one of them still might squeal. He wasn't universally beloved by any means, and didn't given a damn.

Explain it outright, then, but with a canny twist. Tell Marley that Revere let something slip about intending to betray them, once he'd seen the treasure trove. It didn't matter if he made George out to be a lawman or a member of some rival gang, as long as he was dirty, dangerous to their ongoing operation. Seitz was only doing what he thought best for the gang, and who could fault him?

Marley might. And if he did . . . what, then?

Seitz didn't want to think that far ahead, but he'd be ready if and when it happened.

Ready to play his hand and let the chips fall where they may.

It was dark when the *Banshee* reached Timbalier Island and Captain Pickering dropped anchor a quarter mile offshore. Rather than lower skiffs and row to land immediately, Pickering decreed that they should wait for dawn, which meant eating and sleeping on the ship. Ryder was pleasantly surprised to learn there was a cook on board, and supper proved to be a very palatable stew. He hoped that it was beef, but didn't push his luck by asking anyone.

Sleeping aboard was something else. The *Banshee*'s normal crew had berths belowdecks, narrow bunks and dangling hammocks that resembled slings made out of fish nets. No allowance had been made for Marley's men, so they'd be sleeping on the weather deck and hoping that it didn't rain during the night. Ryder picked out a lifeboat for himself and lay down in it, waiting for the clipper's gentle rocking to lull him to sleep.

That took a while, with all the anxious thoughts crowding his mind. He lay with one hand on the Colt Army's curved grip, not really thinking anyone would make a move against him overnight, out on the open deck, but still not absolutely positive. His mind was focused more on what awaited him on shore, tomorrow, or during the journey back to Galveston. If Seitz or Pickering—maybe the two of them together—planned to do away with him somehow, on Marley's orders or without his knowledge, it made sense that they would do it on the island or at sea. Since he had finished half the trip alive, the island got his vote.

And what if he was wrong? What if there was no plot against him after all?

That optimistic notion overlooked last night's attempt to kill him, and his best guess naming Otto as the man behind it. Maybe Otto *and* his boss, in which case getting back to Galveston alive was still no guarantee of safety.

Ryder wondered what Director Wood was doing, whether he'd received the telegrams Ryder had sent him, if he planned to take some action in support of Ryder or leave him to handle the whole operation on his own. The one-sided communication was frustrating, left Ryder dangling with no clue as to when—or *if*—he could expect assistance. Wood was probably afraid to answer, worried that someone in Galveston would intercept his message and deliver it to Marley. Still . . .

Still, nothing. Even if Wood answered his last telegram, he wouldn't know it until he returned to Galveston. Ryder did not enjoy the thought of a message lying around the boardinghouse in his absence, but he trusted Wood to be discreet, if he replied at all.

One of the *Banshee*'s crewmen ambled past the lifeboat, trailing pipe smoke, humming to himself. Ryder observed that he was carrying a Pattern 1853 Enfield rifle, a British rifled musket that had been the South's most common weapon in the recent war. Some Union troops had carried it, as well, though most preferred the Springfield Model 1861 for the interchangeability of its machine-made parts. Either piece would blow a .58-caliber hole through flesh and bone, dropping a man out to five hundred yards.

It came as no surprise, of course, to find the pirates armed. Ryder had estimated twenty-five on board, not counting Marley's crew, which meant near-hopeless odds if Seitz or Pickering were planning to get rid of him. He couldn't count on anyone from Marley's side to help him if the order came from Seitz to put him down, and Ryder doubted whether any would risk aiding him if Pickering decided on his own to lay a trap. Why should they, when the pirate captain kept loot flowing through their hands?

Such thoughts kept sleep at bay, as did the ship's bell, chiming each half hour as the night wore on. Eight bells, Ryder had learned, announced the stroke of midnight and a changing of the guard. Somehow, in spite of his anxiety and the incessant tolling from the bridge, he drifted off before a single ringing note declared twelve-thirty had arrived. The other bells, continuing throughout the night, provided grim accompaniment to his uneasy dreams.

Pale light and bustling activity on deck woke Ryder as the sun began to rise behind Timbalier Island. His first view of the barrier island, lost in early morning haze, showed that it was long and narrow, with an irregular shoreline. He guessed it might stretch close to ten miles from east to west, with fair-sized trees inland, and underbrush around them. Sandy-looking soil told him there would not be much difficulty when it came to excavating shallow graves.

Why make that plural? Because Ryder didn't plan on going down alone if anything went wrong.

Breakfast was more of last night's stew, washed down with coffee in tin cups. Ryder had little appetite but ate his helping, anyway, certain that he would need the energy for whatever might lie ahead. By half past seven, lifeboats had been lowered and the *Banshee*'s crew began to go ashore. Seitz rode the first boat, standing in its bow like old George Washington crossing the Delaware, while Ryder caught the second. Marley's men were not assigned to man the oars, but rather carried picks and shovels for the digging, once they'd landed.

Altogether, Pickering sent twenty men ashore, plus Marley's thirteen, counting Otto Seitz. Four buccaneers stood watching from the clipper's deck, detailed to guard the *Banshee* and presumably make sure the ship did not drift off without its landing party safely back on board. A couple of the men who stayed behind were holding Enfield rifles, while the other two had pistols tucked under their belts.

Expecting trouble?

Ryder knew that the U.S. Revenue Cutter Service had boats stationed around the Gulf of Mexico but didn't know exactly where they berthed or whether they patrolled the stretch of coastline where the *Banshee* had dropped anchor. Like the Secret Service, Revenue Cutters operated on behalf of the Treasury Department, hunting smugglers and enforcing other tenets of maritime law in American waters. They'd been pressed into military duty on various occasions since 1812, and one of them—the USRC *Harriet Lane*—had fought the first naval engagement of the War Between the States, near Fort Sumter, in April 1861.

Ryder didn't expect a Revenue Cutter to save him, wasn't even sure he *needed* saving, and besides, he preferred to gather more evidence against Marley's smuggling operation if he could.

As long as he survived to testify.

Once ashore, Ryder waited with the men from Marley's

group who had preceded him. Seitz paced along the surf line, restless, while the life boats doubled back, took on another load of able bodies, and returned. The *Banshee* crewmen shipped their oars then, dragged the boats well up on shore, and joined the rest while digging tools were passed around.

"This way," said Pickering, who'd ridden in the last lifeboat to reach the island. Seitz walked in his shadow, while the rest of them came straggling along behind, the furthest thing from any kind of military order in the ranks. They hiked inshore for something like a mile, then stopped with Pickering as he examined landmarks, matching them against a yellowed, often-folded piece of paper in his hands.

A treasure map?

In other circumstances, Ryder would have smiled at the idea, or maybe laughed out loud, but there was nothing humorous about his present situation. He had good reason to believe the loot existed, based on items he'd already helped unload in Galveston. The Tariff Act of 1857 had taxed imports at an average rate of 17 percent, now on its way to being doubled by Republicans in Congress since war's end. How much was that, lost to the government in revenue of cargo Marley smuggled into Galveston? On gold and silver? Gems? The silly-sounding ganja?

Thousands, certainly, assuming that the pirate booty was not confiscated outright on discovery.

"This is the spot," said Pickering, grinding a heel in the sand between two live oak trees, set roughly fifteen feet apart.

Ryder half expected to find an X drawn on the ground, after the style of fabled pirate maps from novels he had read in childhood: *Fanny Campbell*, *The Queen of the Sea*, or *The Secret Service Ship*. It was unmarked, however, aside from Pickering's footprint, designating the spot for their digging to start.

"Come on, then!" Pickering bellowed, when no one moved immediately. "Put your backs into it! *Dig!*"

And dig they did, working in relays, following the *Banshee* captain's orders to outline, then excavate, a pit some eight feet long by four feet wide and six feet deep. *A good-sized grave,* thought Ryder, as he took his turn, wielding a spade, careful to step back when the men with pickaxes were swinging. It was sandy soil, all right, but live oak roots made digging difficult until they had been chopped and hacked away.

It anything was buried there, Ryder knew that those roots had sprouted in the meantime, reaching out for sustenance and interweaving to protect whatever lay below them. How long would the treasure have been resting in its hole? If Jean Lafitte had planted it, and he had truly died in 1823—a date disputed, since his corpse was never found—the loot had been underground for at least forty-two years. Plenty of time for trees to sprout, grow tall, and lace the island with a maze of roots. Tack on another decade for the days when the Lafitte brothers had raided British shipping in the War of 1812. What would remain of treasure buried that far in the past?

He knew that gold, silver, and gems would not decay, although the chests or bags that held them might be gone. Ryder supposed they could forget about retrieving any paper currency planted for half a century, but chances were that it would have been printed by some bank long since defunct, in any case. If they found anything, he guessed it would be heavy and would take a fair amount of time for transportation to the *Banshee*.

His thoughts were thus engaged when Ryder's spade struck something solid, with a heavy thunk. He hesitated, then began to scrape the dirt away more carefully, two other men with shovels helping him, until the curved lid of a brass-bound chest had been exposed. Encouraged by the sight of it, and by commands from Pickering, they started digging out around the chest's four sides, until a pair of rotting leather handles were revealed. One of them ripped through on the first attempt to hoist it, and more excavation was required before three men could climb into the hole, standing around the chest, and lift it clear.

It was approximately three feet long, two wide, and eighteen inches deep. The padlock on its hasp had long since rusted shut, but three blows with a pickax shattered it. Seitz moved to lift the lid, but Pickering moved in to shoulder him aside and claim that honor for himself. A moment later, sunlight gleamed on golden coins—hundreds, by Ryder's estimate—untarnished by the years.

A cheer went up, cut short when Pickering began selecting men to take the chest, carry it back to where the lifeboats had been beached, and row it over to the clipper. Those who stayed behind, Ryder among them, would keep digging for a second chest that was supposed to occupy the pit.

They found it fifteen minutes later, raised it in the manner of the first one they had found, and let the captain open it. This time, a rainbow glimmered in the sunshine: rubies, emeralds, and diamonds, some in precious settings, others tumbled loose into the chest. No cheering this time, as a second party was selected for the long trek back to shore.

"Now, we fill it in," said Pickering. "No point in advertisin' what was here."

By *we*, he meant the workmen still remaining, he and Seitz retreating to converse beyond earshot while Ryder and his nine companions sweated through refilling the deep pit, then wiping out all traces of the dig as best they could, scattering sand over the spot.

When they were done and standing idle, Pickering and Seitz returned, taking their time about it, Pickering smoking a pipe. "That does it," he informed them. "All except one little thing."

"One piece of business still needs takin' care of," Otto said. Ryder could feel the short hairs rising on his nape then, as the smuggler's eyes focused on him.

"Bidness?" Harry Morgan echoed.

"I smelled a rat when Bryan brought you into Awful Annie's," Seitz told Ryder.

Bluff it out, he thought. And answered back, "How do you figure that?"

"It's pretty damn convenient, how you showed up just the minute that he needed help."

"Right place, right time," Ryder replied. "Why would I help him, if I meant him any harm?"

"To worm your way inside, maybe."

"Hey, Otto," Morgan interjected, "you ain't makin' any sense."

"Oh, no? You think it's just coincidence he turns up as we go to war with Menefee?"

"He helped us *kill* Jack Menefee," Harry shot back. "Don't tell me you're forgettin' that."

"I ain't fogettin' anything," Seitz said, drawing his Colt. "I'm takin' out the trash."

No time to think about it, then. Snarling at Seitz, Ryder lashed out and slammed his spade into the smuggler's face, then turned and ran.

14

⭐ **C**haos reigned behind him as he sprinted for the nearest tree line, voices jabbering with questions, Otto howling curses with a nasal twang, Stede Pickering demanding that the men still on their feet go after Ryder. He had covered thirty yards, was in among the trees, before they started chasing him. The first shot made his shoulders hunch reflexively, but it was high and wide, the bullet slapping at a tree trunk somewhere off to Ryder's left.

His swing at Seitz had been instinctive, pure self-preservation, but he wondered now if running afterward had been a poor decision. Harry Morgan had been arguing his side with Otto, and the rest of Marley's men, at least, had seemed surprised by Otto's actions. Should he have remained to plead his case after he'd pasted Seitz?

Too late to think about that now.

Clubbing a man who tried to kill him would be normal and expected by the gang, but running once he'd done it would be tantamount to a confession.

"Over here!" somebody shouted, well behind him.

"There he goes!" another cried.

Not voices that he recognized, offhand, but then again, what of it? Any mother's son could drop him with a lucky shot, or slit his throat if he stood still for it. Ryder had to evade them if he could, hold out till nightfall anyway, and hope they'd lose him in the dark.

Another shot behind him, and the bullet came no closer than the first. Combine a moving target with a shooter on the run, and taking down a man was doubly difficult. The woods helped, too, with cover and their shadows. Still, there were eleven men pursuing him, presumably. Call it an even dozen if he hadn't shaken something loose in Otto's skull. Fanned out, advancing steadily, they had a decent chance of overtaking and surrounding him.

As they'd approached Timbalier Island, Ryder had judged it to be ten miles long, at least. Its width and the square mileage of it still remained a mystery. Ryder wasn't convinced that he could run ten miles without a rest, but even if he managed it, he'd find himself cut off, trapped on another beach with nowhere left to turn. They'd have him then, and it would all be over.

Long shadows in the forest told him it was getting on toward dusk, but slowly. If he wanted to survive, Ryder would have to slow down the pursuit. Make his new enemies think twice about the hunt they were engaged in. Raise the stakes for all concerned.

Still running, Ryder pulled his Colt Army and started looking for a place to make his stand. It wouldn't be his *last* stand, hopefully—no imitation of the Alamo—but if he timed it properly . . .

Live oaks and pines were all around him, offering the only cover he could hope to find. He stopped and crouched behind one of the larger trees, heard hunters calling back and forth to one another in the woods before him, drawing nearer by the moment. Ryder cocked his pistol, scanned the ground, waiting for targets to reveal themselves.

The first was someone from the *Banshee*'s crew, bearded and brawny, carrying what looked to be a stubby pepperbox. The little pistol had no barrel in the normal sense, just firing chambers grouped around a central axis. Could be four shots, six, or more, depending on the model, but it would be useful only at the very closest range, compared to fifty yards for Ryder's Colt.

Not that he planned to try a shot from that range in the forest, with the shadows creeping in on him.

Try twenty yards, instead, the pirate blundering along and calling back to others he'd outrun in his enthusiasm for the chase. Feeling no sympathy or urge to spare him, Ryder shot him in the chest and saw him fall, blood spouting from the hole his .44 slug made.

More shouting then, but Ryder didn't wait for any of the others to arrive. When they kept after him—*if* they kept after him—he'd try to snipe another one, and so on, whittling down their will to hunt. With two spare cylinders and one shot gone, he had enough rounds left to deal with all of those who'd stayed behind, but that would be a losing gamble, even if he managed it somehow. The men who'd gone back to the *Banshee* would return for Pickering if Ryder failed to appear, and that would be the end of it.

Hang on, he thought. *Just stay alive for now.*
One minute at a time.

He bwoke ma goddamn node!" Seitz bawled, probing his
blood-caked face with cautious fingertips, then glaring
at Pickering. "Da hell you gwinnin' at?"

Still smiling, Pickering replied, "I never seen you look
so good."

"Weal fuddy!" Seitz was checking his front teeth now,
grimacing as one wiggled under the pressure of his thumb.
"I'm gonna kid 'im!"

"Then we'd better hurry up," said Pickering, "before the
others beat you to it."

Seitz picked up his Colt, spinning the cylinder and blow-
ing sand out of the works as best he could, checking to
satisfy himself the barrel hadn't fouled when he had dropped
it. "C'mod, den," he told the *Banshee*'s captain, setting off
after the hunting party that was chasing George Revere.

It hurt to run, each jolting step driving a white-hot lance
of agony into his skull. It might not be the worst pain he had
ever felt, but Seitz reckoned that it was close enough. Each
burning stab increased his fury, pulled the knot of hatred
in his stomach that much tighter.

He had known that there was something out of plumb
about Revere from the first time he'd met the bastard. Marley
wouldn't listen, but he'd have to pay attention now. Seitz
would have liked to bring Revere's head to him in a basket,
but he didn't want to push it. Find the rat and finish him—
but not before Revere had spilled who he was working for
and why he'd come to Galveston.

Asking the questions could be fun, but that meant catching up with Georgie Boy before the others ran him down

and shot him out of hand. Seitz needed him alive, just long enough to answer certain questions.

And to hear him scream.

The sharp clap of a gunshot up ahead spurred Otto on to greater speed—and greater pain. Trying to keep Revere alive, Seitz bleated out to those who'd gone ahead, "Doan kid 'im! Wade fuh me!"

Long moments later, Otto stood over a corpse, with others grouped around him. It was one of Stede's, which set the *Banshee*'s captain cursing in rare form, using some terms that Seitz took to be nautical. Seitz tried to mask his own sense of relief, assisted in that effort by the throbbing misery inside his head.

He quickly counted those who'd stopped to view the fallen sailor. Four of nine who'd set off in pursuit of George Revere, plus one dead on the ground, left four still on the hunt. Otto had barely finished calculating when another shot rang out, off to the east, and he was running once again, dizzy and nearly sobbing from the pain and the exertion.

Another body on the ground, and three men crouched around it, staring off into the woods. Seitz jostled Harry Morgan as he slid in to a halt and recognized Bob Jacobs stretched out on his back. He only had one eye now, and a bloody socket where a slug had punched the other back into his brain.

"George shot him," Morgan said.

"Still dink he's one ob us?"

"I'm gonna kill him," Harry said.

"You'll do it on your own, then," Pickering informed him, as he joined their group with his surviving sailors. "I'm not puttin' any more of my men on the chopping block for your mistake."

"The hell you mead?" Otto demanded.

"What I *mean* is that I'm sailin' now. You wanna stay behind and hunt this boyo to your heart's content, I leave you to it."

"Jud like dat?"

"You heard me," Pickering replied. "Do what you want on land, but I'm the master of the *Banshee*. And she's sailin' just as soon as I get back aboard her. Come on, men!"

With that, the captain turned away and started trekking westward, toward the beach where they had landed. The remaining members of his party followed, one shrugging for Seitz, to show he had no other choice. Within a few short moments, they were swallowed by the dusk, nearly invisible from where Seitz stood.

It galled him, leaving George Revere alive, but Otto knew that Pickering would sail without him and would not be coming back. It might be days before Marley could find another ship to come and pick them up—or would he even bother? Might it seem a better choice for him to wash his hands of the whole problem?

Let the dead bury the dead.

Slurring a curse, he told his men, "Come odd. We'll let the bastid starb."

Ryder heard the trackers leaving, but he didn't trust it right away. He had nothing to gain by trailing them, except a bullet in the head, but common sense dictated that he see if they were leaving, or if they would camp out on the island, ready to resume the hunt the next morning.

First, before he started trailing them, he swapped the Colt Army's cylinder, two rounds gone, for one still fully loaded. If he walked into an ambush he would have six shots, at least, no fumbling in the dark while trying to reload with bullets flying all around him.

Not that it would matter much, but he preferred to go down fighting if it came to that.

The only light he had to guide by on Timbalier Island was the moon, now, as he made his slow way westward toward their landing beach. Each step he took seemed dangerously loud and grating to his ears, but no one challenged him along the way. No muzzle flashes blasted at him from the shadows as he tracked the smugglers' party back toward shore.

And Ryder saw the reason why as he approached the final tree line, overlooking sand and surf. The last lifeboat had nearly reached the *Banshee*, lamps on deck keeping the oarsmen on a straight course toward the clipper. No one from the crew or Marley's gang had stayed on shore.

Next question: were they leaving, sailing back to Galveston, or would they ride at anchor through the night, then come back looking for him in the morning? Was it worth their time, the risk of being spotted, to remain and run him down, scouring the island end to end?

Ryder walked halfway to the water's edge and sat down on the sand. It didn't matter now if he was visible from the retreating lifeboat, though he doubted it. Plain logic told him that they would not turn around and risk another landing, this time under fire. As far as sniping at him from the lifeboat or the clipper, distance and the cloak of night should keep him safe enough.

For now.

He sat and stared across the moonlit water, watching as the lifeboat reached the *Banshee*, was tied off to hoisting lines, then started to unload its crew. They scrambled up a long rope ladder, one man at a time, until all nine were safely on the weather deck. At that point, other crewmen raised the lifeboat, aided by a block and tackle system, swung it inboard, and prepared to lash it down.

No answer yet to Ryder's question, but he soon received one, as the *Banshee*'s crew began unfurling sails. It didn't take them long, with practiced hands at work. Within a quarter of an hour, maybe less, the clipper had weighed anchor and was underway, gliding eastward, away from Ryder on his lonely stretch of sand, with moonlight on its sails.

His first, fleeting sensation of relief quickly gave way to something more like dread. *Marooned,* he thought, *like Robinson Crusoe.* And how was he supposed to deal with that?

His stomach growled out a reminder that he'd eaten nothing since that morning's breakfast of reheated stew aboard the clipper. It was common knowledge that a man of average size could last a month or more without a meal, before he starved to death. Fresh water was more critical, but Ryder guessed that he could dig for some if necessary, starting where the island's trees and shrubbery grew thickest. Getting off Timbalier Island was his first priority, of course, but that could pose a problem.

Sailing up to it, aboard the *Banshee*, he had calculated that the island lay ten miles from the Louisiana mainland, likely farther. Could he swim ten miles? The thought had never crossed his mind before, and now it seemed a daunting task. Adding the risk of sharks and other predators sharply reduced his prospect of surviving. And if he *could* reach the distant shore, where would he find himself? From what he'd seen of the Louisiana coastline as they passed, it was a maze of rivers, swamps, and hummocks overgrown with jungle. What was waiting for him there, except a wild menagerie of alligators, snakes, and panthers?

Speaking of animals . . .

Ryder decided that the first thing he required, immediately, was a fire. He had a box of matches in his pocket, driftwood on the beach, and there was bound to be some kindling back beyond the tree line. Weary as he was, he rose and set about the task of making camp.

Despite the fire that warmed him, sleep eluded Ryder as the night wore on. Crabs the size of dinner plates appeared from somewhere after sundown, clicking and skittering over the beach around him. They avoided Ryder's campfire, but their shadows lurched across the sand like monstrous spiders, circling him as if they hoped he might dispense morsels of food.

There was no food, of course. Though maybe if they didn't move too quickly he could rustle himself up some of those crabs. His stomach had progressed from growling to a kind of hollow achy feeling. He was thirsty, too, and while that combination likely would have been enough to keep Ryder from sleeping, he was focused on escape. His mind presented fantasy scenarios—building a raft, meeting a kindly fisherman who'd strayed ashore—and quickly moved from there to visions of revenge, confronting Otto Seitz and tracking down the others who had stranded him.

Near midnight by his pocket watch, Ryder heard something he could not identify at first. A chugging sound that brought to mind a locomotive, running in the distance, but he didn't think that sound could carry from the mainland to his camp. Besides, from what he'd seen by daylight, there were only mangrove swamps along the coastline of Terrebonne Bay, no solid ground that would support a set of railroad tracks.

He sat and listened, curious, until he'd satisfied himself that he was not imagining the sound. It seemed to emanate from somewhere to his right, roughly northeastward, drawing closer by the moment on a course from east to west. A steamer, he decided, but with no idea how close it was or how far it would pass offshore from where he sat, beside his meager fire.

Ryder was reaching for another piece of driftwood when he hesitated. Could this be some trick by Seitz or Pickering to draw him out? The *Banshee* had no engine, but could they have found another ship since stranding him and sent it back to see if Ryder would reveal himself? If so, they were approaching from the wrong direction. They had sailed away westward, back toward Galveston, and would have needed hours to return, circling around the island just to dupe him.

No, he finally decided. Not the men who had marooned him—but they could be other smugglers, pirates, outlaws trolling on the Gulf for easy prey. He almost doused the fire, then, but decided it would be a foolish move to hide when help might be at hand.

Some fifteen minutes after Ryder heard the engine for the first time, he saw lights across the water. Lanterns on a ship's deck, clearly, and he started piling driftwood on his dying fire, fanning the low flames with his hands until they caught and leaped into the island's dark, moist air. He tried to judge the ship's size from the space between the lanterns at its bow and stern, guessing around one hundred feet.

Was anyone on watch to see his fire, and if so, would they pay it any mind?

Ryder decided it was worth a gamble. When the ship was opposite his stretch of beach, perhaps three hundred yards offshore, he drew his Colt Army and aimed it skyward, squeezing off two slow and measured shots that echoed from the island's tree line out into the night.

Another moment, and a voice sounded across the water, hollow-sounding, clearly amplified by virtue of a speaking-trumpet. "Ahoy! Are you in need of help?"

"I am!" he shouted back, throat parched, with no idea if it would carry to the ship.

"Stand by!" the tinny call came to his ears, then nothing more except for creaking, splashing sounds. A lifeboat being lowered?

Ryder stepped off from the fire, determined not to make himself an easy target if there was some treachery afoot, his pistol still in hand. Ten minutes later, he heard oars slapping the water, muffled conversation from the boat as it approached the beach. He stood well back, watching the oarsmen drag their boat ashore, noting their uniforms before he put his Colt back in its holster and stepped forward.

Polished brass reflected firelight from the tunic collar of the man who greeted him. "Lieutenant Holland, with the U.S. Revenue Cutter *Andrew Jackson*," he said. "And you, I think, must be Gideon Ryder."

The *Andrew Jackson* was, in fact, one hundred and twenty feet long, a schooner-rigged steamer with three tall masts and a belching smokestack amidships. Its main cabin lay aft, with the lifeboats in their slings, while a pair of three-inch guns on swivel mounts were planted near the bow. No sails were rigged as it proceeded under power toward Galveston.

Ryder ate his first meal within twenty-odd hours, while Lieutenant Holland told the story of his rescue. His telegrams *had* reached Director Wood, and mention of

Timbalier Island had inspired the Secret Service chief to send a cutter snooping in the area, after a decent interval, in case something had gone awry. Holland had not been briefed on Ryder's mission otherwise and gave no indication that he cared to know about it.

"The message," Holland said, "is that you can't expect assistance and you shouldn't trust the local law. Does that make sense?"

"It does," Ryder replied. *Unfortunately.* "I appreciate the lift," he added, pushing back his empty plate, "but I can't risk you dropping me at Galveston."

"I've thought about that," Holland told him. "There's another way to handle it, but you'll be on your own."

"I'm getting used to that," said Ryder.

"If you're sure . . ."

"Let's hear the plan."

"Pelican Island," Holland said.

"Okay. Let's hear a little more."

"It lies north of Galveston proper, connected to the larger island by a plank bridge. Some fishermen have shanties there. Moonshiners, too, we reckon, though we've never actually caught them at it."

"So?"

"So, I was thinking you could go ashore, maybe in uniform, then change into civilian duds and cross the bridge to Galveston, like coming in the back door. I surmise the scurvy rats who left you won't expect you to come in behind them."

Ryder nodded. "I believe you're right."

"Of course, there *is* another way."

"And I appreciate the thought," said Ryder. "But if I come roaring in with your crew, they'll just scatter. We'd be lucky to collect a handful of the flunkies."

"As you like it," Holland said.

"I don't like any of it," Ryder told him. "But I'm in this far and bound to see it through."

"It's your decision," the lieutenant said. "When you get done here, we can fit you for a uniform."

Ryder finished his coffee, set the tin cup down, and said, "Let's get it done."

It was half past five A.M. when the *Andrew Jackson* dropped anchor off Pelican Island, a roughly triangular land mass separated from Galveston's north shore by a narrow strait, spanned by the bridge that Holland had described. Ryder bid his rescuers farewell before the landing party went ashore, with him in uniform. The borrowed clothes fit poorly, but it hardly mattered in the first gray light of dawn, surrounded as he was by other crewmen dressed the same. The fishermen—or smugglers?—who were up and on the move so early made a point of ignoring the revenue officers, even avoiding eye contact.

Ryder carried his civilian clothes and gunbelt tied up in a bundle, tucked beneath one arm as inconspicuously as he could. When the other members of his party fanned out on the pretext of conducting a search, he left them behind, ducked into a dark grove of trees, and changed outfits, leaving the uniform behind. Dressed as himself again, he hiked off toward the south side of the island with its bridge, facing across the strait toward Galveston.

His first stop, he decided, ought to be his boardinghouse. The landlord might be wondering what had become of him, and Ryder didn't want the man disposing of his rifle or his other belongings. Beyond that, he craved a change of clothing, a bath, and a shave, before he went back on the hunt.

It was a different game, now that he had been marked for death by Otto Seitz. Ryder still didn't know if Bryan

Marley was behind that move, but he'd decided that it was irrelevant. Seitz would have given Marley his account of the events as soon as he returned to Galveston. The time for argument had passed.

He had a job to finish. And it seemed he would be doing it alone.

15

Bryan Marley glowered at the two men facing him across the table in Awful Annie's back room. One of his men who'd done some boxing had adjusted Otto's broken nose a bit, but there was nothing to be done about the purple bruises underneath both eyes. Behind him, glaring back at Marley, sat Stede Pickering.

"He hit me with a shovel, in the face," Seitz said. "He killed Bob Jacobs."

"And one of my men, too," the *Banshee*'s captain added. "Stoney Rogers."

"After *you* drew down on him," Marley replied to Seitz, teeth clenched in anger.

"What'n hell was I supposed to do?"

"Leave him alone, goddamn it, like I told you to!"

"Bryan—"

"You started riding him the minute that I brought him in," said Marley, "and for no damned reason."

"But he *ran*. He shot two men!"

"With *them* shooting at *him*. Would you stand there and let somebody kill you without fighting back?"

"You're saying this is *my* fault?"

Marley slammed his fist onto the table, making whiskey glasses dance. "And who else should I blame?"

Beneath the bruising, Seitz wore an expression of amazement. "All the years we been together, if you still don't trust me—"

"*Trust* you? When I give an order time and time again, but you ignore it?"

"There was somethin' wrong with him, I tell you! If you'd seen him—"

"Shut it!" Marley growled. He turned to Pickering. "And you . . ."

The captain rocked back in his chair and aimed a thick finger at Seitz. "*He* told me that the two of you were square on this. I went along with it and lost a good man on the deal. That's it, as far as I'm concerned."

Seitz was half turned in his chair, toward Pickering, staring at each of them in turn. "So I'm the goat? Is that it?"

"Three men down for nothing," Marley said. "You brought it on yourself."

"Brought *what* on?"

"You went behind my back, Otto. Ignored my orders. What do you think I should do?"

Seitz stiffened. "I suppose you'd better tell me."

"If it weren't for all those years you talk about, I'd kill you," Marley said. "As it stands, I can't afford to keep you on."

"For God's sake, Bryan—"

"No. For *your* sake, Otto. Get out while you can. And I mean out of Galveston."

"You run this city now? Is that it?" Otto challenged him.

"Why don't you ask Jack Menefee?"

Seitz pushed his chair back with a grating sound and stood. Beneath the table, Marley kept a Colt Navy aimed at his one-time partner's groin.

"You reckon this is finished?" Otto asked.

"If you come back here," Marley said, "you'd best come shooting."

Seitz seemed on the verge of answering but reconsidered it and turned away, stormed out, and left the two men seated at the table, staring after him.

"Looks like you've made an enemy," said Pickering.

"I don't need friends who go against me."

"True enough. So, how do we stand?"

Marley said, "I take you at your word that you were misinformed."

"All right, then. We'll be heading out this afternoon. I'll be in touch when I have something for you."

"Fair enough. Watch out for Seitz, while you're in port."

"He doesn't worry me," said Pickering. "At least, until he's done with you."

"I'll keep my eyes peeled. Count on it."

"Another glass, before I go upstairs," the captain said. "I fancy there's a red-haired wench out there been givin' me the eye."

"Good luck to you."

Pickering thrust a hand into his pocket, jingling coins. "Luck's got nothin' to do with it."

"You're right, at that."

He watched Pickering drain his whiskey glass, then rise and leave the room. Marley remained, alone, brooding over the trouble Otto Seitz had caused.

He didn't mourn for George Revere, per se, although the

man had saved his life on two occasions. People died in Marley's line of business. It was normal and accepted. What he couldn't tolerate was Seitz, the man he'd trusted most of any in his circle, openly defying him. They *would* be enemies from that point on, as Pickering had said.

Bad blood divided them, and that was only cured by spilling it.

If Seitz returned—*when* he returned—one of them had to die.

Marley lifted his Colt and placed it on the table. He would keep it close at hand from now on, sleep with one eye open if he had to, till the deadly game was finished.

There could only be one winner, and he planned to be the last man standing when the smoke cleared.

After a change of clothes and visit to a barbershop that offered baths, Ryder stopped at a Mexican café where he believed he was unlikely to encounter anyone from Bryan Marley's gang. The fare was unfamiliar to him, but he found that he enjoyed it, wolfing down two enchiladas, a tamale, a chile relleno that proved to be a roasted pepper filled with cheese, and a side dish of beans that the chef called *frijoles refritos*. Thus fortified, with two tequila chasers, Ryder greeted early afternoon in Galveston as he began his hunt.

He had no detailed plan per se, aside from finding Otto Seitz before he tackled any other members of the gang. Their score was personal, and at the same time, Ryder knew the little smuggler's head was full of secrets that could sink the operation if revealed. He wanted more than just a single warehouse filled with loot, though if it came to that, Ryder supposed that he would settle for whatever he could get.

He was desperately short of reinforcements, and

Lieutenant Holland's crew was far beyond his reach, but when they'd parted, Holland had provided Ryder with the name of another Revenue agent whose cutter—the USRC *Martin Van Buren*—operated out of Corpus Christi, some 190 miles southwest of Galveston. Still nine hours away at top speed, from the time Ryder sent the base a telegram, but that was four hours faster than waiting for help from New Orleans, where Holland was stationed.

Meanwhile, anything could happen.

First thing, Ryder took a chance and walked to Awful Annie's by a route that took him to the back door of the bawdy house. Unseen by anyone inside as he arrived, he crept along an alley to the north, finally reached a point where he could scan the street in front, and waited for some drunks to clear the plank sidewalk before he risked a peek into the barroom through one of its dirty windows. From there, he recognized some members of the Marley gang, but couldn't see the boss or Otto Seitz. Mixed in with Marley's men, he spotted several faces he remembered from the *Banshee*'s crew—and Captain Pickering, just now emerging from one of the cribs upstairs.

Which gave him an idea.

He had not hoped to catch the pirates still in port, but now he had an opportunity that Ryder didn't feel he could ignore. Who knew how long the *Banshee* would remain in port, or when it would return? How long until her captain changed the clipper's name again to throw pursuers off her track?

He might be able to prevent that, even put the operation out of business for a time, if he was quick and deft enough. It meant delaying any further search for Otto Seitz, but Ryder was prepared to pay that price.

He left the neighborhood of Awful Annie's as he had approached it, without drawing any notice to himself. The men who could identify him liked to spend their daylight hours indoors, whenever possible, preferring whiskey and the charms of painted women to a sunburn and hard labor on the docks. He hoped the *Banshee*'s crew was of a similar persuasion as he made his way down toward the waterfront, alert to any danger from familiar faces on the way.

He found the *Banshee* without difficulty, tied up to a pier, the gangplank down. Ryder expected guards but saw none on the deck as he approached the clipper. Could it be that all of them had gone ashore? That would explain the gangplank, since there'd be no means of lowering it from the pier, with no one left on board.

And finally, he knew that there was only one way to find out.

With one hand on his holstered Colt Army, Ryder approached the sloping plank and went aboard as if he owned the ship. No one came out to challenge him before he reached the weather deck and stood there listening for any sounds of human habitation on the ship.

Nothing.

It seemed unlikely to him that the *Banshee* would be left wholly unguarded, and he got the answer to that question moments later, when he found a crewman dozing in a hammock toward the starboard side, in shade. Beside him, near his dangling fingertips, an empty bottle stood upon the deck. Ryder retrieved and sniffed it, nearly overpowered by the fumes of rum, and put it back.

If this was Pickering's security, he thought, the ship was his.

A rapid circuit of the weather deck and cabins proved that Ryder was correct; the drunken pirate was the only soul aboard the clipper, other than himself. From what he'd seen at Awful Annie's, Ryder guessed the other crewmen would not be returning to the *Banshee* for a few more hours, at least, but he would finish off the work he'd come to do as quickly as he could, regardless.

First, a search belowdecks.

Ryder did not hope to find the treasure from Timbalier Island still aboard, and he was right in that assumption. Had they stashed it in the same warehouse where he had helped unload the other loot and ganja previously? That was something to investigate, but first he meant to put the *Banshee-Revenant*-whatever out of action, permanently.

If he had his way, this ghost would never ply the seas again.

Well back in the hold he found barrels of tar, presumably used for waterproofing and the patching of leaks while at sea. A tool chest lay nearby, and Ryder rifled through it, settling on a rusty hatchet that he thought should serve him well. Tipping one barrel on its side, he swung the hatchet half a dozen times to smash the lid and waited for the barrel's viscous contents to come dribbling out. Once that was done, he rolled the opened barrel forward through the hold, leaving a trail of tar behind him from the other barrels, like a powder train.

And every bit as flammable.

He knew that fire remained the greatest danger to a wooden ship, whether at sea or moored in port. Fueled by the tar, once it was lit, the *Banshee* would go quickly up in flames, and maybe take the pier along with it. Ryder would have to save the drunken watchman if he could, but first he had to start the fire.

As it turned out, the tar was slow to catch. Ryder wasted a match before he saw a lantern hanging from the bulkhead, smashed it on the deck to spill its reservoir of kerosene, then tried again. This time the flames took hold without delay, spreading along the trail of tar that he had laid, soon lapping at the other barrels in the rear part of the hold, filling the air with acrid smoke.

And it was time to go.

He clambered up a ladder to the weather deck and circled back to reach the sleeping seaman in his hammock. Slapping him repeatedly brought no response beyond a muttered curse, so Ryder hoisted his deadweight out of the hammock, to the rail, and tipped him overboard, into the water. From the shout that echoed back at him, accompanied by thrashing sounds, he knew the man was finally awake.

Going down the gangplank, Ryder took it slow and easy, acting as if he belonged. The first black wisps of smoke were just emerging from the *Banshee*'s hold as he stepped off the pier onto dry land, but then the first pale gout of flame shot skyward, and a sailor working on a nearby vessel raised the dreaded cry of "Fire!"

Two sailors passing on the dock ran to the clipper's gangplank, mounted to the deck, and started calling out to anyone who might still be aboard. When satisfied that no one was imperiled by the flames, they beat a quick retreat and stood apart with others, watching while the fire spread from the hold to upper decks, then climbed the masts and rigging unopposed. Crewmen aboard surrounding ships were busy with their own defenses, no one sparing any time or energy to save the *Banshee* as it was consumed at dockside, gradually burning to the water line.

Ryder remained, watching, until the fire had done its work and guttered out, charred masts collapsing, crushing any structures on the clipper's deck that had not been devoured by the flames beforehand. Turning from the blackened hulk as it began to settle, he was satisfied with one part of a job well done.

But he was far from finished, yet.

Stede Pickering was working on another glass of rum— his sixth, maybe his seventh. He'd lost count and wasn't too concerned about it, since he had a solid head for liquor and the little redhead's amorous exertions had burned off a fair amount of alcohol that he'd consumed before their tryst upstairs. His mood was mellow when the barroom's bat-wing doors flew open and a straggler from his crew barged in, his shirt and trousers sopping wet.

"Captain!" he called out from the doorway, rushing forward. "Come quick! It's the *Banshee*!"

This one, Jonas Walker, had been left behind to watch the clipper, and his presence in the bar could only mean bad news.

"What of her?" he asked, apprehensively.

"S-s-sir," the seaman stammered out, "she's gone!"

Pickering lumbered to his feet and growled, "The hell you say! What do you mean, she's *gone*?"

"Burnt up is what I mean, sir. Burnt and sunk. Gone up in smoke."

Pickering grabbed a hold of Walker's sodden shirt, hoisting the smaller man up onto tiptoes. "Burnt and sunk! Just where in hell were you, while this was goin' on?"

Walker went pale beneath his sailor's baked-in tan. "I mighta fell asleep for just a second, sir. No longer, I can tell you that, when somebody pitched me over the rail."

"Asleep? And then tossed overboard? By who?" Pickering raged.

"I din't exactly see his face, sir."

Pickering pulled Walker close and sniffed him. Mixed in with the smell of sea water, he recognized the pungent scent of rum. "And you were drunk on watch, goddamn you!" he exploded.

"No, sir! I—"

Pickering slammed his fist into the sailor's face and let him drop, unconscious, to the sawdust-littered floor. Turning to face the cribs upstairs, he bellowed out, "All crewmen from the *Banshee*, to the waterfront! No lagging! Last man on the pier's dead meat!"

Trusting the fear his sailors felt for him to roust them out of bed, Pickering turned and bolted from the bawdy house, dead sober by the time he reached the sidewalk and began to run with loping strides down toward the docks. The distant pall of smoke was visible already, growing larger, darker, as he closed the gap, gaining momentum on the downhill sprint.

And it was true, by God.

He'd hoped that Walker was exaggerating, his impressions blurred by alcohol, but that was not the case. Where Pickering had left the *Banshee*—safe and sound, as he'd supposed—a blackened ruin lay partly submerged, the stump of one burnt mast protruding six or seven feet above the water's surface. Pickering stood gaping at the wreckage while his sailors started to arrive, some barely dressed, after their run from Awful Annie's to the docks.

"What happened, Captain?" someone asked.

"The hell should I know? Was I here?" Pickering fought to calm himself and added, "Jonas says somebody tossed him overboard. Next thing he knew, the ship was burning."

"Tossed him over?"

"Who'n hell?"

"Bastard was drunk, all right," said Pickering. "If I find out he set this fire by accident or otherwise, I'll see he takes a week to die."

A sailor that he didn't recognize was standing close at hand and overheard Pickering's comment. Gambling with his own skin, he spoke up to say, "At least both of your men got off all right."

"*Both* of my men?"

The stranger nodded. "One over the starboard rail, the other down the gangplank."

Pickering's assembled men immediately started babbling amongst themselves, their questions batting back and forth until he scowled and shushed them. Turning to the stranger who had spoken, he asked, "Do I take it that you saw this second man come down the plank?"

"As plain as day, friend."

"And could you describe him for me?"

Now the stranger paused for thought, eyes closing for a moment, opening before he spoke again. "I'd reckon he was six foot tall, dark-haired, no whiskers. Young, in my opinion, middle twenties. White, o' course. I do recall he wore a pistol, here." Reaching across his body toward the left hip, for a simulated cross-hand draw.

"Was he familiar to you? Might you know his name?"

"Never laid eyes on him before," the stranger said.

"Thanks, anyway."

That vague description could apply to half the men working along the waterfront, but there was something . . . Wait! The pistol. Pickering had seen a rig like that, just yesterday.

But no. It *couldn't* be.

Raging, he turned his back on what remained of the poor *Banshee*, formerly the *Revenant*, and started back toward Awful Annie's, boot heels clopping on the cobblestones.

* * *

Jonas Walker thought that he was drowning for a second, then he tasted beer and realized someone was trying to revive him from his captain's stunning punch. He came up sputtering, his right eye stinging from the dose of alcohol, his left one swollen almost shut from the impact of Pickering's knuckles.

"Ups-a-daisy," someone told him, as they hauled Walker to his feet. He was disoriented for a moment, then remembered where he was and what had happened just before the lights went out.

Hands steered him toward the bar, where someone handed him a shot glass full of whiskey and he gulped it, gratefully. Walker wasn't used to helping hands and wished that everyone would just leave him alone, but that was not to be.

The leader of the outfit, Bryan Marley, was beside him now, refilling Walker's glass while he plied him with questions. Where had Pickering and all his crewmen gone in such a hurry? Were they coming back, or not?

It seemed that none of Marley's men had heard Walker when he'd told his captain that the *Banshee* was on fire, so he went through it all again, stopping at intervals to wheeze a bit and make a show of wobbling on his feet until the empty shot glass was refilled and he felt fortified enough to forge ahead.

It was embarrassing, explaining how he'd been assigned to guard the ship but had a bit of rum and fell asleep, then woke to someone tossing him over the *Banshee*'s rail. The dunking cleared his head—well, more or less—but by the time he'd dragged himself onto the dock, all sopping wet, the clipper was in flames. Walker had seen ships burn before, and didn't feel like dying in a vain attempt to fight the fire, so he had done the next best thing and raced off to the whorehouse, where he had alerted Captain Pickering and then got knocked out cold.

"You say somebody set the ship on fire deliberately?" Marley asked him.

"Must have," Walker said. "If he was passin' by and seen the smoke, why heave me overboard? I weren't but twenty paces from the gangplank."

"Sabotage," somebody muttered, and that got some of the others grumbling.

Marley shushed them, pressing in on Walker. "Did you see the guy who tossed you over?"

"Nope," Walker replied. "I may'a mentioned I was sleepin' off a wee bit of a bender. He was strong, though, I can tell you that."

Somebody in the group mentioned a name—sounded like "Menefee"—but Marley snapped right back at them, "He's dead, goddamn it!"

"Doesn't mean his friends are," someone else complained.

"Whoever done it," Walker said, "looks like we're stranded here in Galveston until the captain finds hisself another ship. Looks bad for business."

Marley seemed to have a sudden thought, his face taking on an anxious look. "The warehouse! Gabe, take Jack and Willy. Hustle over there and make sure it's all right."

The men he'd spoken to rushed out into the early dusk and disappeared, the barroom's bat-wing doors flapping behind them. Walker stood waiting for another shot of whiskey on the house, but it appeared that Marley had lost interest in him. He was giving orders to the men who still remained, directing some to gather weapons, others to go off in search of gang members who weren't already at the brothel. Walker understood that they were making ready to defend the place—or maybe go to war.

He leaned against the bar and thought about that for another moment, weighing his alternatives. There was no point in volunteering to help Marley and his men, after he'd just confessed his own ineptitude. Likewise, he couldn't count on any mercy from his captain or the crewmates he'd let down. There must be *something* he could do in Galveston, while waiting for a berth aboard some other vessel, but the thought of being killed or badly injured in a shooting war held no appeal for Walker.

On the other hand, if he got out of there while Marley and his people were distracted . . .

Walker saw them huddled at the far end of the bar, all deep in earnest conversation. There would never be a better time, he thought, and ambled casually toward the door.

16

★**R**yder approached the warehouse cautiously, convinced that Marley would have guards stationed around it to protect the loot deposited in recent days. He was correct but found the two lookouts detailed to watch it posed no problem, since their throats were slashed from ear to ear, their bodies dragged inside the warehouse and concealed there.

Ryder saw that much because the broad front door was standing open to receive him. Pistol drawn, he ducked inside to stand above the corpses, listening to sounds that emanated from the shadowy interior. It sounded like one man, or two at most, opening crates and pawing through their contents, likely seeking treasure he or they could haul away on foot, without a team and wagon.

Ryder had not counted on a robbery in progress, much less double murder. He had come to search the warehouse with no plan fixed firmly in his mind, aware that he could not abscond with much of Marley's loot himself, uncertain whether anything he carried off without a warrant qualified as evidence. He'd planned to have another look around, at least, maybe consider treating Marley's cache as he had done the late *Banshee*, but now he faced a different proposition altogether.

He cocked the Colt Army, half wincing at the hammer's sharp metallic sound, but if it carried to the looter farther back inside the warehouse, it did not disturb him. Or them. Ryder moved as quietly as possible, placing each foot with caution on the concrete floor, avoiding any scuffs to give himself away. It seemed to take forever, moving down one aisle between two rows of wooden crates, the person he was stalking still unseen and one row over to his right. The stacks of merchandise concealed Ryder from his intended prey, as it hid him—or them—from Ryder, but it made him wonder how he would, in fact, confront the prowler after all, without forewarning him.

When he had reached a point directly opposite the sounds of avid searching, he decided it was only one intruder after all. A pair would certainly be talking now, even in whispers, as they rifled through Marley's loot for some specific prize. One man would make things easier, but there was still the problem of approaching him. Unless . . .

The crates nearest to Ryder, standing like a wall between the burglar and himself, were stacked in an arrangement mimicking stair steps: one crate on top, with two beneath it, three beneath the two, and so on, down to six across the bottom row. Holding his pistol and his breath, Ryder began to climb the barricade, expecting each move that he made to cause some creaking sound that would alert his target on the other side. The crates were sturdy, though, and made no sound before he reached the top, leaned over, and looked down into the next aisle—

Where he had an unobstructed view of Otto Seitz, kneeling, a Bowie knife beside him on the floor that he had used to pry the lid off of a crate that he was rifling through. Gold coins jingled though his plunging hands, Seitz dumping them around his knees as if they had no value. Digging deeper. Seeking . . . what?

Ask him? thought Ryder.

Suiting thought to action, he immediately rolled across the topmost crate and dropped into the aisle behind Seitz, landing in a half crouch, with his six-gun leveled. Seitz spun toward him, reaching for the knife instinctively, then froze at sight of Ryder and his Colt Army.

"It can't be!" Otto blurted.

"Guess again."

"Awright." Seitz rocked back on his heels, hands on his knees, the Bowie still within his reach. "You're back with Marley, eh? He sent you here? And now you've got me."

"Some of that's correct," Ryder replied.

"I guess you're tickled that he threw me out. I tried to tell him you were rotten, but he still blames me."

"You feel like getting even with him?" Ryder asked.

"The hell is that supposed to mean?"

"I need corroborating evidence to prosecute him. Play your cards right, we can probably convince a local judge those boys you killed back there went down in self-defense."

"I *knew* it! You're a goddamned copper!"

"Secret Service," Ryder said, correcting him. "I guess it's all the same to you."

"I shoulda stayed behind and killed you when I had the chance."

"Should have but didn't. Now it's on the other foot. One chance to save yourself from stretching rope."

"See you in Hell first." Otto sneered.

Instead of reaching for the knife, he whipped a hand behind his back and came out with a small revolver, cocking it before he had a chance to aim. He got no further with it, then, as Ryder shot him in the chest and slammed him over to the concrete floor, twitching his last before the echo of the shot had died away.

First thing, Ryder doubled back to check the street outside for passersby who might have heard the gunshot. He found no one, which was reassuring to a point but obviously did not mean that he was in the clear. He felt time slipping through his fingers now, as he considered how to stage the scene.

His first impulse, immediately banished, was to summon the police, identify himself, and tell them what had happened. Understanding how things seemed to work in Galveston, however, he projected what might happen if he got hold of the *wrong* police, maybe wound up in jail on murder charges, while the coppers ran to Bryan Marley with a warning. Even if the lawmen took his story and credentials at face value, there was no reason for Ryder to believe that they would help him round up Marley's gang.

No. He would stake his hopes on the Revenue Cutter from Corpus Christi, make sending that telegram his next priority. But in the meantime, Ryder needed to arrange the shooting scene, to place the full responsibility on Otto Seitz.

Otto had made it easy for him, to a point. The knife he'd used to slit the throats of Marley's guards lay on the concrete floor beside his corpse. He'd wiped the blade after the killings, but that was a problem easily resolved. If either of the murdered lookouts had a pistol on him, Ryder thought his plan should work.

Unless somebody caught him in the midst of fixing it.

Ryder strode to the warehouse door and closed it, then had a look at Otto's body, making sure the bullet from his Colt Army had not come out the smuggler's back. With that confirmed, he left no blood trail dragging Seitz along the aisle where he had died, back toward the bodies of the former comrades he had slaughtered. One more trip to fetch the Bowie knife, and he was ready for the final bit of playacting.

It was a grisly job, but Ryder got it done. After discovering that both of Marley's warehouse guards were armed with Colts—a Walker .44 and an older .36-caliber Paterson—he chose the corpse whose weapon matched his own revolver's caliber and left the other one alone. He hauled the body he'd selected six or seven feet off from the other one, and didn't mind the bloody drag marks this time, thinking they could be interpreted as evidence of struggling. From what he'd seen of the police in Galveston so far, he thought them likely to accept the easiest, most obvious solution they could find to any incident.

Next, Ryder had to fire the dead man's Colt Walker, a risky business, since a second shot might bring police before he'd slipped away. Taking the pistol from the dead man's belt, Ryder went back to check the street again, saw no one passing by, and ran back to the far end of the warehouse, where he fired the gun point-blank into a bale of ganja. He would be surprised—make that amazed—if any Galveston patrolman found that slug, or even spied the small hole in the burlap sacking.

Jogging back to dead man's land, he finished setting up

the scene. The Colt Walker, one chamber fired, he pressed into the murdered watchman's limp right hand. Next, Ryder wiped the Bowie's heavy blade across the lookout's gaping throat, before he placed it into Otto's hand and pressed his still-warm fingers to create a fist of sorts. The worst bit was arranging Seitz and his dead victim in a grappling pose, the Colt Walker wedged in between them where it might have slipped after a fatal shot was fired in self-defense.

Ryder stepped back and studied the tableau he had created. It would not deceive an expert, diligent detective, but he counted on the local coppers being lazy and slipshod. They'd want to close the case as simply as they could—and if they doubted his arrangement of the corpses, what was their alternative solution? Ryder checked to verify that nothing of himself remained for the police to find. Once Otto and the others were identified, any suspicions that still lingered would be aimed at Bryan Marley and his crew.

It was the best that he could do for now, in any case, and *now* was all that mattered. Getting out, away from there, before another pair of watchmen showed up to relieve the ones Otto had slain, or someone else showed up to ruin everything.

One final check along the street, in both directions, and he fled, leaving the warehouse door as he had found it on arrival, open to the world.

Whoever turned up next was in for a surprise.

Stede Pickering was halfway back to Awful Annie's when it hit him. He stopped dead in the middle of the street, his crewmen piling up behind him, jostling one another. "Damn and blast!" the captain swore.

"Whatsa matter?" someone asked him.

"That lubber on the dock," said Pickering. "When he described the fella comin' off the *Banshee*. Who'd that sound like? Anybody?"

"Anybody, sure," one of his dimwit crewmen answered, shrugging.

"Damn it! Think of someone who we've seen just recently." When that failed to produce a glimmer anywhere among them, Pickering added, "Someone who might bear us a grudge."

"Old Seitz was steamin' after Marley kicked him out," one of them said.

"Not him. He doesn't look a damn thing like the man who was described," said Pickering.

Blank faces all around him.

"Christ all Friday!" he exclaimed. "Are all your brains so soused you can't remember yesterday?" Still nothing, so he spelled it out for them. "It sounds like George Revere."

"Him from the island?" one of them inquired.

"That don't make sense," another said. "We left him, din't we?"

"Left him, sure," said Pickering. "We didn't *kill* him, though."

"That can't be right," a balding pirate groused. "It's more'n two hunnerd miles of open water, comin' back."

"Longer than that, if he went overland somehow," a scar-faced sailor added.

"Lotsa guys look purty much the same," a one-eyed buccaneer allowed.

"That's true enough," said Pickering. "But who among 'em has a grudge against the *Banshee* and her crew?"

That stumped them for a moment, then a skinny redhead said, "Awright, but *how* would he get back here?"

"Doesn't matter how he done it," Pickering replied. "The

question's whether Marley knew about it and they's in this deal together."

"What deal?" asked the cyclops.

"Burnin' up our ship, you idjit!"

"Why'n hell would Marley go along with that?" the red-head challenged. "He's been our best customer, these past two years."

"But he was het up when he heard we left Revere on Timbalier, weren't he?" Pickering reminded them. "Kept sayin' how the boy had saved his neck, not once, but twice."

"So, this Revere comes back somehow," said One-eye, "*and* he talks to Marley somehow, while we's all together at the whorehouse?"

"Why not?" Pickering replied. "The hard part's gettin' back, but once he's here, what's stoppin' him? Was any of you watchin' who came in and out?"

The redhead sniggered. "Only once I got upstairs."

"Shut up! If I'm right," Pickering continued, "Marley either knows Revere is back in town and burnt the *Banshee*, or he oughta know. We need to find out which it is, and quick."

"We goin' back there, then?" asked Scarface.

"Goddamn right, we are," said Pickering. "But first, we have to make another little stop."

"For what?" one of his crewmen asked.

"If you could think straight for a second, you'd remember that our guns, most of 'em, went up with the clipper. I ain't bustin' in on Marley and his bunch," said Pickering, "unless we're all well armed."

"You know someplace in town to get more shootin' irons?" asked One-eye.

"This is Texas," Pickering replied. "Guns ain't the

problem. What we need is cash to buy 'em with, so ever'body turn your pockets out and show me what you got."

It didn't come to much, after the hours spent in revelry at Awful Annie's. Truth be told, they were well short of what he thought they'd need to supplement the knives and few pistols his men had brought ashore from the *Banshee*. Pickering knew a man who dealt in guns and had a shop nearby, but if he quibbled over price . . . well, that would be *his* problem this time, wouldn't it.

Nothing would stand between Stede Pickering and his revenge. Not money, not the local coppers, and for damn sure not a lousy bunch of cowards whose idea of fighting was to sneak around behind a captain's back and burn his ship.

Someone would pay for that insult. In blood.

F rom the warehouse, Ryder made his cautious way back to the Western Union office and dispatched a telegram to Corpus Christi. Requesting help forced Ryder to identify himself, and since he'd gone that far, he played his other hole card at the same time, mentioning Director Wood by name. As a precaution, he stood waiting while the telegram was sent and the acknowledgment came back. Whatever happened after that—say, if the clerk ran off to warn somebody from the Marley gang—at least he'd done his best.

And any way he looked at it, the pot was coming to a boil in Galveston.

From Western Union, Ryder made a quick but cautious circuit of the waterfront, watching for any members of the *Banshee*'s crew and spotting none. He buttonholed a passing stevedore and asked if anybody from the clipper's crew had come to view the wreckage yet, receiving a description of a man who had to be Stede Pickering, arriving on the scene with something like a dozen men, then storming off again.

Where to?

The dock worker could only shrug at that, but Ryder knew from conversations he had overheard that Pickering and company had no lodgings in Galveston. When they delivered cargo to the port, they spent their idle time ashore in the pursuit of booze and women, then slept off the binge aboard their vessel. When they *had* a vessel.

Now, where would they go? Back to the cribs at Awful Annie's? Or would the disaster that had overtaken them persuade the buccaneers that they had best find someplace else to stay, while they considered their next move?

Ryder could not begin to list all of the brothels, bars, and cheap hotels in Galveston. The only starting place that he could think of for a search was Awful Annie's, with the danger it presented if he should be spotted there by anyone from Marley's gang or Pickering's. It would be helpful, once his reinforcements had arrived, if he could find all of the miscreants together in one place, but that posed problems, too.

He didn't know how many men would be aboard the USRC *Martin Van Buren* when it arrived, or how they would be armed. Pitting that crew against two fighting gangs, perhaps three dozen men in all, could spark a battle that was bound to draw police—but to assist which side? The best thing he could do, Ryder supposed, was make his cautious way to Annie's place, try to discover who was there, and hope that all of them were drinking heavily enough to put them out of action when the time came.

Nine long hours, at a minimum.

More than enough time, Ryder thought, for any drunk to sleep it off and have his wits about him when the law arrived.

Unless he found some way to thin their numbers in the meantime.

Nothing had occurred to him as he set off for Awful Annie's, moving through the gray light of an early dusk. He calculated that the cutter couldn't possibly arrive before the clock struck three A.M., and that would be if nothing slowed it down. He would devise some kind of plan before the night ran out and hope he didn't wind up paying for the effort with his life.

Ryder had left his Henry rifle at the boardinghouse, thinking that it would make him too conspicuous, walking around the city's streets. Now he regretted that decision, but did not think he could spare the time to go back for the long gun. If the *Banshee*'s crew had made for Awful Annie's and persuaded Marley's men to seek new quarters overnight, for safety's sake, he ran the risk of losing them entirely while he went back to his room.

He would make do with what he had, the Colt Army with two spare cylinders. Beyond that, if it came down to a fight with melee weapons, Ryder had his switchblade, but he knew it wouldn't do much good against a mob of cutthroats.

Neither would his badge, unless he somehow managed to get help from the police.

Not likely, he decided, judging that the coppers would most likely let a battle run its course before they waded in to risk their own lives.

Mopping up was always easier than taking sides.

Pickering's gun dealer, as he'd expected, wasn't keen on parting with his merchandise on credit. Neither was he in the mood to offer discounts, nor to rent his guns out for the evening, accepting promises that they would be returned.

Pickering soon grew tired of arguing about it, drew his pepperbox revolver, and demanded satisfaction on the spot. That worked, all right, but got him thinking about coppers, so he had one of his men escort the dealer to his shop's back room and slit his gullet.

Dead men tell no tales.

The shop was well stocked, and since most of their old arsenal had gone down with the *Banshee*, Pickering gave his men free rein to arm themselves. Those lacking pistols had their choice of Colts—Dragoons, as well as 1851 and 1861 Navy models—along with the the Remington Model 1858, the Smith & Wesson Model 1, and the double-action Starr revolver. Pickering himself collected a LeMat .36-caliber with a nine-round cylinder and a separate 16-gauge smoothbore barrel for buckshot.

Most of his crewmen also went for long guns, including a mix of Spencer repeaters, Springfield's Model 1861, and Enfield's Pattern 1853. Again, Pickering claimed what he regarded as the best piece for himself: a shortened carbine version of the Colt revolving rifle, chambered in .44 caliber with a five-shot cylinder.

"Don't stint on ammunition, either," he advised them, as they rummaged over shelves, one man detailed to guard the door. "No tellin' when we'll have another chance to shop for cartridges and powder."

Some of them, by then, were grabbing sabers from a rack behind the counter, slicing at the air with them and growling until Pickering commanded them to sober up and act like men preparing for a fight, instead of children on a holiday.

In terms of arms and numbers, Pickering imagined they should do all right against the Marley gang. What troubled him was going up against his adversaries on their home ground, where a natural advantage lay with the defenders.

Yet another disadvantage would be laying siege to Awful Annie's, where the enemy had cover and his men would be compelled to risk their skins on open streets. Darkness would help a bit, in that regard, and also the advantage of surprise, if he could keep it. Still, storming a building was a chancy proposition, on a par with boarding hostile ships at sea.

Except, of course, the building would be stationary. Neither it nor any of its occupants could sail away.

But, like a ship, it *could* be set on fire.

"We'll take those lanterns, while we're at it," Pickering directed, pointing toward another shelf. "Just leave 'em dark for now. I'll tell you when to light 'em up."

Some of his men saw what he had in mind, smiling and moving to collect the six or seven lanterns, checking to make sure their reservoirs were amply filled with kerosene. Pickering had them leave the shop in twos and threes, with intervals of time between them to avoid attracting undue notice on the street. They would seem strange and savage as it was, armed to the teeth with swords, pistols, and rifles, but he didn't want them looking like an army on the march, making their way to Awful Annie's.

Most of all, he didn't want to get police involved until their work was done, or nearly so.

And after that . . . well, what the hell. Those uniforms they wore weren't bulletproof.

Pickering was the last man out, locking the door behind him to forestall discovery of the arms dealer's corpse. After tonight, Pickering would have burned his bridges here in Galveston and wasn't sure exactly how he'd make his way to some more friendly port. Perhaps he and his men—those who survived the night—could steal a small ship from the waterfront and sail away. If not, they'd have to travel overland, avoiding lawmen till they reached someplace where they weren't recognized and bargains could be struck.

And if it all went wrong, if this night proved to be the only time that he had left, at least Stede Pickering could use it striking back at someone who'd betrayed him. He could teach a lesson that would be remembered, after he was gone.

Truth be told, he'd rather be a *living* legend, but nobody lived forever. Better to die fighting than lie down and waste away.

With that in mind, he reckoned Galveston would be as good a place as any for a grand rip-roaring end.

17

★ **O**n his way to Awful Annie's, keeping to the alleyways and shadows, Ryder heard a grumbling,
growling sound approaching from the east. Accompanied
by noise of tramping feet, he recognized it as the echo of an
angry crowd in motion, and paused in an alley's mouth
beyond the reach of lamplight while he watched and waited
for the mob to come within his line of sight.

Another moment passed before their marching shadows
fell across the street in front of Ryder, then he saw the leader
of the group and recognized Stede Pickering. Most of the
others straggled out behind their captain in a rough parade
formation, were familiar to him from his one-way trip
aboard the *Banshee*. All of them were armed with rifles,
pistols, plus a wide variety of sabers, swords, and knives.

Going to war, unless he missed his guess.

But war with *whom*?

The only thought that sprang to mind was Bryan Marley

and his crew, though Ryder couldn't figure out why Pickering would turn against his business partner. Not unless the captain blamed Marley for what had happened to his clipper. And if Pickering believed that . . .

Ryder thought he might not need those reinforcements, after all.

He waited for the mob to pass him by, gave them a block's head start, then slipped out of the alleyway and followed them. There was no question. Pickering was headed for the brothel where Ryder had seen him earlier, before he'd gone to torch the *Banshee* at the waterfront. Two blocks before they reached their destination, Pickering hissed at his men for silence, then proceeded with the nearest thing to stealth a crowd of angry men can manage on their way to facing death.

This wasn't what he'd planned, but being heavily outnumbered, Ryder figured he should seize whatever opportunity he had to thin the odds against him. Bryan Marley was his primary concern, the one he wanted to arrest above all others and deliver to Director Wood. Whatever happened after that—a deal worked out between them, or a quick trip to the penitentiary—was no concern of Ryder's.

He still hoped to bring Marley in alive, for trial, although that raised a whole new set of risks beyond the mere act of arresting him. Would Galveston's police cooperate with Ryder, or conspire to liberate the smuggler who'd been bribing them for years on end? In the alternative, could Ryder trust the county's sheriff or the Texas Rangers for assistance? Houston was the nearest town to Galveston of any size, some fifty miles away—another seaport where, for all he knew, Marley might well have friends in power.

Never mind, he thought, and tried to concentrate on what was happening right now, without distractions. Marley wasn't in his hands yet, and might never be. They both had to survive this night, before Ryder could see his mission through.

A half block short of Awful Annie's, Pickering stopped short and issued orders to his troops. Ryder was too far back to overhear him, but he saw three men duck down an alley on the brothel's eastern side, while two more ran around the southwest corner. They were covering all exits, making sure that no one could escape.

Ryder slowly advanced along the north side of the street, moving from one shop doorway to the next. Pickering's men were focused on their target, paying no attention to the neighborhood around them as they found the best cover they could, their rifles aimed at Annie's door and windows. With his Colt Army in hand, Ryder crept up behind them, waiting for the battle to commence.

S ay that again," Bryan Marley responded. "You're not making sense."

"I swear it's the truth," Tommy Rafferty answered. "I seen it myself."

"He ain't lyin'," Ed Parsons chimed in.

"Just *repeat* it, will you!" Marley snapped.

"It was Otto. He kilt Jim and Billy, but Jim got a shot in 'im as he was dyin', it looks like."

"Why in hell would he do that?" asked Marley, already half sure of the answer.

"You kicked him out, din't you," said Parsons. "I figger he took it real hard."

"Mebbe thought he could pick up some cash for the road," Tommy offered. "You know how he was."

"Tried to rob us," said Marley, and then something

clicked in his mind. "The warehouse! You just left it unguarded with dead men inside?"

Ed and Tommy exchanged startled glances. "Well, we—" Tommy started to say.

"Get back over there, you idjits!" Marley raged. "Somebody could be looting it right now!"

Parsons and Rafferty broke for the bat-wing doors, then stopped dead just inside them, staring at the street. "Bryan," Tommy called out, "you better have a look at this."

"What is it now, for God's sake?" he shouted back, moving reluctantly across the barroom, toward the exit. He could feel his men and some of Annie's girls tracking his progress, all afraid to make a peep when he was in a fury.

Halfway to the door, he halted, frozen by the echo of a voice he recognized. "Marley!" it bellowed. "Bryan Marley! Show yourself, you scurvy bastard!"

Moving to the door, he pushed Parsons and Rafferty aside. "Is that you, Pickering?" he shouted back, already certain of it.

"Who else would it be?" the captain answered.

Marley saw eight or nine armed men outside, crouching behind whatever objects offered partial shelter—water troughs, a wagon parked across the street, one at the nearest corner. All of them were armed with rifles, as was Pickering, the only man who stood before him in the open.

"What's the problem, Stede?" asked Marley.

"You know goddamn well," said Pickering.

"I heard your ship was damaged."

"Damaged, hell! It's gone, as you well know."

"All right, it's gone" Marley replied. "What brings you here, dressed up for war?"

"Oh, now you're playin' innocent? Is that the deal?"

"Make sense, will you?"

"Your man was seen leavin' the *Banshee*, just afore she burnt," snarled Pickering.

"My man? *Which* man?"

"Your precious George Revere!"

"You're either drunk or crazy," Marley said. "You left him on Timbalier Island, if it hasn't slipped your mind."

"We left 'im, but he's back," said Pickering. "Your bosom friend."

"You think he burned the clipper?"

"I jus' tole you he was *seen*."

"By who?" Marley demanded.

"By a man with eyes, is who."

"Let's say that's true," Marley replied. "I ain't admitting it, but say you're right. What makes you think I sent him to your ship? Seems like he had reason enough to hate you, on his own account."

"Don't even try talkin' your way around this, Marley. Time and time again you've told me nothin' happens in the Port of Galveston without your say-so."

"Stede, be sensible. You don't—"

The shot cracked past his face before Marley could finish, clipped the top curve of the bat-wing doors, and sprayed his cheek with wooden splinters. Diving backward, out of sight, he flipped a poker table on its side and ducked behind it for the extra cover.

Marley shouted to his gunmen, "Let 'em have it! None of 'em goes home alive!"

Stede Pickering was shouting, "Who did that? Who fired that shot?" when pistols blazed from Awful Annie's two front windows, smashing glass and forcing him to run for any cover he could find. Ryder, well out of range from that barrage, edged forward, ducked into the nearest alley running north-south from the sidewalk where he was, and moved along the narrow passageway toward the rear of the brothel. Rats scurried out of Ryder's way, and garbage shifted underneath his boots as he proceeded, following the path that three men from the *Banshee* had already taken to their posts.

Behind him, more gunfire was hammering the street, glass breaking, bullets rattling as they struck the brothel's clapboard walls. That racket signaled Pickering's rear guards to make their move, a crashing at the back door as they stormed it, kicking through and rushing on inside. The next shots that he heard were muffled, coming through the wall immediately to his left. Ryder picked up his pace, making more noise than he preferred, but feeling fairly confident no one would hear him with the battle under way.

How long before police arrived in answer to the gunfire? They'd been slow the night he went with Marley, on the raid against Jack Menefee, but that was no reliable predictor for the present case. It wouldn't do for him to waste a moment, when he might wind up arrested with the smugglers and their former friends-turned-enemies. Ryder was sure he wouldn't last the night if he was jailed with either group—and that might happen, he supposed, even if he arrested Bryan Marley and identified himself to the authorities.

As Ryder reached the brothel's northeast corner, he paused once again, wishing he'd gotten off the *Southern Belle* at Tampa, with Irene McGowan, when he'd had the chance. It was too late for anything resembling a happy ending now, he thought, cocking his Colt Army before he eased around the corner, watching out for stragglers from the *Banshee*'s crew. None challenged him, and he saw no one as he approached the back door of the whorehouse, standing open in a haze of gray gun smoke.

Across that threshold, Ryder knew that life-and-death decisions would be mandatory. On the other hand, if he retreated, hid somewhere and let the battle run its course, then who would be any the wiser? No one back in Washington expected him to stand between two warring gangs, did they? His mission had not been to die in Galveston, but rather to break up a smuggling ring. Couldn't he wait and see if Pickering accomplished that, himself?

The answer from his conscience came back, clear and unequivocal.

The word was, *No.*

Should he announce himself as being from the Secret Service? Would it matter, now that battle had been joined between the gangs? Ryder decided on the spot that it would be a foolish risk, drawing attention to himself in such a way that both sides might join forces to eliminate him.

Nice and quiet, then, if he could manage that.

He stepped through Annie's back door, moved immediately to his left, and pressed his back against the wall. Whatever happened in the next few moments, at least nobody could shoot him in the back.

From where he stood, Ryder was forced to lean right for a view along the hallway leading from the back door to the barroom, past the entrance to a small kitchen and other doors he took for storage rooms or closets, possibly a small office. The hooker cribs were all upstairs, but he passed along the corridor, trailing the *Banshee* crewmen who had led the way inside.

And where were they?

Based on the shouts, the cursing, women's screams and gunfire, they had reached the main saloon and gaming room, surprising Marley's men who hadn't thought to block the rear approach. Ryder wished he could still the tremor in his gun hand as he closed the gap between the back door and the barroom, where a second battle had erupted, only yards away.

No one had 'fessed up to firing the first shot at Marley, and Pickering no longer cared who had done it. They were down to killing now, and only one side could emerge victorious—that was, if either of them did. Hunched down behind a water trough that was already leaking from two bullet holes, Pickering aimed his Colt revolving rifle, squeezed the trigger carefully, not jerking it, and sent a .44 slug on its way into the whorehouse.

Hitting what? Most likely nothing, but at least he'd made some noise.

The men inside were fighting back with pistols only, so far, though he guessed they likely had some long guns stashed somewhere inside the place. Shotguns would be a problem, when his people tried to enter, but he didn't plan to lead the way himself. Old Mother Pickering had raised some cutthroats, it was true, but none of them were idiots.

Speaking of men, he wondered what had happened to the bunch he sent around behind the brothel, hoping they would stand their ground and block the way for anyone who tried escaping through the windows or back door. A better deal, for Pickering, would be if they had made their way inside of Awful Annie's, killing some of Marley's boys or at the least distracting them while Pickering arranged a charge at the front door. With all the racket, it was hard to tell, but even one man on the inside could play hob with the defenders.

Pickering triggered another shot that whistled through

one of the shattered street-side windows, going God knew where inside the barroom. That done, he called out to several of the crewmen nearest to him, drawing their attention briefly from the fight.

"Jubal! Eric! Nosey!" The latter's name was something French, but he was nicknamed for his trait of butting in when others talked. When they had turned toward Pickering, he said, "We need to get inside there. Rush the front door on my signal. Pass it on!"

None of the three looked happy with that order, but they hastened to obey, knowing a bullet in the back might be their payment if they balked. Before another minute passed, the rest of Pickering's men on the street were ready—or as ready as they'd ever be—to charge at the saloon and try to force their way inside.

Could be a massacre, thought Pickering. But on the other hand . . .

He shouted, "Now!" and cranked off two rounds from his Colt rifle in rapid fire, adding some cover as his men cut loose with everything they had. For some, that meant a single rifle shot, before they clawed their pistols free and ran headlong toward Awful Annie's bat-wing doors. The two men armed with Spencers pumped the lever actions on their rifles, laying down a steady fire as they burst out from cover, joining in the charge.

One took a hit and fell, sprawling across the wooden sidewalk, nearly tripped the man behind him, then that second man was through the swinging doors and lost to sight. The others followed swiftly, shouting incoherently and firing shots at anything that moved.

Pickering counted off ten seconds in his head, then followed them inside.

* * *

Bryan Marley had begun to sympathize a bit with dead Jack Menefee. The siege of Awful Annie's had surprised him, made him wonder whether Pickering had soaked his brain in too much rum and lost his mind entirely, but that didn't matter now. They were surrounded in the brothel and, worse yet, some of the *Banshee* crewmen were inside. He hadn't paid attention to the back door—hell, he hadn't stationed any guards at all around the place—and now he was regretting it.

It was amazing, how the world could shift in nothing flat. One moment, he and Pickering had been the best of friends, drinking and whoring together; now, they were at each other's throats over a stupid accusation that Marley had sent George Revere, of all people, to burn the *Banshee*. Revere, who should have been still stranded on Timbalier Island, thanks to Otto Seitz. And Otto, once his trusted right-hand man, was dead now, after killing two of Marley's men in a botched robbery.

It was too much. He didn't even want to think about the treasure storehouse, left unguarded. Not while he was busy fighting for his life.

Three of the gunmen who had come in through the back door were behind the bar, rising by turns to fire around the room. They'd shot the barkeep first thing, and they had his shotgun now, aside from any others weapons they had brought along with them. A fourth intruder had been gutshot in the early moments of the skirmish. He was lying on the threshold of the hallway leading to the kitchen, Annie's office, and the back door, through which Marley was expecting more invaders anytime now.

What he needed was a new perspective on the battlefield,

a view from higher ground. And that, in turn, might offer him a chance to slip away unnoticed in the general confusion. Some might call that cowardice, desertion of his men, but Marley's first concern had always been self-preservation. Friends might come and go—take Otto as a prime example—but he had only stayed alive this long by looking out for number one.

His first step was to find a way upstairs. That offered him a better vantage point for fighting, plus more windows he could possibly escape through, if raiders didn't have them covered from below. And even if they *did*, Marley imagined that his odds of taking down one lookout, then escaping, were a great deal better than if he remained downstairs, hemmed in by shooters to the front and rear.

Marley was moving, ducking bullets from the street and watching out for Pickering's three men behind the bar, when someone in the outer darkness shouted, "Now!" A storm of gunfire peppered Awful Annie's bat-wing doors and shattered streetside windows, forcing Marley down to hands and knees, then driving him to wriggle on his belly like a lizard, making for the stairs. Passing Harry Morgan, Marley heard his squawk of pain, felt warm blood splash his cheek before he crawled on by.

He reached the staircase, started scrambling toward the second floor on knees and elbows, as the gunmen he had seen outside burst through the brothel's swinging doors. One leaped in through an empty window frame, then tumbled out again, backward, when one of Marley's people shot him in the chest.

"The lamps!" somebody shouted, and a fireball streaked across the barroom, bursting when it hit the old piano, spreading flames.

Marley could not afford another moment's hesitation

now. He had to get upstairs and find a way out of the house before it all went up and he was cooked alive.

Ryder was halfway down the hall when Pickering's frontal assault began, the sound of shots and shouts redoubled in the barroom up ahead. He saw a lantern tossed and tumbling to explode in leaping flames and knew the building wouldn't stand for long unless somebody doused the fire.

His sense of urgency increased, Ryder approached the doorway to the barroom, stepping past a wounded gunman who was writhing on the floor, clutching his stomach, dark blood pulsing from between his fingers. At the threshold, Ryder crouched and peered around the room, looking for Marley, glimpsing him just as he reached the second-story landing. It was thirty-some-odd feet from Ryder's present position to the stairs, with nothing close to decent cover on the way. He'd have to trust in speed, and as he braced himself to run for it, Ryder wasn't convinced that would be good enough.

Get on with it!

He bolted from the doorway, startling one of Marley's men who'd crouched behind an upturned table. Ryder recognized the face but couldn't put a name to it. The shooter gawked at him and cried, "You're dead!" but raised his pistol anyway, to make it true.

Not yet! thought Ryder, as he fired his Colt point-blank into the smuggler's chest.

A bullet plucked at Ryder's left sleeve and kissed his biceps with a wasp's sting before flying on to strike the room's west wall. He didn't know which side had fired the shot and didn't care. A pirate's gun would cut him down the same as one of Marley's if he slowed his pace and made an easy target of himself. One saving grace was the confusion that surrounded him, men firing almost randomly around the barroom, Annie's girls squealing in counterpoint to the staccato gunfire. The bar's piano was consumed by fire, and now a second lamp had burst behind the bar, flames threatening the shelves of liquor there.

As Ryder reached the stairs, Annie herself came rushing down to meet him, cursing like a sailor as she witnessed the destruction of her livelihood. Brandishing a Colt Dragoon revolver, she passed Ryder on the staircase without glancing at him, charging into battle like a Norse berserker while her place went up in flames. More gunfire echoed from the staircase and beyond it as she reached the ground floor, screeching as she waded into battle.

Ryder focused on the stairs in front of him, keeping his head down, straining for a glimpse of Marley on the second-story landing. Wherever he'd been going, Marley was no longer visible from Ryder's limited perspective. Ducking another shot that came within an inch or so of furrowing his scalp, Ryder pressed on to reach the landing, where he stretched out on the floor.

Smoke from the barroom stung his eyes, obscuring his vision. Ryder knew that rising flames would reach the stairs and balcony before much longer, making his pursuit untenable. Whatever hope he had of finding Marley, taking him alive, was swiftly running out. It crossed his mind that he might already be trapped, retreat cut off by fire and well-armed enemies, but from his nights with little Nell he knew the brothel's upper floor had windows that could serve as exits in a pinch.

Assuming he survived that long.

Staying beneath the smoke, Ryder began to crawl along the balcony.

18

★ Stede Pickering was having second thoughts about his plan to burn the brothel, but they came too late. His men were all inside there now, at least the ones who hadn't been shot down on the approach, and he could see flames racing all along the bar and wall behind it, where the shelves of bottled liquor served as extra fuel. He'd meant to use the stolen lamps only if Marley's men had kept them off the premises, but someone from his crew had lit the blaze after they got inside.

Idjits.

His problem now: should he attempt to call his people back before they fried, or leave them to it? What would a heroic captain do? And who in hell had ever labeled *him* a hero?

If they'd been at sea, storming another ship, he would have known exactly what to do. The captain goes down with his vessel—or, at least, does what he can to make sure everybody else is off before he goes over the rail himself. But this was dry land, in the middle of a city, probably with coppers on their way to find out what was happening.

So, stay and fight? Or cut and run?

Was it a matter of honor or self-preservation?

All alone so far, outside the whorehouse, Pickering paced back and forth, watching the fire and battle through the shattered street-side windows. He was looking right at Frankie Drake, one of his men, when someone shot him through the head and splashed the wall behind him with what looked like bloody oatmeal.

Drake had not been any kind of special friend, but Pickering felt something snap inside him. In another heartbeat, he was charging through the bat-wing doors, looking for targets through the smoky haze that filled the barroom. Smoky, and it was *hot* in there, like standing in the fierce draft from a blacksmith's forge. Pickering ducked after a bullet whistled past his ear and found that it was somewhat easier to breathe, once he was belly down against the floor.

It had been foolish to come in. He saw that now and was about to turn, wriggle beneath the bat-wing doors and back into the street, when someone clutched his arm.

"Captain! You came!"

Turning, he recognized the face of Jonas Walker, bruised where Pickering had slugged him earlier, yet strangely pleased to see him. All that Pickering could think to say was, "Where in hell is Marley?"

"Gone upstairs, I think," said Walker. "Captain, this whole place is goin' up. We need to get out while we can!"

"Get out, then," Pickering replied. "I've still got work to do."

Foolish, he thought, but how could he let Jonas Walker of all people make him quit the fight? Walker, who'd been assigned to guard the *Banshee* but had let her burn.

Pickering jerked his arm free of the frightened sailor's grasp and started crawling toward the stairs. He felt ridiculous, diminished, but it was the only way to reach his goal with bullets flying overhead and smoke fouling the air above knee-level. He was bent on killing Marley now, if it turned out to be the last thing that he ever did.

He reached the stairs at last, but didn't have a chance to start the climb before a slug splintered the newel post mere inches from his face. The angle of the shot told Pickering the shooter was above him, on the second-story landing, so he swung his Colt rifle in that direction, looking for a target. Spotting one of Marley's men, an empty muzzle-loading pistol dangling in his right hand, while he raised another in his left, Pickering found his mark and slammed a bullet through the smuggler's chest.

"Take that, you prick!" he snarled and started up the stairs.

The smoke upstairs was thicker now, and Ryder's plan to stay beneath it wasn't working out. A glance into the barroom, down below, showed him a little slice of Hell on Earth, with flames climbing the walls now, bodies scattered everywhere, and the survivors still doing their best to kill each other, some pairs grappling hand to hand. He saw one figure lurching toward the bar, the curved blade of a saber run completely through his abdomen, pitch headlong into crackling fire around the bar.

It was a nightmare scene, and Ryder tore his eyes away from it, returning to his quest for Bryan Marley. The cribs stretched on in front of him, most of their doors closed, but he didn't know if there'd be time for him to search them thoroughly. Burning to death for Marley's sake was definitely *not* a part of Ryder's plan.

He heard a shot behind him, from the general direction of the stairs, immediately followed by another. Turning back in that direction, Ryder thought he saw a body drop, but the pervasive smoke prevented him from seeing who it was.

An enemy, no doubt of that. He had no friends at Awful Annie's now.

Likely, not even little Nell.

Ryder approached the first crib's door, reached up and turned the knob, pushing the door open from his position near the floor. Smoke from the barroom slipped in ahead of him, providing cover, while he braced himself for gunfire from within. When nothing happened, Ryder ducked across the threshold, huddled with his back against a little chest of drawers, and scanned the room.

Empty, besides its well-used bed and single straight-backed chair.

Ryder retreated to the doorway, glanced both ways along the balcony, then darted toward the second crib in line. Again, the doorknob turned without resistance and he entered in a rush, half crouching in anticipation of a bullet that was not forthcoming. Yet another empty room yawned at him, its musty aroma soon banished by wood smoke and gun smoke. Ryder wasted no more time than necessary to make sure he was alone, then moved back toward the balcony.

Just as he got there, Nell emerged from the third crib in line, holding a handkerchief over her nose and mouth to filter out some of the rising smoke. She saw Ryder and stopped short on the threshold, gaping at him even as the smoke brought tears to her green eyes.

"George? You—"

Whatever she'd meant to say was cut off as an arm circled her throat, trapping the words inside her. Bryan Marley edged into the open, clutching Nell before him as a human shield, his six-gun's barrel visible over her shoulder.

"She was about to say you should be dead," Marley declared.

"I'm hearing that a lot," said Ryder, up on one knee now, his own eyes tearing from the smoke.

"Stede says you burned the *Banshee*."

"Couldn't help myself," Ryder acknowledged.

"And he thinks I put you up to it." Which clarified the raid on Awful Annie's.

"That one never crossed my mind," said Ryder, wondering if he should feel remorse for all the blood that had been spilled as a result.

"Otto swore there was something wrong with you. I still don't get it," Marley said.

"I'm with the Secret Service," Ryder answered back.

"The what?"

"It's new. A part of Treasury." He felt vaguely ridiculous, delivering a lesson in the middle of a gunfight.

"So, you're like a copper?"

"Right."

"And now you're planning what? To take me in?"

"That's it," Ryder agreed.

"Like hell," said Marley, as he raised his piece to fire.

Marley was looking for a window to escape from when he'd blundered into Nell. The first crib he had tried, the window had been nailed shut for some reason that he didn't understand and didn't have the time to think about. Trying the second crib, he'd peered outside and found the drop intimidating, but a glance off to his right showed him a pile of garbage heaped roughly below the next window in line. That led him to the third crib, and he'd been about to exit when the closet door opened behind him, bringing him around, his Colt Navy leveled to deal with any threat that might confront him.

"Bryan?" Little Nell had seemed surprised to see him in her room. "What are you doing here?"

"Just leaving," he'd replied and turned back toward the window, reaching for it with his free hand.

"Wait a second! Will you help me?"

"Help you how?"

She startled him by sobbing then. "To get away," she said. "Don't leave me here to burn!"

"Come on, then," he had said, impatiently, and raised the window's lower sash. A gust of cool, fresh air had chilled his face and made it easier to breathe.

"I can't!" she'd said.

"Why not?"

"It's just . . . I'll fall."

"And that's the damn point, isn't it? A short drop to the ground, instead of cooking. Even if you snap an ankle—"

"God, don't say that!"

"—even if you *do*, it's better than the fire."

"I can't jump out the window!"

"Fine," he'd said. "I'm going. You do what you have to do."

"Goddamn you, Bryan!"

She had bolted for the door, clutching a handkerchief over her face, then stopped dead in the open doorway, saying, "George?"

And that was how he'd come to find himself staring at George Revere, hearing the man he'd trusted—who had saved his life not once, but twice—saying he was some kind of copper for the federals, planning to clap Marley in jail.

"Like hell!" he spat, shoved Nell along the balcony in front of him, and blazed a shot toward where Revere was kneeling with his own pistol in hand.

He missed, of course, too hasty with it, but Revere held off on firing back since Nell was in his way. Marley gave her a shove, putting his weight behind it, snarling as he turned and dashed back through her crib to reach the window he had opened moments earlier. He'd seen that it would be a tight fit for a man his size, but what choice did he have, with George outside the door and Awful Annie's burning out from under him?

The awkward part, he found, was going out feet first, so that he wouldn't break his neck. One leg was fine, but when he tried to swing the other out across the windowsill, the sash jammed painfully against his chest. Cursing, hoping to buy another moment, Marley fired a second shot back toward the door and balcony beyond it. George still didn't try to shoot him, which seemed inexplicable, unless he'd tangled up with little Nell somehow.

Marley was halfway through the window now, sliding by slow degrees, the sash scraping his belly while the sill gouged furrows in his back. It hurt like hell, but he was almost there. If he could just—

The drop came suddenly, surprised him in a way, despite the fact that he'd been straining for it. Marley plummeted to land in stinking trash that slithered out from underneath his feet on impact, dumped him on his back, and knocked the air out of his lungs. He felt the Colt Navy slip from his fingers, wheezed a curse, and scrambled after it while he was struggling to breathe.

* * *

Ryder had ducked the shot that Marley fired in his direction, more or less, and rolled aside in case a second followed it. Instead, Nell stumbled toward him, nearly fell into his arms as Ryder tried to brace himself. She wasn't heavy, but momentum rocked them backward, Ryder nearly falling over, knowing he'd be vulnerable to a killing shot if Marley caught him on his back. Instead of using Nell to shield him, Ryder rolled her clear and struggled to his feet, mindful that he was in a cross fire now, between the door to Nell's room and the barroom battleground below.

When no one cut him down from either side, he took a cautious step in the direction of Nell's crib, where he'd enjoyed himself—and her—on several occasions. Now, it was a snake's den that he entered only at the risk of mortal danger.

Scrabbling noises and the sound of muffled cursing told him Marley must be trying for the window. Crawling out, he'd likely turn his back to Ryder and the doorway, judging distance for the leap, and during that time—

Ryder had been just about to look around the doorjamb when another pistol shot rang out. It smacked against the wall and made him jerk back in surprise, clutching his Colt Army. He tried to frame an argument that would encourage Marley to surrender, but he couldn't think of anything offhand. He had no deal to offer, no concessions for the leader of the gang he'd been assigned to crush. It would be prison or a rope for Marley at the judge's pleasure, if he got that far.

Ryder was braced to rush the doorway when Nell clutched his belt and drew him backward. "George," she said, "don't risk it. Everyone's gone crazy!"

Looking at her, Ryder knew she wasn't trying to deceive him. She was in a panic from the shooting, Marley's handling of her, and the spreading fire below them.

"Let's get out of here!" she pleaded. "We can make it!"

Ryder disengaged her fingers. Told her, "You go, while you can. I've still got business here."

"He'll kill you," Nell said, reaching out for him again.

He shoved her back and snapped, "Go on!" Seeing the disappointment in Nell's eyes, mixed up with fear, he was disgusted with himself but had no time to think about it.

Charging through the door behind his Colt, he found an empty room. Ryder rushed over to the open window, peered outside, and was in time to see his quarry roll out of the alley trash heap, scooping up some object that could only be his pistol. Proving it, Marley spun back to face the second-story window, squeezing off another shot that struck the windowsill and splintered, stinging Ryder's chest with tiny bits of lead.

Too close for comfort.

Ryder raised his Colt as Marley bolted down the alley, but he held his fire, put off by shooting Marley in the back— and not at all convinced that he could make the shot, regardless. Muttering a string of curses, pistol holstered now, he gripped the window frame and wriggled into space, then plummeted through darkness and the stench of smoke.

Stede Pickering crouched on the brothel's second-story balcony, peering through smoke that nearly blinded him, feeling the heat from roaring flames below. The place was groaning now, as fire devoured its underpinnings, and he wondered if the tremors he felt rising through his feet and legs came strictly from his own uneasiness or if the building was preparing to collapse. A gruff voice in his head warned

Pickering to flee, but he crept forward, rifle probing at the smoke in front of him.

A crack of gunfire from the landing made him stop and duck. The bullet did not reach him, but he wasted precious moments waiting, started forward once again, then stopped short at the echo of a second shot. Mouthing a silent curse at his own cowardice, Pickering willed his feet to move and had advanced ten feet or so when he collided with a woman rushing toward him, through the smoke. He sidestepped, caught her with an arm around her slender waist, and held her fast.

"Who's back there?" he demanded, giving her a shake to clear the dazed look from her face.

"Bryan and Georgie," she replied.

"Would that be George Revere?"

The little hooker bobbed her head. "They're killing one another!"

"Not if I get to 'em first," said Pickering. "Which room?"

"Mine," she replied, as if that told him anything.

Another shake, harder this time. "Which one is that?"

"The third one down!"

"Get outta here," he said and spun her off behind him, toward the stairs.

He passed two open doorways on his left, pausing at each to check for lurking enemies, then moved on to the third. No shooting now, except for what continued in the main saloon downstairs. Pickering wondered if the girl had lied to him or if the two men he was hunting had eliminated one another.

Why would they do that, if Marley had dispatched Revere to burn the *Banshee*? Pickering had no idea and didn't aim to stand there wondering about it, if they were within his reach and still alive.

If they were dead, so be it. But he wanted ironclad proof before he left the burning whorehouse.

And his problem, now, was moving from the spot where he stood rooted by a sudden pang of fear. It struck him that if Marley and Revere were in cahoots against him, they could easily have told the girl to spin a tale for Pickering and make him walk into their waiting guns. He still had not worked out why Marley would have turned against him, but it didn't matter now. The die was cast—and dying was the last bit that remained, for one or both of them.

Pickering found his nerve and cocked his rifle, charged the doorway with a loping stride, braced for whatever he might find inside the crib—except the empty room that mocked him. Furious, he checked under the bed, knowing before he did that two men couldn't fit beneath it, then stood up and saw the open window leaking smoke into the night.

Damn it!

He started for the window, then experienced another tremor rising through his lower body. Not a case of nerves, this time. The house was definitely breaking up around him, crumbling as its ground floor was consumed. Pickering turned back toward the doorway, took one step, then cried out as the floor split underneath him and he plunged, howling, into the hungry flames.

Ryder landed on his feet, then lost his balance, tipping over to his left as garbage slid and shifted out from under him. He landed hard but kept a tight grip on his pistol, rolled clear of the stinking refuse pile, and wound up on his knees, facing along the alley toward the point where he had last seen Bryan Marley. Firelight from the brothel helped him spot his target, running with a limp but making decent time, nearly a block away from Ryder.

Try a shot, or follow him?

Ryder lurched to his feet, nearly went down again, but found his balance somehow and ran after Marley, trash and gravel crunching underneath his boots. He caught his second wind, gained speed, and had begun to close the gap when Marley reached a corner up ahead, turned to his right, and disappeared. Ryder kept after him, aware of how much racket he was making in the process, then slowed down as he approached the corner, wary of a trap.

Decisions.

Every second that he waited, listening for receding footsteps, gave Marley a greater lead. The problem: Ryder's ears were ringing from the recent gunfire and commotion back in Awful Annie's, coupled with his jarring leap out of the second-story window, and he couldn't tell if Marley was retreating or if he was just around the bend, lying in wait.

One way to tell, he thought and lunged into the open, belly down and rolling with his Colt Army extended for a hasty shot if need be. Marley wasn't huddled in the shadows, though. Instead, Ryder could see him running for his life, a block or more down range and widening his fair head start.

Ryder knew cursing was a waste of breath and energy but did it anyway, while he was rising to his feet once more, rejoining the pursuit. He didn't know where Marley might be headed, wasn't sure he could keep up, but knew that he was bound to try, even if he collapsed in the attempt. It all came down to this, the risks and lives that he had taken to arrest one man, before his quarry could escape and start all over in some other port, with new accomplices.

After a few more blocks, it finally occurred to Ryder that

his man was heading for the treasure warehouse. Whether Marley hoped to hide out there, or simply bag enough loot to get started in another place, it made no difference. If Ryder let him slip away from Galveston, it could be months before he found his man again—if ever. Failure on his first job for the Secret Service, when he'd come this far, was unacceptable.

He ran, lungs clearing finally of all the smoke he had inhaled at Awful Annie's, laboring to match his pulse rate and the running pace he held by sheer determination. Any moment now, it seemed that he might trip over exhaustion, sprawling headlong into lassitude, and lose the race. Ryder could not have said what kept him on his feet and moving forward, other than his stubborn will.

They must be halfway to the warehouse now, he reasoned, maybe even closer. In a few more moments he would glimpse it, see the spot where he'd killed Otto Seitz in self-defense and staged the scene to blame it on his adversary's victims. Wondering if Marley knew about those killings yet, he ran on, wishing that he could gain some ground or, better yet, see Marley trip over a stone.

That didn't happen, but he *did* make out the warehouse, finally. Its door was closed now, Marley drawing closer to it with his limping stride, now rolling back the door and disappearing into midnight shadows. Then the pistol cracked in front of Ryder and he saw its muzzle flash, skipped awkwardly aside as Marley's bullet struck the earth between his feet.

"All right!" the smuggler shouted, sounding breathless from his run. "That's far enough!"

19

★ "Your operation's finished," Ryder called to Marley.

"This one, maybe," the reply came back. "But I can always start again. You're finished, period."

He had a point. Ryder was stuck on open ground, under the gun. His only cover was the night itself, and the long shadows cast by faint moonlight from the adjoining warehouses. The Colt Army felt heavy in his fist.

"It doesn't have to end like this," he said.

"For you, it does," Marley replied. "Why couldn't you leave well enough alone?"

"I have a job to do," said Ryder, thinking that it sounded weak, under the circumstances.

"So, you've done it, right? No *Banshee*, anymore. You've broken up two gangs and put me out of business, for a while, at least. Why don't you let it go?"

"And leave you with a warehouse full of treasure? How would that sound, back in Washington?"

"The hell do you care?" Marley challenged him. "Most of this stuff was stolen from the Spanish or whoever, when our daddies were both still in short pants. No one's claiming it but me."

"And Uncle Sam."

"To hell with him. What did he ever do for me or mine?"

"I'm not here to debate a lot of politics," said Ryder. "And the War Between the States is over, far as I'm concerned."

"The wrong side won," said Marley.

"But they *did* win. And the law says you pay taxes on whatever you're importing."

"Jesus!" Marley barked a rasp of laughter. "That's what this is all about? You're just a goddamn tax man?"

"No. The Secret Service deals with frauds against the government."

"The *Yankee* government."

"The only one there is, from here on in," Ryder replied.

"So, how 'bout you just take some of the swag and give it to your uncle, while I take the rest?"

"They might work out a deal with you. It's not for me to say."

"What *do* you say, then?"

"Come with me and get yourself a lawyer. Make the best deal that you can. The pile of loot you're sitting on, who knows? They just might let you go."

"With nothing left to show for years of work."

"For years of stealing," Ryder said, correcting him.

"That *is* my work!"

"You might want to consider changing that."

Another bitter laugh. "Easy for you to say. Hey, tell me something, will you?"

"If I can."

"You saved my life two differ'nt times," said Marley.

"Why'n hell'd you do that, when you could've just stood back and let me die? Less work for you that way, as I see it."

"My job's to bring you in for trial, not kill you."

"Let the Yankees shame me, eh? You figure there's a jury here in Texas that'll find me guilty?"

"Beats me," Ryder said. "But if you're right, why don't you just throw down that Colt and come along with me?"

"Because I still lose everything! Your precious uncle robs me blind, regardless."

"It was never yours to start with."

"Hell it wasn't! Who else sweated like a field hand just to get it here? Who took the chances? Who spilled blood to make it happen?"

"Sell that to the jury, you'll be home and dry."

"I like my chances as they stand," Marley replied, emerging from the deeper shadows of the warehouse. "Do you want to holster up and draw, or just start shooting?"

"Please yourself," Ryder replied.

"Well, since you put it that way—"

Marley raised his Colt Navy, as Ryder threw himself to one side, hit the dirt and rolled, his pistol out in front of him. Ryder fired once, just as Marley did, and heard the .44 slug zip through empty space where he'd been standing just an eyeblink earlier. His first shot may have missed, as well, but number two took Marley in the chest and staggered him. The smuggler fired another round as he was falling, wasted on vast darkness overhead.

Ryder got to his feet and took his time approaching Bryan Marley. He could see the Colt Navy where it had fallen, ten, maybe twelve inches from his adversary's hand, but reachable. He didn't want to fire again, so circled wide around Marley to reach the pistol, kicking it away.

Marley smiled up at him and wheezed, "You cheated, Georgie."

"Were there rules?"

"Jus' one. I'm s'pose to win."

"You had a long run. And it's Gideon."

"What is?"

"My name."

"Funny, ain't it? I don't even know . . . who . . . killed me."

"Marley? *Bryan*?" There was no response, and Ryder saw the smuggler's eyes already glazing over, taking on that dusty look that's never found in life.

He dragged Marley inside the warehouse, leaving him with Otto and the two men Seitz had killed, then closed the door and started back toward Awful Annie's through the maze of darkened streets.

The place was burned out to a hollow smoking shell when Ryder got there, people standing in the street and gaping at the ruins, coughing when the night breeze shifted, carrying the smoke their way. The fire department had arrived in time to save adjoining structures, though the walls of Annie's next-door neighbors had been badly scorched before the flames were watered down. The odor that assaulted Ryder's nostrils was a mix of wood smoke, soggy ash, and roasted meat.

Police were on the scene by now, milling about and questioning spectators. Ryder moved around the fringes of the crowd, avoiding men in uniform, alert for any sign of the patrolmen he had pistol-whipped a few nights earlier, eavesdropping where he could. The witnesses he overheard were telling variations of a single story: men with guns had stormed the brothel, then the place went up in flames. Some claimed they'd seen people escaping from the fire, but couldn't offer any names. In passing, Ryder heard one copper tell another that he reckoned more people had gone up in the blaze than managed to get out.

That roasting smell.

Ryder felt sickened as he circulated, watching out for any faces he might recognize. Awful Annie should have been there, certainly, if she'd survived—unless, perhaps, she feared involvement with the law and had decided that discretion was the better part of valor. None of Marley's crew were present, that he saw, nor any from the late *Banshee*.

All up in smoke?

He was about to leave and head back to his boarding-house, hoping to get some sleep before he had to meet the USRC *Martin Van Buren*, when a small voice at his back said, "Georgie?"

Turning, he was face-to-face with little Nell, her cheeks darkened by soot, except where tears had left clean tracks. Her hair was wild, eyes red from weeping, smoke, or both.

"You made it out," she said.

He nodded. Said, "I'm glad you're safe."

"What's safe?"

"Alive, then."

Lowering her voice to a near-whisper, stepping close enough to touch him, she asked, "What's become of Bryan?"

Ryder wondered whether he should bluff it out, play dumb, but then decided not to.

"Bryan didn't make it."

"He's . . . in there?"

Ryder saw nothing to be gained from going into details, there and then. Instead, he simply told her, "It was quick."

"Lucky for him. Wish it was quick for me."

"You don't mean that," he said.

"Oh, no? The hell are you, to tell me how I feel?"

Before he could respond, she turned and left him, vanishing into the crowd. Instead of lingering, Ryder departed in the opposite direction, ducking down the first alley he came to, hurrying along to reach the next street parallel to where the mob had gathered. There, he slowed his pace again, considered making for the Western Union office, sending off another telegram to Washington, but decided it could wait till morning.

Sleep was what he needed now, if he could manage it. Tomorrow, early, he would send a message to Director Wood, tell him the job was done after a fashion, then he'd meet the cutter coming in from Corpus Christi and direct its officers to Marley's treasure trove.

Assuming that it wasn't cleaned out overnight.

He doubted that would happen, though, with Marley's gang and Pickering's both slaughtered in the fight at Awful Annie's. Anyone who'd managed to survive, if they were fit to travel, would most likely be intent on getting out of Galveston before first light. He could have sent the coppers off to Marley's warehouse, but that would have meant a night in custody, at least, and might have guaranteed the loot was gone before the *Martin Van Buren* pulled into port.

Tomorrow would be soon enough.

Sufficient to this day was all the misery he'd seen.

The Western Union clerk was dozing in his chair when Ryder got there, jolting him from dreamland with the small bell hung above the office door. He gave Ryder a message blank and tried to hide a yawn behind his hand while Ryder filled it out, sticking to basics. He would have to file a full report in time, but didn't feel like sharing all the details with a stranger who would charge him by the word, then maybe share the contents of his telegram with God knows who in Galveston.

When he was done, he waited for the message to be sent, saw it acknowledged, then retrieved his copy from the clerk and stuffed it in his pocket prior to settling up the bill. The groggy clerk, if he leaked anything, would have to reconstruct the terse message from memory before he passed it on.

From Western Union, Ryder made his way on to the waterfront and stopped in at the Customs house. He showed his badge, identified himself, and asked if there was any word about the cutter coming in from Corpus Christi. The officer on duty told him that the *Martin Van Buren* was expected shortly, whatever that meant, and directed Ryder to the pier where it would dock upon arrival. Stevedores and fishermen were busy at their work when Ryder reached the water's edge and settled down to wait.

He spent the better part of forty minutes idling on the dock, before the cutter pulled in, jockeyed for position, and was made fast to the pier. Ryder was waiting quayside when the crew began to disembark, led by a young lieutenant who introduced himself as Joseph Pulaski. The lieutenant verified Ryder's credentials, then picked two seamen to remain aboard the cutter and ordered the other fourteen into formation on the pier. Pulaski wore a holstered Colt Navy, while each of his men was armed with a Spencer repeating rifle.

Ryder led them to the warehouse where he'd left four dead men yesterday. The place was undisturbed when they arrived, but had acquired a rank aroma overnight. Pulaski scowled over the corpses, then instructed several of his men to drag them into daylight and fresh air.

"You say you found them this way?" he asked Ryder.

"All but him," Ryder replied, nodding to Bryan Marley's body.

"I've heard of that one," said Pulaski, "but I never had the pleasure. You were lucky that he didn't kill you."

Ryder let it go at that and led Pulaski on a guided tour of the warehouse, watching the lieutenant's eyes go wide as he examined Marley's cache of treasures. Most of it was still in crates, except for what he'd found Seitz picking over yesterday. Around them, Ryder heard Pulaski's men exclaiming over one thing or another, sometimes whistling softly to themselves as more loot was revealed.

"I can't begin to estimate what all of this is worth," Pulaski said, when they were finished with a cursory inspection. "Several hundred thousand dollars, easily. I wouldn't be surprised if some of it wound up in a museum."

Ryder pictured the Smithsonian in Washington, opened five years before Abraham Lincoln was elected president and the United States plunged into turmoil. He imagined some of Marley's stolen objects on display there, if the rogues in Congress could be kept from picking over them beforehand. In the short term, he was looking forward to Director Wood's reaction when he saw the treasure trove and started working out its value.

Maybe that would cancel out the fact that Ryder had no one in custody for trial.

"How did you plan to move all this?" Pulaski asked him.

"Hadn't thought about it," Ryder answered honestly. Railroads in Dixie were a fright after the war, with many of the tracks destroyed, repairs and new construction hanging fire until the readmission of the former Rebel states could be resolved. That narrowed down the choices to a ship or travel overland, which would require a train of wagons even if they left the normal merchandise and ganja there in Galveston.

"We could take it back to Corpus Christi, I suppose," Pulaski said, "but that's moving it farther from the capital."

"I'm waiting to hear back from my director," Ryder told him.

"As am I, from Secretary McCulloch."

"That would be my boss's boss," Ryder replied.

"Maybe they'll have you guard it on the trip back East."

"Be just my luck," said Ryder. Then, remembering the difference between his life in Washington and what he'd seen of Texas, so far, he decided there were worse things than a turn on guard duty, if it would take him home.

When Lieutenant Pulaski had finished a rough inventory of loot at the warehouse, he left most of his men on guard there, bringing one along on their trek to the county sheriff's office. Ryder was gambling on the sheriff as an intermediary with the Galveston police and was relieved to have two officers in uniform supporting him.

At least, this way, he couldn't simply disappear without a ripple.

Sheriff Roy Winstead was six feet tall and barrel-chested, with dark hair going gray around the temples. He'd been cut at some point, with the scar bisecting his right eyebrow at an angle and continuing down to the outside corner of his eye. He chewed a dead cigar while listening to Ryder's tale—the parts of it that Ryder chose to share—and then dispatched one of his deputies to fetch the chief of Galveston's police department.

That turned out to be a sharp-faced Irishman, Sean Doherty, who brought a couple of his officers along for company. According to the decorations on their uniforms, one was a captain and the other a lieutenant, but the chief wasted no time or breath on introductions. Ryder told his story once again, careful to be consistent, then sat back and waited for the locals to respond.

Chief Doherty spoke first, saying, "It seems you've wreaked a lot of havoc here in Galveston."

"How so?" Ryder inquired.

"We've had a ship burned at the wharf, and then a tavern where they're still counting the dead. Now we've got four men murdered at this warehouse—"

"One, I understand, was shot in self-defense," Pulaski interjected, "while the rest killed one another."

"So *he* says," the chief replied, clearly unhappy with the interruption.

"Have you any reason to dispute it?" asked Pulaski.

"Not yet. But you can be sure that I'll be looking into it."

"The warehouse stands on county land," said Sheriff Winstead. "If there's any lookin' in to do, I'll be the one to do it."

"I suppose you'll want to hog the merchandise, as well?" Doherty challenged.

"I can put your mind to ease on that score," said Pulaski. "Everything inside that storehouse is the fruits of smuggling, meaning a conspiracy against the U.S. government."

Doherty snorted back at him, derisively. "Conspiracy, my ass."

"Evading import duties for a start," Pulaski said. "That's federal. Defrauding Customs and the U.S. Treasury."

The sheriff cleared his throat. "If there was a reward . . ."

"You'd have to take that up with Washington," Pulaski told him. "What I understand, most of the loot was stolen off of foreign shipping, more than fifty years ago. You'd have to trace the ownership, first thing, and even then you can't claim a reward unless you're able to return the items.

Which you won't be, while they're held in federal custody. Try writing to the State Department if you think you've got a case."

Ryder was pleased to sit and watch the argument play out around him, thankful that he wasn't forced to answer any of those questions on his own. The less that Chief Doherty and Sheriff Winstead focused on him, the better he liked it.

"Damn it," Doherty was saying, "I don't like the way we're being pushed aside in this. I represent the law in Galveston, and—"

"Chief," Pulaski interrupted him again, "you needn't worry. I'll be sure to note in my report that Marley's gang accumulated all this loot while you were busy . . . um . . . investigating them."

"Hold on, now!"

"I suspect the Secret Service may want to discuss your methods. Agent Ryder?"

"Hmm. I wouldn't doubt it," Ryder said, making an effort not to smile.

"Hey, now!" said Doherty. "We can't watch every ship that comes to port. That's down to Customs, anyhow."

"That's settled, then," Pulaski said. "We'll have no more discussion about shares, rewards, or any other foolishness."

The chief and his two escorts rose, red-faced. As he was stalking toward the exit, Doherty rasped out, "I don't know why you bothered calling us at all."

"Consider it a courtesy," Pulaski said, to his retreating back.

The sheriff's laugh was muted, like a hiss of steam escaping from a leaky radiator. "It was worth my cut, just watchin' that," he said. "But seriously, fellas, if there's any chance to get a piece before you take the lion's share . . ."

* * *

From Sheriff Winstead's office, Ryder went back to his boardinghouse, to fetch his rifle and the personal effects still waiting in his rented room. Pulaski had gone off to make arrangements for a team and wagon, planning several trips between the warehouse and the waterfront until he'd salvaged Marley's treasure and secured it aboard the Revenue Cutter. Ryder was supposed to join them at his leisure, understanding that the *Martin Van Buren* meant to leave for Corpus Christi by sundown, at the latest.

One more voyage over water, and he hoped that it would be his last.

En route to claim his Henry and the rest of his belongings, Ryder heard his stomach growling and remembered that he'd had nothing to eat since supper, yesterday. The Mexican café where he had dined last night was on his way, so Ryder stopped in there for a steak they called carne asada, with a side order of tamales, rice, and beans. He washed the whole lot down with beer—*cerveza* in the native tongue—but passed on the tequila, since he meant to keep his wits about him.

No time yet to celebrate.

It took less time than Ryder had imagined, clearing out his room and settling his final payment to the landlord. On his walk back to the waterfront, he thought about Director Wood and how he might react to the conclusion of his work in Galveston. The lack of an impending trial, he thought, might work to his advantage, since there'd be no risk of anybody paying off a judge or jury to derail the wheels of justice. As to any mixed emotions Ryder had about the fate of Bryan Marley, he supposed that he would learn to live with them.

He stayed alert during his final stroll through town,

keenly aware that some of Marley's men might still be circulating through the city, scheming to recover loot they saw as theirs, perhaps seeking revenge for the demise of Marley and their crew. No one but little Nell had heard Ryder proclaim himself a lawman in the fight at Awful Annie's, but she might have talked to others. And, he knew, there was a nagging possibility that Doherty or one of his corrupt policemen could have spread the word, from simple spite.

With that in mind, he kept the Henry rifle in his left hand, while his right was free to draw the Colt Army, the portmanteau he'd brought from Washington slung from his shoulder by its strap. His watchfulness turned out to be a waste of time, since no one challenged him along the way, and Ryder was relieved to reach the pier without another fight.

Pulaski showed up moments later, with a second wagonload of crates from Marley's warehouse. They attracted some attention, but his rifle-bearing seamen kept the gawkers at a distance. Ryder was about to join them, shifting cargo from the wagon to the cutter, when Pulaski stopped him, handing Ryder a flimsy envelope printed with the legend WESTERN UNION TELEGRAM.

"A messenger brought this while you were gone," Pulaski said.

Ryder opened the envelope, unfolded the message inside, and perused it. The telegram read:

```
JOB WELL DONE STOP PROCEED CORPUS CHRISTI
STOP AWAIT ORDERS RE KNIGHTS OF RISING
SUN STOP WOOD
```

Ryder showed Pulaski the telegram and asked him, "Any idea what that last bit means?"

"A Rebel outfit," said Pulaski. "Never heard of Appomattox. Are you going after them?"

Ryder could only shrug. "You know as much as I do. Maybe."

"Well, good luck then," the lieutenant told him. "Better you than me."

PETER BRANDVOLD

"Make room on your shelf of favorites:
Peter Brandvold will be staking out a claim there."
—Frank Roderus

THE GRAVES AT SEVEN DEVILS

BULLETS OVER BEDLAM

COLD CORPSE, HOT TRAIL

DEADLY PREY

ROGUE LAWMAN

STARING DOWN THE DEVIL

RIDING WITH THE DEVIL'S MISTRESS

.45-CALIBER FIREBRAND

.45-CALIBER FURY

.45-CALIBER REVENGE

"Recommended to anyone who loves the West
as I do. A very good read."
—Jack Ballas

"Takes off like a shot, never giving the reader a
chance to set the book down."
—Douglas Hirt

Don't miss the best Westerns from Berkley

. . . .

LYLE BRANDT
PETER BRANDVOLD
JACK BALLAS
J. LEE BUTTS
JORY SHERMAN
DUSTY RICHARDS

. . . .

penguin.com

M10G0610

Penguin Group (USA) Online

What will you be reading tomorrow?

Patricia Cornwell, Nora Roberts, Catherine Coulter,
Ken Follett, John Sandford, Clive Cussler,
Tom Clancy, Laurell K. Hamilton, Charlaine Harris,
J. R. Ward, W.E.B. Griffin, William Gibson,
Robin Cook, Brian Jacques, Stephen King,
Dean Koontz, Eric Jerome Dickey, Terry McMillan,
Sue Monk Kidd, Amy Tan, Jayne Ann Krentz,
Daniel Silva, Kate Jacobs...

You'll find them all at
penguin.com

Read excerpts and newsletters,
find tour schedules and reading group guides,
and enter contests.

Subscribe to Penguin Group (USA) newsletters
and get an exclusive inside look
at exciting new titles and the authors you love
long before everyone else does.

PENGUIN GROUP (USA)
penguin.com

M224G0909